You make

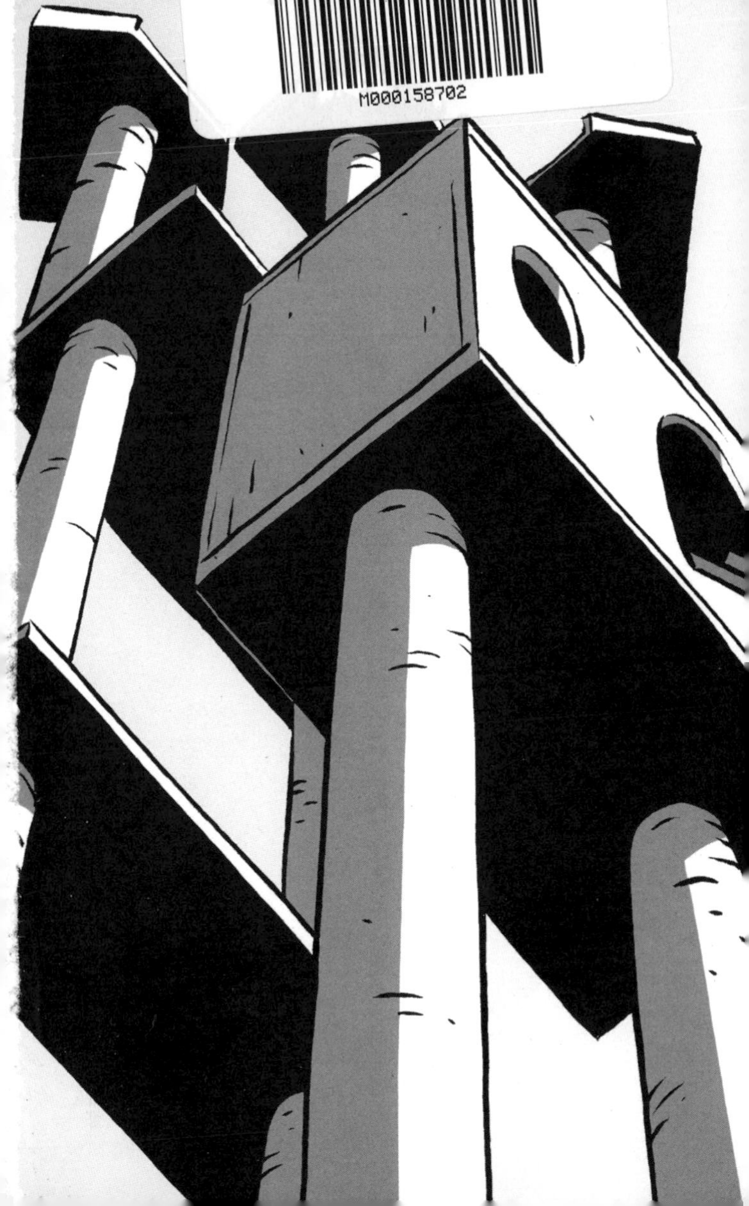

Books by the Same Author!

A

PICK·A·PLOT!™

BOOK

#3

You Are a Kitten!

WRITTEN & ILLUSTRATED BY SHERWIN TJIA

© Sherwin Tjia, 2015
Designed by Sherwin Tjia
First Edition

Library and Archives Canada Cataloguing in Publication

Tjia, Sherwin, author
    You are a kitten! / Sherwin Tjia.

(Pick-a-plot ; 3)
ISBN 978-1-894994-97-2 (paperback)

    1. Graphic novels. I. Title. II. Series: Pick-a-plot! ; book 3

PN6733.T55Y68 2015   741.5'971   C2015-903871-5

Printed and bound in Canada by Gauvin Press

Conundrum Press
Greenwich, Nova Scotia
www.conundrumpress.com

Conundrum Press and the author acknowledge the financial
assistance of the Canada Council for the Arts, and the Government
of Canada through the Canada Book Fund toward this publication.

For my family.
Those by chance
& those by choice.

WARNING!

Do not read this book beginning to end like a normal novel. You make the choices! You pick the plot!

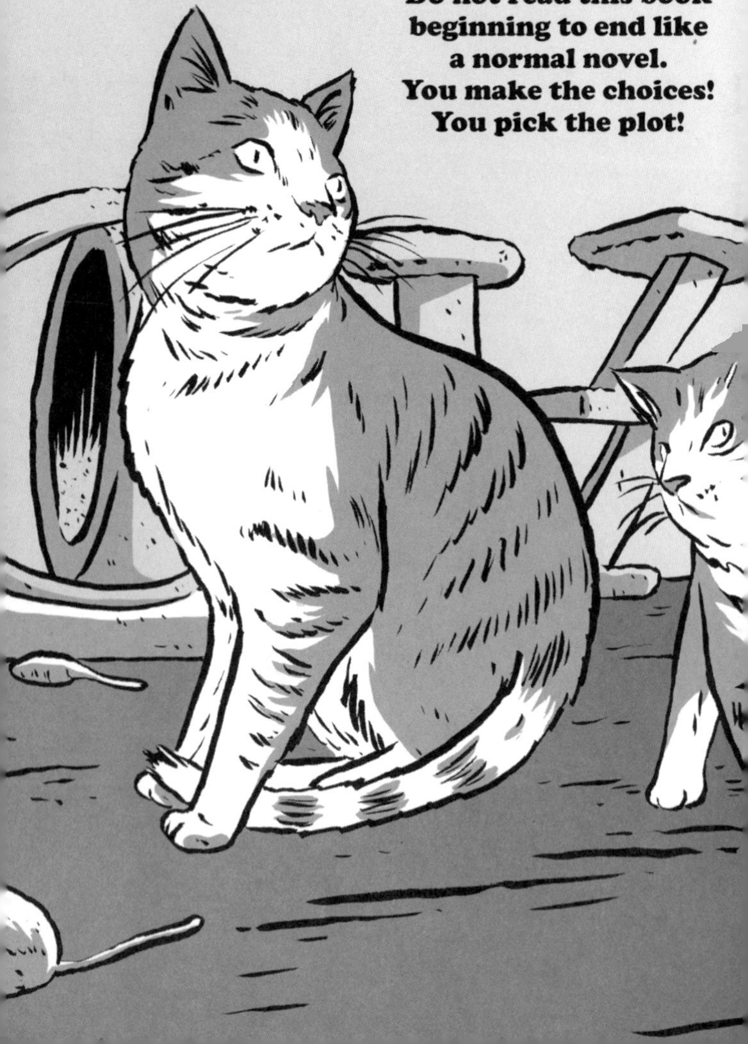

As you move through this book you will occasionally be asked to make choices. Once you've made your choice, follow the instructions and turn to the page indicated. Your choices will shape, influence and direct what happens to you!

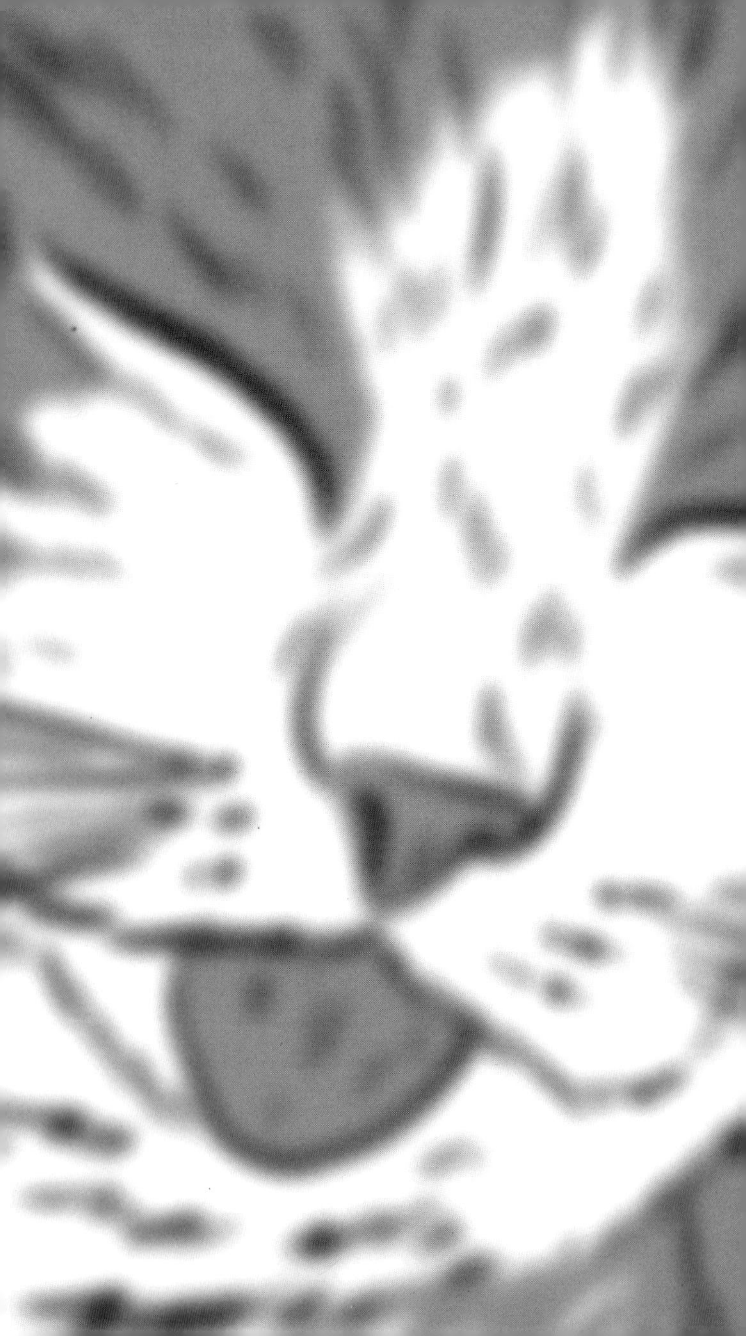

It's cold.

You don't like it.

You want the other thing.

Everything's cold. Your whole body is *chilled.* You cry out in fear and exasperation. It's all you can do.

But then the other thing is back, though it doesn't envelop you. It's just a taste of the former warmth that you enjoyed. It's molten hot on your cold cheek. It's repeated lapping that moves across your face and forehead, then travels down your neck and chest, and over the rest of you.

You cry out again. Your voice is a dull, inchoate noise mingling with the low-level buzz.

And after awhile it's not so cold anymore. Something large and warm is close by, radiating heat, and you move toward it. You are aware of other bodies, also warm, also moving around you. You follow a deeply satisfying smell toward her.

Mom.

Under her fur, the soothing *lub-dub* of her heart pulsing against your face. The rhythm is a faint echo of the same beat that used to surround you, that was your whole world. It feels so far off now.

Her tongue comes again, licking at your ear. This time you cry out in appreciation. More. You want more of this.

A moment later, something simultaneously soft and stiff makes its way into your mouth. Instinctively, you suck on it and the most deliciously warm fluid seeps onto your tongue. You put your paws out around it and press down. More milk floods your mouth. You drink it down greedily.

2

You don't like being out here.

Everything used to be warm, and calm and nice, but Mom's milk mitigates the awfulness.

And after a little while, you're full and satisfied.

The other bodies around you are still and asleep. They press against you, keeping you warm.

After licking your lips to taste the last of the milk, you sleep too.

~ ~ ~

"Tupac," the low, male voice says. "Call him Tupac."

"Why Tupac?" the higher female voice replies. Your ears prick up at the woman's tone. Hearing is still a new thing for you, and you've discovered that you have a harder time picking up the lower baritone of the man. Except when he yells. Which he does a lot.

"Doesn't he *look* like a Tupac?" the man says.

"Wait, what are you saying? Because he's black?" The man laughs.

"That's racist," the woman says.

"It's funny," the man chuckles. "C'mon, you have to admit that it's funny."

"It's not funny. It's racist! And black cats already have a hard enough time getting adopted."

"Wait, you're serious?" the man says. "Now *that's* racist."

"We're not calling him Tupac."

"Which ones are you keeping again?"

"The black one and the orange one."

"Which orange one?"

"There's only one orange one."

"There are two orange ones."

"No there's not."

"Sure there is."

A movement beside you. Your brother is lifted up and away. Suddenly there is a cold gap on one side. You mewl in complaint.

"Him?" the woman says. "I wouldn't call *that* orange."

"He's orange," the man declares definitively, voice rising. "C'mon. He's fucking orange."

Despite the loss of your sibling, you try to get back to sleep. But the loud voices rouse you. You hope they stop talking soon.

"Whatever," the woman says.

Your brother is dropped back down beside you. He pads around a little bit on the blanket before settling. You lean into him and he leans back.

"What I don't understand," the man says, "is how the same cat can give birth to orange and black cats. Aren't they all supposed to be the same colour?"

"Sometimes a litter can have multiple fathers. When a girl's in heat, she'll send out this pheromone and she'll mate with a lot of different toms."

The man is quiet for a moment.

"Makes sense," he says, "that *you* would know a lot about that."

Now the woman is quiet.

"Fuck you!" she screams.

Your ears prick up. Uh oh. Sometimes the man and the woman argue for a long time. You hope this isn't one of those times.

"That was *one* time! You were being a *jerk!* And that was over a *year* ago!"

"So you're saying it's *my* fault!?" the man bellows back. "That you were a slut?"

You flatten your ears and are now fully awake.

~~~

Tupac is nibbling at your tail and you let him. His little teeth are sharp, but he never bites hard anymore. You've smacked him enough times that he knows your limits. As you know his. All around you the rest of your littermates are in various stages of sleeping, playing or tumbling over each other.

When your mom jumps back over the high wall of the pen, you immediately get up, raising your tail in greeting. Hers is raised high in return. You wobble over to her. By now you can take a number of steps before falling over. And every day it feels like you can go longer and longer before you have to pick yourself up. But it's fun. It's a game.

Your mom bends her head to bump her nose with yours, then gives your forehead a couple of licks. Your nose pulses as you sniff her mouth. She just ate something. It is a fascinating smell, earthy and pungent.

She flops over onto her side and as a group, you and your siblings sidle up to her. You go to your particular nipple to feed. Over time, it just worked out that way – you each have your own spot.

The days pass by in a beautiful rhythm. The pen is your playground. You feel like you could do this forever, even as you notice something deep inside you that wants to know what lies over the wall.

Where does your mom go? The warm sunbeam that visits every morning, that crosses the floor of the pen, that climbs the wall then disappears. Where does *that* go? You are curious.

Later, Tupac nudges you awake from your post-feed stupor. He wants to play.

You look around and your mom is gone. The other kittens are still slumbering in a pile.

You stumble after Tupac. He leads you to the wall. He's been trying to climb it. It's made of a slick, smooth plastic material. But with his nascent claws, he's been managing to scrabble up. He sinks his claws into the wall and actually gets a foothold. But halfway up, he falls back to the blanket that carpets the floor of the pen.

He rolls back onto his feet. His tail swings back and forth and he runs over to your side, nudging you.

He wants *you* to climb the wall.

If you decide to take a turn, move to page 8.

If you think you'd rather let Tupac try again, turn to page 10.

You try to move under the bed, but the man's hand blocks you.

"Where are you going?" he asks. "How'd you get out?"

The man tries to grab you. You get a terrible feeling from him. Something's wrong. He is wrong. He's going to shout and be scary, like the lightning and thunder you've seen outside the living room window.

"Why are you doing what you're not *supposed* to be doing!" the man shouts.

He charges you and you run back out into the hall.

The heavy thud of his feet rattle the floor underneath you as you gallop toward another doorway.

As you enter, you jump intstinctively. An oddly-shaped structure stands in your way and you hope to get to the top of it.

Full of adrenaline, you pounce higher than you ever have. Your mom would be so proud!

Amazingly, you reach the top of the structure! But it's slippery, and weirdly, there's a giant gaping hole, which you fall into!

Splash!

The man cackles as he looks down on you in the toilet bowl.

"Hey shithead," he chuckles. "Living up to your name, I see?"

Spitting, you are cold. You have never been this cold before. You've never had so much water on you before. You move to get out of it, but the walls of the small pen are slippery, and it's difficult for your claws to get a grip.

You cry out.

Suddenly, your mom is there! She stands on the

toilet bowl edge. Her head bends down to try to get a hold of you, but then the man grabs her and she is gone.

"No, no," the man says. His arm reaches over and pulls down the lid, leaving you in darkness.

You hear your mom screaming at him.

Small thuds as the man walks away.

Your mom jumps up onto the toilet lid. She's crying. With her claws, she tries to lift the lid, but can't.

It's so dark where you are.

You try to climb out, but the walls are too slippery. Your head keeps falling under the water's surface. The cold, and the dark, and your tiredness all contribute to making it easier to let go than to struggle to keep aloft.

After a while, your ears fill with fluid and you can't hear your mom anymore, but by then it doesn't matter.

THE END

You have just used up one of your lives. You have eight more! Feel free to reincarnate on page 1 and make different choices! See another ending! Pick another plot!

8

Following the same path as Tupac, you dig your claws into the vertical surface. Paw over paw, you haul yourself up. You can hardly believe it when you reach the top! Your hind feet scrabble on the slick surface as you mount the edge and then promptly tumble down the other side.

Once you regain your feet, you look around. The room is large. You knew it was large before, but now you can see the contents of it. Various pieces of furniture are arrayed along the edge of the room, and a grey fuzzy carpet lies under your feet. Your claws pick at it happily.

Oh! It's *Mom!*

She sits sleeping along the arm of the pale blue floral couch, eyes closed, head low.

Opposite her is a big screen with moving images, the volume low.

On the floor in front of you is the sunbeam. You have never seen it outside of the pen. You have more time in the blessed sunbeam if you want it!

You hear Tupac scritching at the wall on the other side, making another attempt.

You can go anywhere. The sudden plethora of options is a little overwhelming.

If you decide to wait for Tupac to make it over, turn to page 15.

If you decide instead to venture out into the room to see what wonders it holds, turn to page 16.

You decide to stay put.

The sunbeam reappears a while later, but it doesn't stay.

You nap. All of this being outside is very exhausting.

The shift of the sliding door awakens you.

"Oh god!" The woman is there, looking panicked. She gasps in relief to see you. Slowly, she bends down. With a trembling hand she shakes a small colourful bag. Curious, you go over to it. A pungent scent. You don't know what it is, but you really, really like it. She shakes the bag and a couple nuggets fall loose onto the concrete. You move over to them and inhale deeply. Your tongue flicks out and tastes one. You bend down and take one into your mouth. You try to chew, but the nugget is very hard. You like it in your mouth, however. You suck on it, your saliva coating it.

"Gotcha," the woman breathes, as she scoops you up and brings you inside.

Oh no! As she lifts you, the nugget falls from your mouth! You cry in protest.

Inside, the woman drops you back into your pen and then closes the sliding door. You mom is there to greet you. She comes over to you, worriedly, and licks you. One by one, all your other siblings come over to smell you.

You smell different. You are different.

All of a sudden, the playpen feels very small.

In a few moments, you're going to find a corner and fall asleep, exhausted. You won't realize it, but your mom will come over and put an arm over you, and she will sleep too. Also exhausted.

Turn to page 23.

Gamely, Tupac tries to climb the wall again, making new marks with his claws as he ascends. But halfway up, he seems to lose his nerve. His head swivels in panic and he shoots a glance back at the ground. But then, not knowing what else to do, he keeps going!

Finally, he reaches the top and you see him disappear. He squeaks as he gets to wherever he went. Then it's quiet.

You are half-compelled to follow when Tupac suddenly reappears! But this time, not by himself.

Your mom has him by the scruff of his neck as she jumps into the pen and drops him gently on the gathered blankets. You go over to him and sniff him. Has anything changed? Has *he* changed? Tupac doesn't smell any different, but he's quiet.

All of a sudden he's on his feet again, and wandering around the playpen, looking for something to do. He jumps up onto the first step of the cat tree — a series of connected, rising platforms — making his way to the top.

You look back at the tall wall, Tupac's claw marks are faint lines in the smooth white surface.

Over the next few hours, you nap a little and play a little and occasionally you glance at the tall wall.

If Tupac could make it — maybe you can too.

But the playpen is such a warm and wonderful place. You are loathe to leave it.

If you decide to savour the playpen a little longer, turn to page 23.

If you are obsessed with what's over the wall, scramble up it on the next page.

When you climb the wall, you give yourself a running start. Or at least as much of a running start as you can manage, because it hasn't been that long since you even *learned* to run.

And actually, the running start doesn't help that much, but it's doing wonders for your spirits as you make your way up and over the top of the wall!

After a short drop you land on your haunches. You look around. There's no sign of any living thing, and no sunbeam either. Still, there's plenty to explore.

As you venture further into the room, a tall shadow appears to your left. The man, with a white bag in his hand appears from the outside and opens the sliding door.

As he steps inside, he suddenly notices you.

"Jesus, kitty!" he exclaims, dropping his bag.

The bag startles you and you jump a few inches into the air.

"Dude," the man bends down, reaching for you. "Get back in your pen."

You are freaked out! If you freeze and do nothing,
turn to page 18.

To run out the still-open sliding door,
turn to page 12.

If you bite the man's hand as it closes in,
bear down on page 19.

Deking around the man's feet, you run out the sliding door!

Immediately you are out of your element, as you stumble down to the concrete asphalt of the porch. Not to be deterred, you keep moving, but stop when you encounter the field of green fur.

Your nose pulses as you take it in. What is this? It has a powerful smell and tickles your whiskers.

Behind you there is a sliding noise.

You turn, and see that the man has shut the door.

He stands there, staring at you. He waves lifelessly at you.

Suddenly, your mom comes into view at the man's feet. She paws frantically on the glass. Her mouth opens in a loud cry. It's muted, but you can hear it through the door.

The man bends down and lifts her, still crying, out of view.

You stand there in the field of fur, staring at the glass door.

Will he come back?

It's frightening out here, and you don't move.

You don't feel safe. It's way too bright, and a low hum suffuses the air. Everything's moving, including you. An unseen force occasionally blows across your face, like cold breath, and moves across the green field you're in. So many movements! It's hard to know what you should be afraid of.

Time passes and you move back to the door. You feel safer here, underneath the awning. You paw at the door, peering through the glass but neither your mom nor the man are to be seen.

Moments later, you move back to the field and have an amazing discovery.

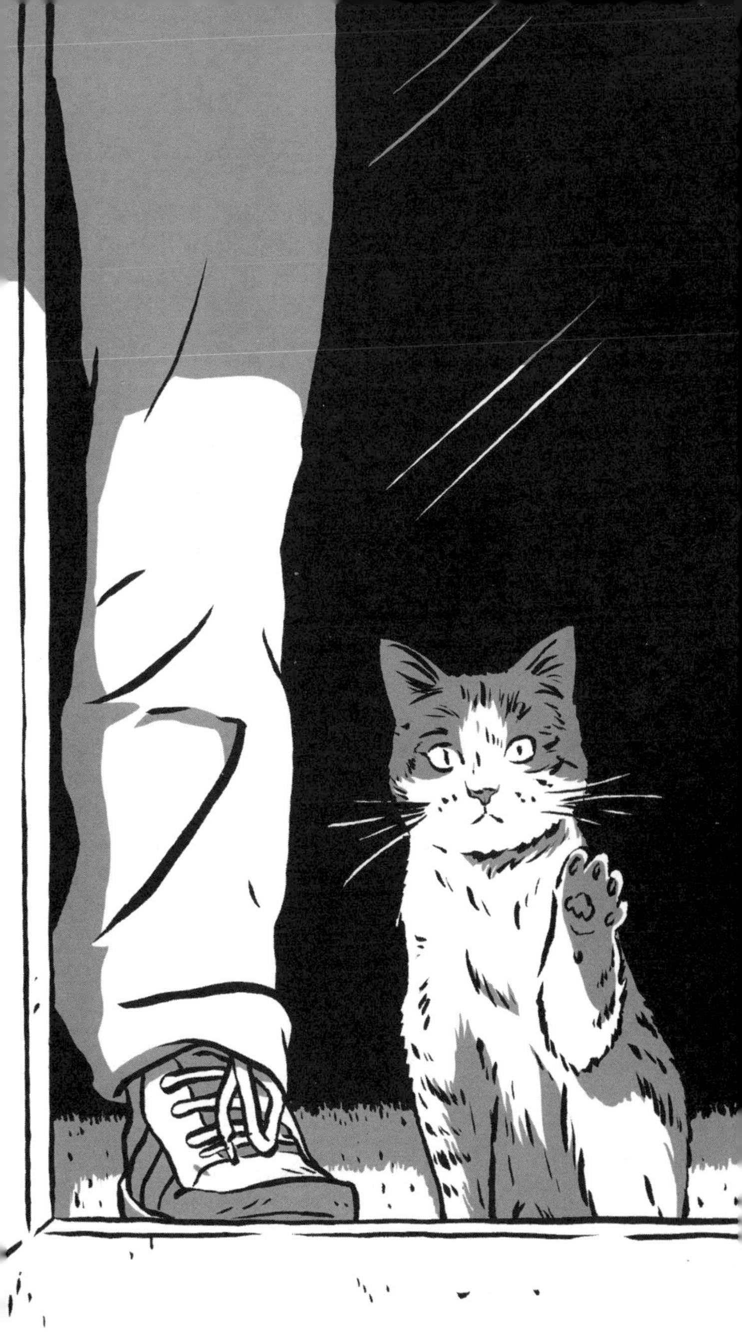

14

Out here, the sunbeam has *grown*. It's everywhere!

Until now you've only known the sunbeam by its daily journeys through the playpen and into the larger room beyond. It was a specific, focussed band of warmth, and when it was gone, it was gone until the next day, if it even decided to visit. But now you realize that it's everywhere. The thing in the world that most closely approximated your mom's love is not this limited quantity, but generous and infinite.

Love is everywhere.

For a long time, you bask in it. Outside, it's not nearly as warm as it is inside, but it comforts you as you squint into its overwhelming light. Soon however, a fleecy white surface covers the sky, and the sunbeam disappears.

It begins to get cold. And barely perceptibly, darker. You don't like this.

What do you do?

If you decide to stay put, and hope that the man will come back and let you in, turn to page 9.

If instead you decide to take this opportunity to explore a bit, and venture out into the world, turn to page 149.

You look up at the wall as Tupac's furry black ears make an appearance. Proudly he mounts the edge, but immediately falls! What's worse — while letting out a terrified squeak, your brother falls onto *you.*

You dig yourself out from underneath him. Being a kitten is a rough and tumble kind of life, so you are used to this sort of thing, but breaking Tupac's fall was a little much.

As Tupac pauses to take in the entirety of the room, you notice something.

Uh oh.

Your mom wakes at Tupac's squeak. Her eyes widen, and immediately she drops down from the couch and moves over to you. She gently bites the scruff of your neck and she jumps easily back into the pen, dropping you.

A moment later Tupac is returned to the pen as well. She gives both of you head nuzzles and licks.

Out of nowhere, one of your sisters jumps on your tail!

You run wildly, and she chases you with the same freneticism.

Minutes later, the wall and the outside world are completely forgotten.

Turn to page 23.

Moving quickly, you sneak past your snoozing mom. You can't get over how cavernous the room is. You never even saw all of it.

As you make your way forward, you stumble into the sunbeam.

Everything is bright and white in it. Tiny motes of dust float around you, and you half close your eyes to revel in it. Special and warm, the sunbeam is the closest thing to your mom's warmth.

But then, a distant noise snaps you out of your reverie.

The room you are in leads to a long hall with various doorways. You leave the sunbeam to indulge your curiousity. Sticking close to the wall, you peer around a corner into one of these doorways.

The man sits in a chair, at a desk. His hands move on the desk and you can't see what he's doing, but you hear a minute clicking noise.

The man grunts to himself, disgusted.

"I can't believe..." he mutters. "This isn't... this is such bullshit. She just... she's fucking around again."

Curious about the room, you make your way in. There's a large bed here and you are very interested in the vast dark space underneath.

At the movement, the man glances over at you.

"Fuck!" he swears. "Fucking cats!" Abruptly, he pushes the chair back from the desk.

You freeze.

For a moment you consider dashing underneath the bed, but then the man starts clucking with his tongue, making a friendy noise. His face, which had been a grimace of anger a moment ago, settles into an impassive mask.

"Kitty," his voice goes singsong. "C'mere, shithead."

The man slides out of the chair and onto the carpeted floor. On his knees, he shuffles slowly toward you.

He beckons with his hand, fingers flicking and mesmerizing.

Would you rather ignore him and keep exploring the room? Turn to page 6.

If you would prefer to pounce on the hand, as if it were prey, jump away on page 19.

18

The man grabs you around your tiny body and lifts you into the air. You cry out. It's always terrifying to be so high up.

You are brought close to his face and he peers at you.

"Goddamn cats," he mutters. Slowly his grip increases pressure until you're uncomfortable.

Your meow is muffled. It's hard to breathe!

"Don't stray, shithead." The man releases his grip and you can breathe again.

You are dropped back into the pen.

Your mom is there. She is tense. She licks your fur for a long time before you are calm enough to take a nap.

Such excitement!

Turn to page 23.

Before you can do anything, however, the man's hand darts at you, quick as a lightning strike. Immediately, he has a hold of you.

You struggle, mewling, but his grip is unyielding.

He walks you to another room you have never been in before, where he opens a drawer and rummages around for something. All you hear are crinkly rustles.

Suddenly, your mom is there below you.

Mom is meowing at the man, pawing at his pants. With his foot, he pushes her aside.

The man snaps open a white plastic bag and then tosses you inside.

Now your mom is hissing. You don't know if you've ever heard her make that sound before. Something is really wrong.

The bag is kind of nice. It cradles you, and the gentle swing is calming.

"Fuck this," the man whispers. "Fuck you. Fuck everything."

After a moment, the sound outside the bag is different.

Your mom is gone. Instead, you are hearing a generalized hum, and tiny, intriguing chirps in the background.

The air is cold. Not unbearably, but colder than you are used to. And a short gust of wind swirls into the bag you're in, tickling your whiskers.

What is going on?

Turn to page 20.

20

After hearing a loud thunk, it's quiet again. Are you back inside? The man has hung the bag up on a hook, and you move around the slippery interior trying to get upright. To your delight, you discover that your claws, tiny as they are, are more than sharp enough to tear through the bag's skin, which you do now.

Suddenly, there is a huge growl.

You freeze.

In the bag, you sway and are flung around. You have never experienced anything like this. It's not the man moving you — it's something else. You are *in* something that's moving. Once you've determined that the growl wasn't made by anything threatening you, you cut away at the bag, creating a shredded opening wide enough to see through.

What you see amazes you. It's almost too crazy to process.

You are moving at an incredible speed. The outside world is blurry and zipping along furiously fast.

You close your eyes for a moment. The bag sways gently. You thump occasionally against the window.

At one point, the vehicle stops, and you peek through the hole again. A car sidles up to you and there are people inside! A woman glances over at you, then looks away. A moment later, she takes another look, and frowns.

You're off again. The woman slides out of view.

You drive for awhile longer, until the man eases the car to a stop.

The low growling — which sounded like a purr — ceases.

"Well shithead," the man says from the front of the vehicle, "last stop."

You peek out your eyehole.

You see a moving surface, glittering in the sun.

In the front of the car, the man keeps talking, but you get the feeling that it's not to you. He takes on a familiar taunting tone — the kind he adopts when he's talking to the woman.

"Hey," he says, "it's me."

A pause.

"You'll never guess where I am."

The man gets out of the car, opens the back door and lifts the bag you're in. You shift around uneasily. You were just getting used to the gentle sway.

"This isn't a game. *You're* the one playing a game. And guess what — *you're* the one who left their email open this morning."

You're outside again. You hear a high, distant cry. You don't know what it is. In addition, there's a low, generalized rustling sound.

"Yeah, so I *know!* I saw those emails! What's going on? I thought we were okay?!"

The man is shouting. You flatten your ears and cower in the bag.

"*I'm* not the asshole here! Remember that! I *loved* you!"

The man takes a few steps. The air is moist.

"You're the one who's making me do this! I want you to see I'm serious about this!"

The man swings the bag. No longer a gentle sway — you are pressed into the bottom at the end of every arc. You don't like this. It's uncomfortable.

"Do what? You'll find out — when you come home and *apologize* to me."

The man makes an inchoate scream.

There is a sudden, intense acceleration. You feel

ill. You don't know which way is up or down anymore. Your stomach lurches. At the end of the bag the man's hand is a taut fist, knuckles white as he spins and hurtles you —

A split-second later, you realize that you're in the air, unleashed from the man's hand.

But that moment of calm is short-lived as you slam into a floor of flowing water!

Turn to page 24.

Days pass by simultaneously slowly and quickly in the playpen. Over time, you master jumping from one cat tree to another. Mom teaches all of you to hunt by having you pounce on a toy mouse. The man and the woman argue a lot. Their heated exchanges occasionally compete with the thunderstorms that terrify you and the other kittens.

And one miraculous day, the playpen walls are removed. At first, none of you dare to venture past the point where the walls once stood, but once Tupac trots over to the sliding glass door and looks out, you all go crazy and run around. Soon, the rest of the apartment is your playground, and this seems like a natural and utterly appropriate growth of your territory. You learn the wonders of the space underneath the bed, and discover the marvel of the bed itself, this giant plateau of soft and grippable land.

And then a day later, you decide to expand your territory even more — when the woman opens the sliding door to have a smoke, you dart out between her legs!

"Hey!" the woman yells, dropping her cigarette.

But she's too late. You run out into the yard and underneath the fence. By the time she makes it out there, you've already ducked underneath another fence and have hidden in some bushes. She searches for you for a long time, shaking treats, even bringing your mom outside on a leash. But you elude them all. Finally, they go back inside and you move back towards the alleyway.

Now your territorial expansion and curious exploration can begin!

Turn to page 184.

For a moment, you can't think — stunned as you are from the shock of hitting the water.

You've fallen from the very top of the cat tree before, but then only onto the springy and forgiving blankets. You hit the river a whole lot harder, and it takes more than a moment to shake the cobwebs out.

And then when you do, panic grips you. You are colder than you have ever been, and only the pale thin membrane of the bag prevents the freezing, teeming tide from getting at you.

The steady, terrifying thrum of your own blood beats in your ears. Small plumes of condensed air stream from your nostrils. You don't know what these clouds are. You have never encountered them before! You want to cry but you are too shocked by your circumstances to do anything.

But after a moment, when nothing happens, you calm down. The sound of your panting echoes in the bag. You shiver uncontrollably, but the panic subsides.

A sudden homesickness seizes you. You want to be back in your cuddlepile — inhaling the familiar smells of all the other kittens. Even the slight annoyance when one of your sisters kicks you in the head with her hindleg; you want more than anything to feel that now — every single being that comprises your entire world warming you. How can you get back to them? You don't even know if that's *possible*.

All you know is that water is slowly filling the bag from somewhere underneath you.

It might be from the eyehole you made!

Suddenly, a huge beast fills your vision. It screeches a loud warning in your face. Its wings beat furiously, keeping it aloft. Instinctively, you throw your paws up. Can you attack it? The wind from its wings fan the thin bag, collapsing the walls.

You're sinking! You need to make a decision!

If you want to claw your way out,
scrabble furiously to page 34.

If you decide to just stay still and do nothing,
curl into a fetal ball on page 42.

Or, if you cry out for your mommy,
peal petulantly to page 129.

You extricate yourself from the towel. Your fur is all floofy, but dry. You stand on the towel and try to figure out how you're going to get down to the ground. It's a long way.

As the man purrs, his chest rises and falls and the rhythm is comforting. You move down his body to the couch.

Oh, you think. *You like this. You could get used to this.* With your claws in the couch, you discover you can navigate with extraordinary facility. And though the distance between the couch cushions and the floor is disconcertingly far, you manage to climb down most of the way, only falling a little bit near the end.

The smell of the other cat is strong here. It's a very different scent than that of your mom, or anyone else in your family. It hovers over everything in the room like a fog.

There is a room just off the room you're in. You're curious about it because a sunbeam shines in through the window there.

You walk over to it and a thin breeze draws your attention to an additional discovery: there is a tiny port in a tall door here. It's not very far off the ground, and with a little jump you can access it. Reaching up, you push upon it, experimentally, and it gives way.

The smell of the other cat is *very* strong here. Everything is telling you that you should leave. Your instincts tell you not to get caught here. This cat flap might be your way out.

If you decide to use the little door to escape the house, turn to page 149.

If you'd rather take your chances inside, go to 40.

You watch the creature swim. It's rather hypnotic, the way it sways and shimmies.

When it sees you, it turns away. But it always turns back round and gets close again. An almost endless rhythm.

"I don't think he's gonna do it," the man whispers.

"I can't look," the girl says, hands over her eyes. "Tell me when it's over."

You put one paw up on the pan, to get a closer look, but your weight almost tips the pan up and onto you!

You jump back. Water splashes onto you, and spills all over the floor.

"Eli!" the girl screams. "Is Eli okay?"

The man laughs.

"Okay, okay," he concedes. "We'll try something else."

Turn to page 28.

The man comes over and takes the pan away. Wait! Where is the creature going?

The man leaves you alone with the girl, but she doesn't look at you. She is staring at a rectangular wafer in her hand. She taps on it with her finger. What is so interesting?

You spend the next few moments licking the water off yourself.

Abruptly, the wafer makes a noise. Then it stops, and the girl brings it up to the side of her face.

"Federal Bureau of Missing Cats," she says quickly, as if it were one long word.

There is a brief silence while the girl bends her head slightly and presses the wafer into her ear.

"Oh, hi Ms. Xeroulis... yeah. No, we need a blanket, or a favourite toy... the idea is that it's a familiar smell, so if we get a sighting, we can respond to it and smell familiar to your animal... okay, yeah. We can pick it up tomorrow, sure... Okay. Thanks! Thank you! Yeah, good-bye."

The man returns carrying something in his arms, which he unfolds onto the floor. When it is finally set-up, you see that it is a kind of pen. It reminds you a little bit of the playpen from home, except the walls of this one are clear, and the available room is about half the size of what you're used to.

"Did you get a call?" the man asks the girl. "I'd already set up the forwarding."

"Oh yeah. That was Ms. Xeroulis. She has a scent sample ready. I told her we can pick it up tomorrow."

"Oh that's good," the man replies, disappearing back into the house. "We'll be in that neighbourhood tomorrow anyways."

When the man returns, he has his hands clasped

together, as if he were holding a treat.

Could it be a treat? You are instantly interested and you follow his hands with your eyes.

He moves over to the pen, then loosens his grasp, dropping something small and grey down into it!

You stare, transfixed.

At first it doesn't move. The creature stands stock-still for what seems like forever. Then it straightens up and looks around, shiny black eyes taking everything in, nose pulsing and whiskers trembling. When it sees you, it scampers to the other side of the pen. But there is nowhere to escape to. It's visibly agitated.

"Oh god," the girl says.

The man kneels down beside you and brings his hand over to your face. You sniff it. You smell the creature. You find the smell very intriguing, though it's unfamiliar.

You press your nose against the glass, and watch the creature. Unconsciously, you crouch down, trying to lower your profile.

Gently, the man lifts you up, and drops you into the pen!

Now there is nothing standing between you and the creature. You watch as it moves back and forth along the far wall. When it hits a corner, it tries to climb it, but the walls are smooth and clear.

The man moves closer to it, and then with his hand, he pounces quickly on it!

It makes a squeaking noise.

When you hear it cry, something inside you leaps.

The man holds the creature down for a moment, then lets it go.

"Like that, kitten. That's how you do it."

On the far end of the pen, the mouse is trying to

jump out. It can get halfway up the wall, but then falls back to the floor.

The man moves his hand over to you so you can smell the creature on it.

"Go get it!" he urges.

If you leap on the man's hand, turn to page 36.

If you go pounce on the mouse, turn to 32.

If you decide to do nothing, turn to page 52.

You wake up on top of the man. He is still purring.

Upstairs, Sofia is crying. It is a sad, mournful sound. She lets out a howl which arcs and peters out. She pauses to catch her breath, then does it again. Will she ever stop?

The man doesn't seem to hear it, but you can, and it's bothering you.

Why does the cat hate you so much? You think you know why. This whole house is her territory, and you don't belong here. And yet, you're here on the man's chest, and she's upstairs locked in a room.

You didn't ask for this. You didn't ask for *any* of this!

You want to show the man you're upset. You want to wake him up. You want him to do something about Sofia. You want to go home to your family. You want to see your mom and Tupac again, and cuddle in the kittenpile, snoozing in the sunbeam. You just want things to be wonderful again.

You're going to show the man how you feel.

If you pee on him, find release on page 57.

If you go hide and never come out, turn to 84.

If you decide to scratch his face, turn to page 86.

You decide to go for it and pounce!

But you jump more into the *air* than at your terrified prey, and the girl bursts out laughing at your antics.

"Oh, he's so cute!"

You land awkwardly after your leap and lose your balance, running into the wall and steadying yourself against it to remain upright. Looking around for the mouse you discover that it has already scurried to the other side of the pen.

But the scent of it — so close — has given you renewed vigour. It practically *reeks* of fear.

Your blood thrums at the scent.

This time, as you move in, you watch carefully. At the last second, it scrambles to the right and you move with it, only leaping once you are close enough to snag it with your claws and bring it to your mouth.

And you have it!

You are amazed by the size of it — it doesn't even all fit in your mouth.

"He's got it!" the man crows.

The mouse throbs, its furiously beating heart pulses against your tongue.

You bite down to eat it.

As you do, it squeaks, and a warm fluid fills your mouth.

Your teeth aren't very large, but they are sharp. Soon the beating heart of the mouse slows, then stops.

"Oh, gross!" the girl says. "Joe, this is gross. You've got to stop this."

"I guess you're right," the man concedes. "He's probably not old enough yet for solid food."

You chew on the mouse flesh. It's rather tough in some parts. Still — this is the biggest thing you have ever caught! You feel amazing!

Then the man is there, tugging on the mouse's limp tail.

"C'mon kitten," he urges, stroking your back and pulling on the mouse, "let it go."

He wants it! He wants your prize! You bite down harder, and emit a low growl.

Despite her squeamishness, the girl laughs at this. "Oh, he's a little lion!"

Finally, you release your jaws. As the man pulls it away, you get a glimpse of your handiwork — the lifeless thing has all these puncture wounds in it, and its eyes are cloudy and still.

Your first kill. You marvel at this development.

"Are we done?" the girl asks.

"Not quite yet," the man grins. "One last test. Or *treat,* depending on who you ask."

Turn to page 54.

34

Furiously, you dig at the white skin of the bag with your nascent claws. Small as they are, they're sharp as new razors. But immediately river water springs in! The fluid floods the bottom of the bag.

You recoil from the wet tide, but there's nowhere to go. Your paws are wet, your tail is wet. Even your ass is wet.

You cry out in desperation and fear. And you hear a loud screeching cry in response.

The beast is still out there! It swoops in for the kill!

You stare at its terrifying face, but then it does something totally unexpected —

It grabs the loops of the bag in its beak, and with a powerful push of its wings, it drags you aloft!

Turn to page 147.

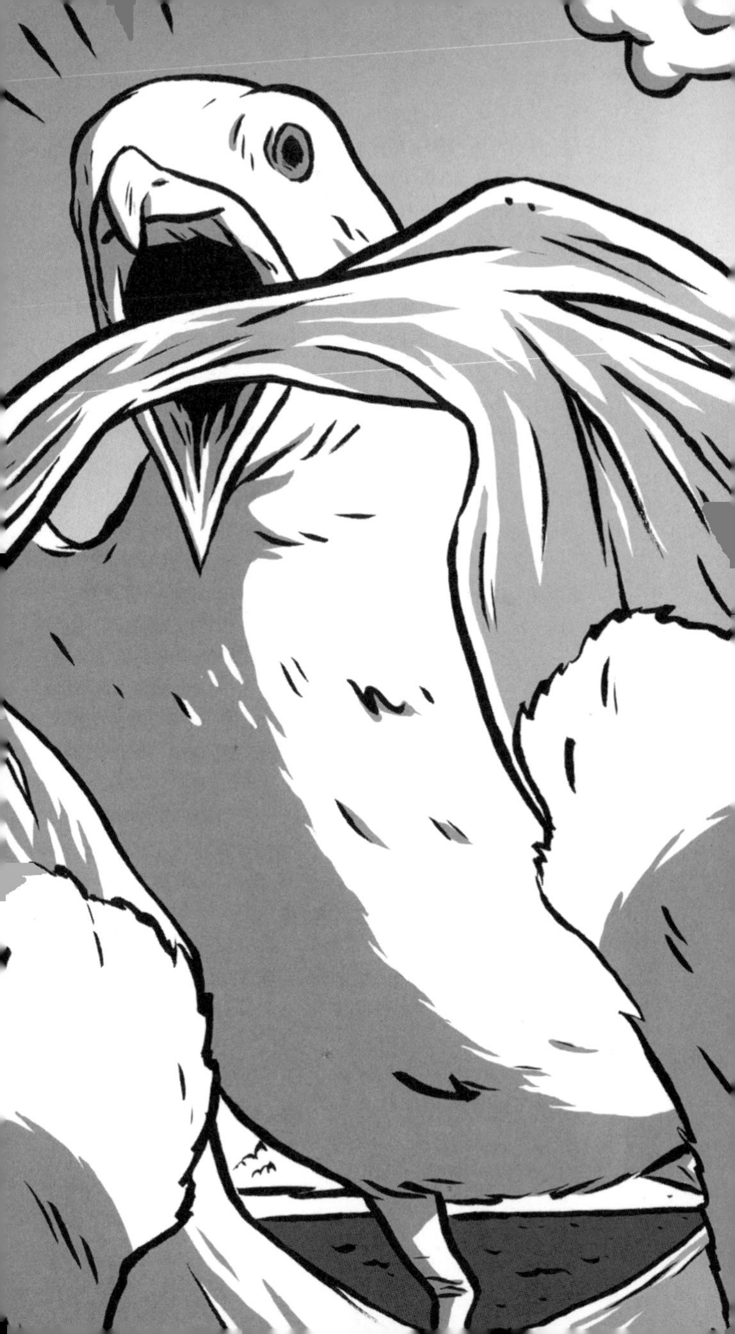

36

You pounce on the man's hand! You gnaw at his wrist and wrap your paws around it.

"Ah!" the man shouts, then jerks his hand back.

Behind him, against the wall, the girl laughs.

Then the man chuckles too.

"Well, at least he's learning *some*thing," he says, then points at the mouse. "But you need to attack the *right* thing."

Do you leap on the mouse?
Turn to page 32.

Or, you can decide to do nothing
on page 52.

When you wake up, you're not sure where you are.

You feel like you've slept forever.

You realize you're cradled in a box of some kind. You like it a lot, this box. Underneath you is a soft white padding that you've covered in baby-fine kitten hair.

After a moment, you try to get out of the box. It's difficult, because you were sleeping on your back, but you manage to shift your weight enough to tumble out.

Beside you is a door with a sizable gap at the bottom of it. On the other side you hear the man purring.

You reach underneath the door, and scrape your claws against the other side.

The man stops purring momentarily, but starts again a minute later.

Then you have the sudden, unmistakable awareness that you are being watched.

The fur on your neck stands on end and the odour of the other cat floods your nostrils. The other cat is close!

You feel it looking at you.

If, though you are afraid, you turn to look, move to page 74.

If you decide to pretend you smelled nothing, claw again underneath the door on page 53.

If you decide to just go back to sleep, turn to 78.

38

You are only dimly aware of what happens next as you move in and out of consciousness.

The man is slapping you on the back, trying to force water out of your mouth.

Then he tilts your head back, holds your jaw shut and breathes into your nose.

His mouth is so warm. Water drips from his lanky hair and tickles your whiskers.

Finally you are on your side. You can feel the hard ground against the length of your body. He presses and releases your chest. Is he kneading you? Sometimes your siblings do this to each other, when mom isn't around to do it to.

You cough.

You blink. Your eyes flutter open and everything is blurry.

It hurts to inhale. You immediately start shivering.

The man picks you up, cradling you in his arms.

Suddenly, you are inside.

Or rather — you're inside something moving. You jolt into motion. You're used to it by now, and anyway, you don't have much choice.

"Thanks for cranking the heat," the man holding you says.

"No problem," another man says from the front of the vehicle. "It's your dime."

You pass out. All this is too much to take.

When your eyes open next, you're in a warm towel. The man holds you against his chest. He is purring loudly. You're feeling a lot better now — warm and dry. But you're very hungry.

You glance around the room you're in. There is the distinct scent of another cat.

*If you decide to explore the room,
and maybe find food, turn to page 87.*

*If you want to play with the purring man,
turn to page 50.*

*If you are interested in meeting
this other cat, turn to page 26.*

Leaving the cat flap behind, you move to explore the rest of the kitchen. In a corner, there are a couple of bowls that smell very interesting.

One has water in it! Thirstily, you lap at the fluid. When you're sated, you sniff at the other bowl. Dark, crusty food cakes the bottom corners of it. A few nuggets remain.

You are still new to solid food. You've tried it, but it hurts your mouth. The wet food the woman occasionally gave you was really good, though.

You draw a nugget into your mouth with your tongue and give it a munch. It's still very hard, but you swallow it. Then you go back to the water bowl. The food is very salty. It does, however, remind you of your mom. The way her mouth would smell sometimes after she ate.

Suddenly, there is a loud, high sound that echoes through the entire house.

Ding-dong!

You freeze.

The man in the other room groans awake. You watch him rise on the couch, then shrug on his pants as he ambles to the front door and opens it.

Turn to page 43.

Thankfully, when you enter the house, Sofia isn't there.

You are so angry at her though that you go to the kitchen and eat from her bowl. She'll be mad at you, but you are so mad at her that you envision yourself fighting back, howling and hissing at her. So much so that she gets scared and backs off and leaves you alone forever.

You drink from her water bowl as well.

The memory of the man lying still in the street haunts you. It was weird how still he was. Not breathing. Not purring. Nothing.

You jump up onto your computer desk seat again. It's covered in your orange hair. Sometimes the man cleans your hair off of things, but never from this chair.

You nap for a bit, exhausted.

Then, you hear a sound!

It's Sofia, but she merely jumps up onto the couch and curls up in a corner. She never even looks at you — which is good.

Hours and hours pass.

The sunbeam is streaming through the front windows when you awake.

You hear a noise at the front door.

Turn to page 133.

Against all your instincts, you try to calm down. You close your eyes and settle into a small little ball. You are cold, but calm.

The bag drifts fitfully along the river. Where will it take you?

You're aware that water is coming into the bag from somewhere.

Thankfully the beast is gone. You can still hear its cries, but from a distance.

Then the top of the bag collapses down in a gust of wind. The breeze tickles the tips of your ears and you squint into the bright air. You yelp in frustration and desperation.

On the shore, you see a figure. He is blurry and unfocused, but he clearly turns at your cry and sees you.

"Oh my god!" you hear him yell.

He drops something off his back and kicks some things off his feet.

As water fills the bag and you feel it saturating your fur, you see the man dive into the river!

You let out one more cry before you go under.

Cold envelops you. You *inhale* the cold. You try to cry out again but you can't.

Turn to page 38.

A dark-haired girl walks in, and closes the door behind her.

"How come you didn't answer your cell?" she asks the man.

"It was wet," he answers. "I'll have to get a new one. We'll have to use yours for the time being — have the hotline calls forwarded. Is that okay?"

"Sure. But wet *how?*" The girl dumps a bag on the floor and flops down on the couch. "Did you drop it in the toilet?"

The man walks out of the room and into the kitchen, calling over his shoulder. "I forgot to take it off me when I jumped into the river!"

"What?! What hap — " The girl gets up and starts for the kitchen, when she sees you. "Uh, Joe. You have a strange cat in here."

The man emerges from the kitchen drinking something from a large jug. He looks at you. "I know."

You don't like this — everyone looking at you. You move underneath a low table and look for a hiding spot. Maybe under the couch? You hadn't noticed until now how attractively low and dark it was. But you'd have to cross the entire living room floor to get there, and you feel exposed enough.

Still — after a second's hesitation, you run as fast as you can under the couch. There, that's better, you think as you slide into its safety.

"He was in a plastic bag floating in the canal," the man says. "I have no idea why or how. But I heard him crying, and so I jumped in the river to get him."

The girl laughs. "You're crazy. What were you doing out there?"

"My morning walk. Normally I don't go down that far. Kitten's lucky."

The girl is now sitting on the floor. Her movements are very slow. She is trying not to look directly at you, but you can tell she is monitoring your general direction. Now she slides onto her belly and starts slowly inching over to you. One of her hands is outstretched.

The man laughs.

Now the girl makes eye contact, then looks away again. She makes a little clucking noise with her mouth. "Kitten," she sings, "hello, kitten. Pleased to meet you..."

Eventually she reaches you and you sniff her outstretched hand.

"Hey honey," she whispers. "I'm Dashiell."

The girl scoots a little closer and you let her pet you. She seems nice and her hands smell nice too. Gently, she pulls you toward her, then, without warning, she lifts you into the air, rolls on the floor, and hugs you to her chest! "Woop!" she sings.

You panic momentarily, meowing loudly, but the girl continues stroking your back, and everything becomes stable again. You settle on her chest and calm down, but not completely. Too many abrupt happenings here.

"Wow," the girl says, looking you over, "he's really young."

"Yeah," the man concedes. He sits on the couch and continues drinking from the jug. You wonder what's in the jug. You want to drink it too. "That makes me sad. I'd say he's on the borderline. He might still be nursing. His teeth are barely in."

"What are you going to do? Do you think Sofia will take to him?"

The man snorts.

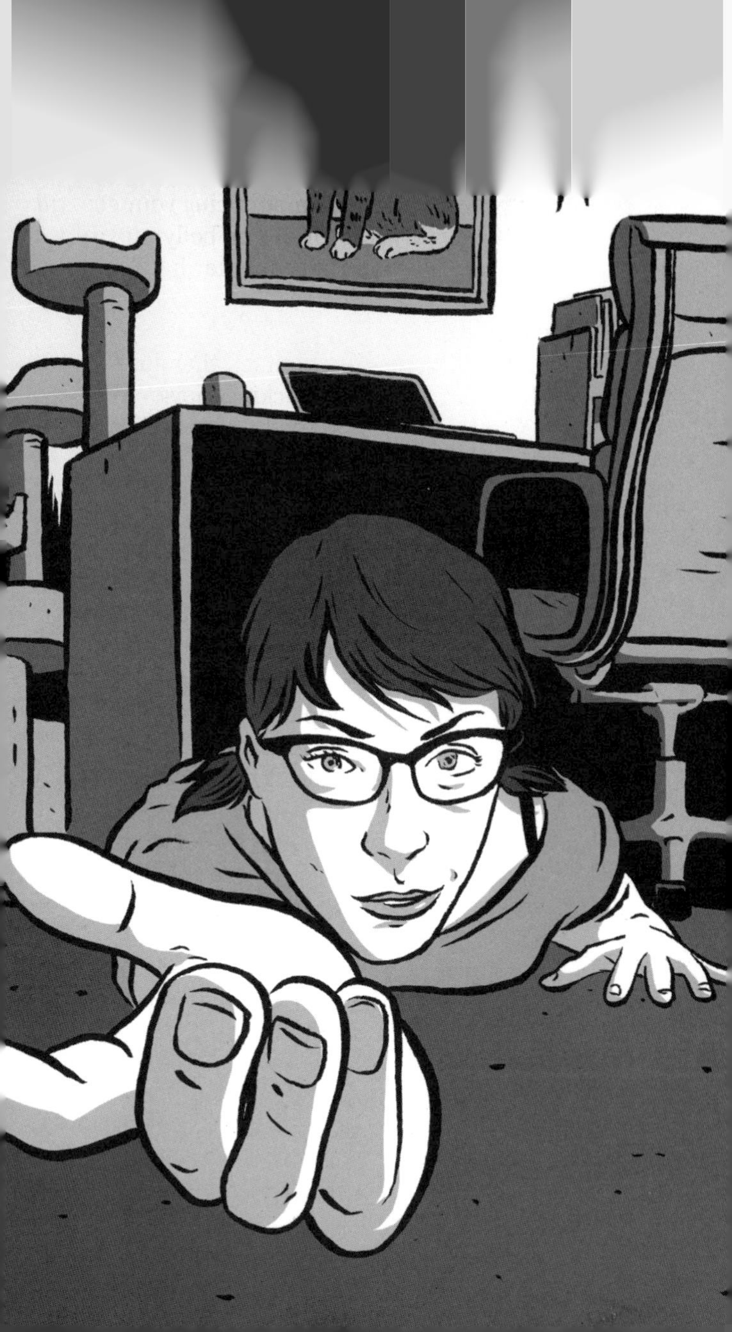

46

"Sofia? She's a little jealous. You know that. You remember when I catsat for Tori last year? I came home smelling like another cat..."

"What are you *talking* about?" the girl scoffs. "Coming home smelling like other cats is your *job*."

"Yeah, but those are mostly superficial smells. And I keep all the scent samples in the garage. I spent a lot of *time* with Tori's cat."

"Where *is* Sofia, anyway?" the girl asks, looking around.

"Dunno," the man replies. "Out."

The man takes a final swig and puts the jug down.

"I may," he begins, "have to teach this one to hunt by myself. I can tell he's used to people. He's okay being handled, but someone has to teach him to hunt, like, before it's too late. And it might be already."

The man gets up.

"C'mon," he calls over his shoulder. "Bring him to the garage."

"Wait," the girl says. She holds you gently to her chest with one hand, while using the other to prop herself up. "Are we not patrolling today?"

The man opens a door to another room.

"Maybe. If there's time. But I can't really leave him alone with Sofia. Not yet, anyway."

The girl gets up and carries you into the other room. You're nervous.

It's cooler here. And darker. But the man yanks on a cord, and then the room is very bright.

"Dash, put him on the floor. I want him to get comfortable."

The girl places you on the ground, then steps away.

You don't like this, being all out in the open. You

move toward some tables and boxes against the wall.

"Aren't you afraid you're going to lose him in all your junk?" the girl asks the man.

"Not when he sees what wonderful toys I have for him."

The man places a shallow pan on the floor, then grabs a hose from the wall. He brings it over and fills the pan with water.

You back even deeper into the shadows while he does this.

When the pan is full, the man puts the hose away and goes back into the house.

"You're crazy, you know that?" the girl calls after him.

After a minute, the man returns with a mug. He kneels down by the pan and then dumps in the contents. You see a flash of orange.

"Oh god," the girl says. "Is that Eli?"

The man nods. "Sorry."

"Aw jeez," the girl pouts.

"They're called feeder fish for a *reason,*" the man says. "C'mon, let's back off a bit."

The man and the girl go to the wall and sit on a bench.

You are curious about the pan, and what's in it.

After a little while, you venture over.

"He's doing it!" the girl whispers.

"Shh!"

You stare at the little swimming thing in the water. It seems to sense you, because it swims away, but there's nowhere for it to go.

Soon, it ventures back, but then it senses you again, and once more moves to the other side of the pan.

48

You circle the pan, following it.

"I love this part," the man says. "This is the best."

"I love it less," the girl says pointedly. "I might like it more if only it weren't Eli."

"How come you like him so much?" the man asks.

"I dunno. Maybe 'cuz his name is *Eli*," the girl responds. "The second you give something a name you start to love it."

The creature moves nervously in the pan.

What *is* that?

You are full of conflicting emotions.

If you want to catch it, turn to page 58.

If you just want to watch it swim for now, turn to 27.

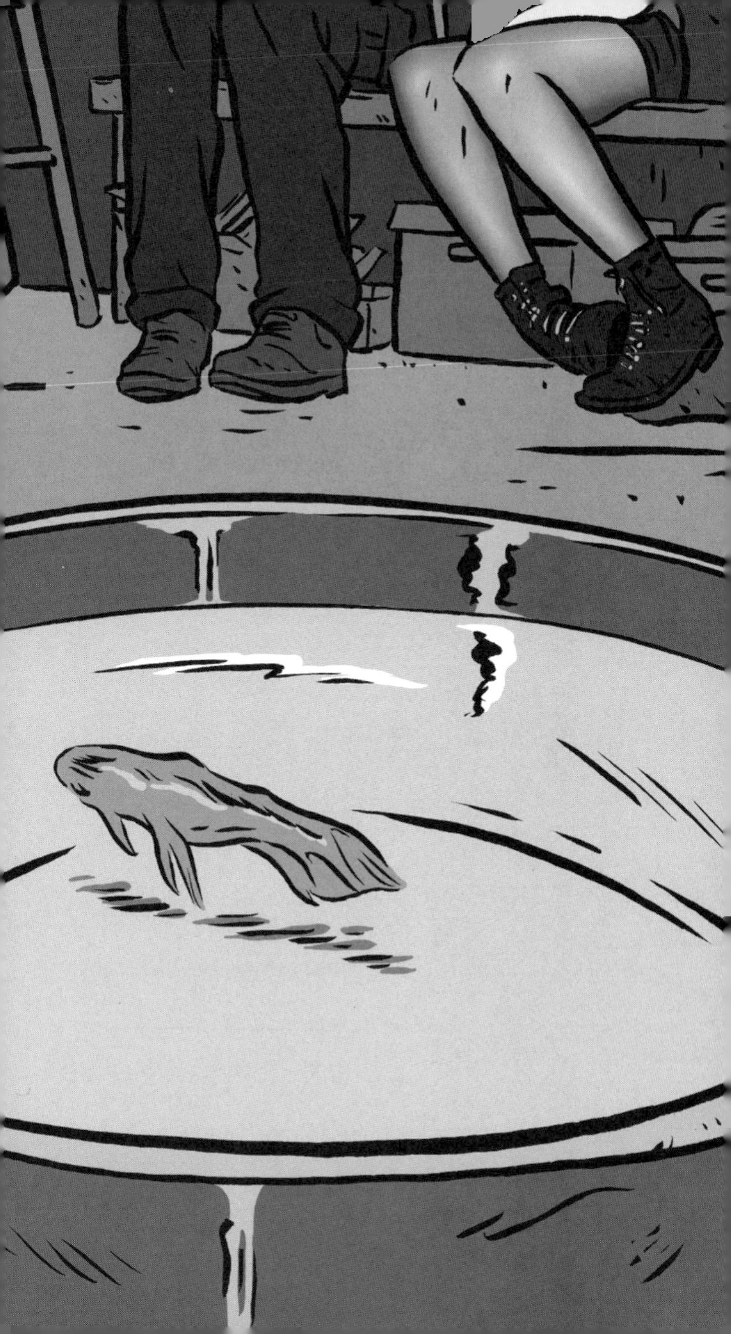

Once you're out of the towel, you move up to the man's face.

When you sniff his chin, he stops purring. His breath catches for a moment, but he keeps breathing steadily. You feel his exhalations like gentle breezes on your whiskers. You lick his chin. It's stubbly, and your rough tongue scrapes against it in a way that is pleasing to you.

A moment later, the man is purring again.

There's something on his face. You don't know what it is. A kind of structure resting on his nose. Maybe you could climb it.

You step up onto his mouth and pull at the thing.

Suddenly, the man moves. The purring stops. His head turns and you almost fall off!

You drop back to his chest, and the structure on his face falls and clatters on the floor!

"Wha — " the man touches his lips, then his face. He looks at you through half-closed eyes, then he glances at the fallen structure on the floor. With one hand, he strokes your back.

With his other hand, the man reaches down to the floor and picks up the structure, placing it back on his face.

"So, what are we gonna do with you?" the man murmurs to himself, smiling at you.

Suddenly, a loud, high sound echoes through the entire house.

Ding-dong!

From his hand, you bolt from the man's belly down to the floor. In your frantic need to find cover, you don't even notice how far you've jumped.

You find safety under a table, and you watch the man look over at you. He's laughing.

"Jesus, are you gonna do that every single time the doorbell rings?"

The man gets up, pulls on some pants, then pads over to the front door, which he opens.

Turn to page 43.

52

You stay on your side of the pen and the mouse does the same.

The mouse doesn't relax, but you do. Quietly, you observe it and make no move toward it.

"C'mon," the man urges. "Go for it."

You lick your paw and your chest, cleaning yourself. It's something you've watched your mom do.

"It's okay, kitten," the man says, drawing a soft hand along your forehead. "I know that this is probably very new and terrifying for you. Some cats don't hunt. It's not for everyone."

"So are we done?" the girl asks.

"Not just yet," the man says. He picks up the mouse and drops it in a cup, keeping his hand overtop. "I've got a trump card. La *crème de la crème*. I think it'll be impossible for the kitten *not* to get at least a little excited."

"This is weird, you know," the girl chides, "what you're doing — setting up this weird, cat gladiator arena thing."

"More like a *cat*iator arena?" the man allows himself a wry smile. "I prefer to think of it as a cat*muse*ment park."

The man leaves the room with the mouse, then returns a few moments later to deal with the makeshift playpen.

Turn to page 54.

With your arm still underneath the door, you scratch at the other side again. Maybe the man will wake up, and come play with you.

You can feel the other cat's eyes burning a hole in the back of your skull. You feel its breath along your back.

A harsh hiss fills your ears.

Despite yourself, you turn your head to see it...

Turn to page 74.

While the man folds up the pen, you wander around the garage. Along the far wall, you notice all these transparent bricks. They smell of faint chemicals, and are covered with a light dust.

You are surprised to discover that each brick has a small creature suspended inside it.

"You like that?" the man asks. He comes over and kneels down beside you. He points at different animals, in turn.

"These are all Sofia's. That's a hamster. Dunno where she got that one. Those are mice. That big one's a rat. Two crows. That one might even be a vole. That's a pigeon head. I don't know where the rest of it went — all I found was the head."

One brick doesn't have an animal in it; it has a small, red leaf.

"Haha," the man laughs. "That one? That was Sofia's first 'kill'. She got that one when she was just a little older than you are now." He pats you on the head.

"You are the weirdest man," the girl says.

"I know," the man says. "But this is what you do if you love cats."

"Is it?" the girl asks, a note of skepticism in her voice.

"Can you play with him?" the man asks her. "I'm going to prepare his *Final Challenge*."

The girl laughs. "Sure."

While the man busys himself with a small closet in the back, the girl comes and sits with you. She has a set of keys on a lanyard, and she shakes the long lead in your face. You jump on it, snagging the line as she whips it past you.

Finally, the man shuts the closet door at the back,

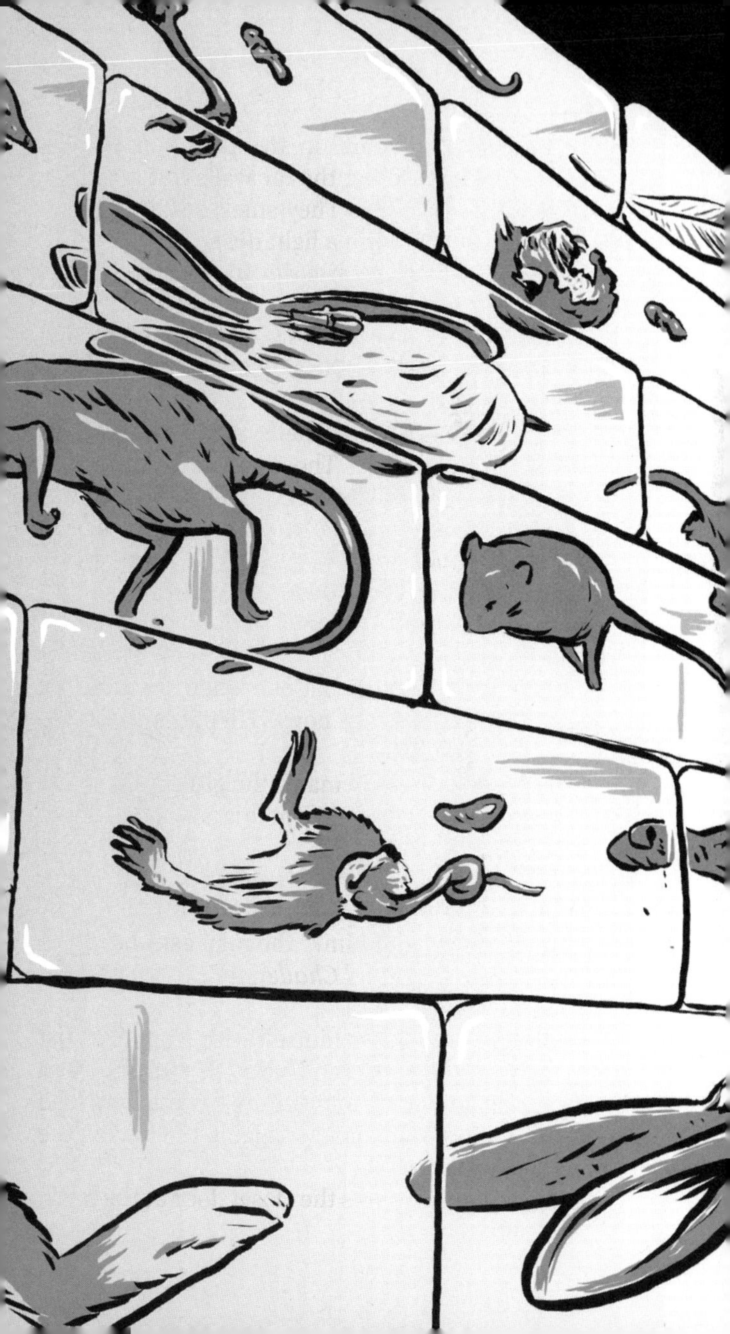

56

and smiles.

"It's ready," he says. "Bring him over."

The closet door has a small cat flap at the bottom and they place you right in front of it.

"Step on through, kitten," the man says. "This is a threshold that you have to cross yourself."

You pause. This is odd and weird and terrifying. There is something in the closet, and you don't know what it is. You don't want to go in. You don't feel safe.

"Aw jeez," the man mutters. "C'mon kitten." He nudges you with his foot.

"I thought you said he has to cross it *himself,*" the girl chides.

The man shrugs. "Fuck it." Without warning, the man pushes you through the cat flap with his foot!

You stumble into the closet and look around the bare room. There's nothing on the floor, but you sense a motion above you.

A bluebird sits on a perch high above you. It shifts its footing, nervously.

The room is quite dark, lit only by a small window — also high above you. There is a motion in the window and you see the man and girl's faces pressed up against the glass, staring down at you.

"C'mon kitten," the man says, voice muted. "Get the bird. You have to jump!"

If you decide to go after the bird, take your first jump on page 67.

If you're tired, and would rather stay still, hoping this will all end soon, turn to page 72.

Relaxing your bladder, you pee on the man's shirt. Then you walk gently down his belly and jump onto the couch.

He stops purring, and brings his hand over to the wet spot, patting it. He scratches it idly for a moment, then his eyes flutter open.

"What?" The man looks around confused. He glances at the ceiling. Then he spots you. You meet his gaze.

"Aw jeez," the man gets up. "Kitten!" He lifts you up and carries you into the kitchen and puts you on the floor. Then he peels his shirt off and pushes the wet spot into your nose. You back away.

"No!" he bellows. You startle at his sudden volume change and run back into the living room.

"Fuck," the man swears, wetting a paper towel and wiping his chest. "I need to find you a home."

The man disappears upstairs and you climb back up onto the couch, where you find a quiet corner and sleep.

Ding-dong!

The sound rouses you, but unlike last time, you don't run in panic. You are getting used to it.

The man comes downstairs and opens the front door.

The girl laughs as she steps inside. "What are you wearing?" she asks the man.

"Sofia's homicidal. She tried to kill the kitten last night. We got to bring him with us."

Turn to page 59.

58

You approach the pan and raise your paw, watching the creature. When it swims near, you bat at it!

But you miss.

Ripples spread across the surface of the water, and the backsplash gets all over your fur.

"Oh god," the girl says, "don't let him kill Eli."

"How's he going to learn then?"

"I *know* you have other things. Use one of those. Just not *Eli*."

The man sighs.

"Okay."

Turn to page 28.

The man comes over to you on the couch and picks you up. Holding you by the armpits, he slides you down along his chest facing outwards.

"Can you make sure his tail goes through the hole?" he asks the girl.

The girl is too busy laughing to respond, but she comes over and adjusts your feet and tail so that you're seated comfortably in a harness. When you're well-situated, she folds up a panel and clips it in place. It forms a kind of outside pocket that the man's strapped to his body.

"What is this? A baby bjorn?"

"It's a kitten bjorn," the man smiles. You feel the vibrations in the man's chest as he talks rumbling against your back. It's a nice little massage.

"Where'd you get something like that?"

"I had it made with that other outfit."

"What other outfit?" the girl asks.

"The Catnip Suit."

"What's that?"

"Oh that's right," the man chuckles, "you hadn't been hired yet. The Catnip Suit was this harebrained notion I had when I started this business. It's what you think it is."

"A suit made of catnip?"

"Close. A suit with a million pockets. Well, actually just pants. Pants with a million cargo pockets sewn all along and all around the legs. I'd pack all of them with fresh catnip in the mornings and then start walking in the alleys."

The girl laughs. "Did it work?"

"All too well," the man responds, shaking his head. "At one point I had like, thirteen cats chasing me."

"You must have looked like the Pied Piper of cats!"

The man chuckles. "It was nuts. They were chasing me and trying to climb up my legs. It was completely impractical. Eventually I had to just ditch the pants."

"Wait — you were just in your underwear?"

"Well, I ditched them close to home. Hours later, I went to get them back, but they were gone. Some drugged-out tom must've dragged it away."

"Where did you get the catnip?" the girl inquires. "That must have been expensive."

"I grew it in the backyard, actually. The entire garden was one crop. The only problem was — every morning there'd be like, eight cats, all lolling about, high as kites. It upset Sofia to have so many interlopers in her territory, so I killed all the catnip with bleach and vinegar."

Gravity keeps you sitting snugly in the harness, and you kind of like it. What you lose in personal mobility and agency is made up for in the view. You are not used to seeing the world from this height, and it strikes you that this must be how humans see the world. The girl glances at you.

"So cute!" the girl shrieks, then pulls out her rectangular wafer from her pocket. "Lemme take a picture."

"Aw jeez," the man demurs, but dutifully stands as the girl lifts the wafer to her face. What is she doing?

Suddenly, there is a bright white flash.

You blink and look away.

What the hell was that?

"Alright," the man says. "You ready?"

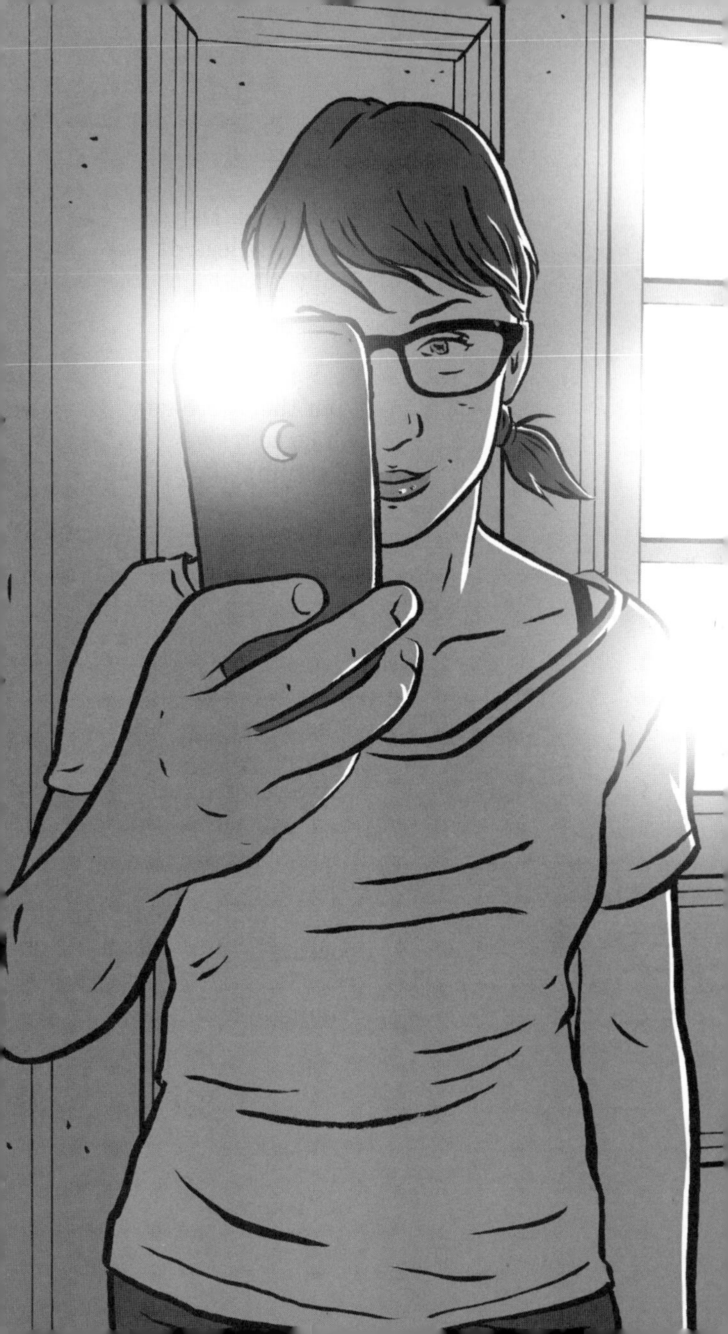

The girl nods.

"Oh shit," he says.

"What's wrong?"

"Sofia's still locked up in the bathroom upstairs. Could you go up and let her out? I'd do it myself, but I don't want her to see me with the kitten like this."

"Sure. I'll meet you outside."

The man shrugs on a backpack and walks out the front door. He goes down a short path and stands on the sidewalk, beside the street. You watch a car pass. Across the street a tree full of birds is chirping. You want to go and chase them. Suddenly, the harness which seemed so nice and comforting is a confining restraint. You fidget to get out.

"Kitten!" the man puts a hand over your belly, "Please!"

When the girl comes out, the man turns to her. "How is she?" he asks.

"None too pleased, as you might imagine," the girl says, "but she'll have the house to herself to chill out."

The man nods and they start walking.

The whole day is like this — a lot of walking. Fortunately, you're not doing any of it. You're just along for the ride. And it is a terrifying widening of your perception of what the world is. You had no idea the world was this vast. It is overwhelming. Because it's so much new information, throughout the day you take periodic naps.

The humans stop a lot. They put up posters. They take down posters. They take photos of other people's posters. They walk up streets and down alleys.

Around noon they stop by a house.

"Hey Ms. Xeroulis," the girl greets the woman

who comes to the door.

"Oh my," the woman makes eye contact with you and grins. "Who do we have here?" She brings her hand over to your cheek and gives it a rub.

"He doesn't have a name yet," the man explains.

The humans talk some more before the woman retrieves a small blue blanket. It is covered in cat hair and smells strongly of another cat. The girl pulls a clear plastic bag from her backpack and puts the blanket inside. Then she writes on the outside with a smelly marker.

Why are they doing this? Are they going to bring another cat back to the house? Isn't Sofia enough? The smell of the other cat unsettles and upsets you.

Soon, you leave the house, and the man and the girl turn down an alley.

The girl looks at her wafer and strokes her finger along its lit screen.

"Who's down this way?" the man asks.

"We've got two possibilities," the girl murmurs. "Booger and Sandwich."

"Who are the owners?" the man asks.

The girl pulls a small notepad from her jeans pocket and flips through some pages before she speaks.

"Booger is owned by a woman. Sandwich by a man."

"So I'll take Sandwich," the man says.

The girl nods. She puts the notepad away, then pulls a small container of food out of her backpack and starts shaking it. You look at the container. Is it treats? If it's treats, why isn't the girl offering you any?

"Booger!" she calls out in a clear voice. "Booger!"

"Sandwich!" The man and the girl start walking slowly down the alley. "C'mere Sandwich!"

As they move, they are constantly looking. Behind trashcans, under bushes, around fences. And every few minutes they'll stop, absolutely still. They won't speak or move for an uncomfortably long time.

"Did you hear something?"

"I think that was a baby crying."

Then they'll move again, shouting the same things over and over.

"Whoa," the girl stops. She puts a hand on the man's arm, then points down the alley. You follow her gesture and see a cat hanging out at the far end. She pulls off her backpack and reaches inside.

"You have your zoom lens?" the man asks.

The girl nods. She pulls out an enormous camera and lifts it to her face. She presses a button a few times, then she pulls out her wafer and turns the camera to it.

"Hurry," the man says.

"I know," the girl says. "I'm just time-stamping and geo-locating us."

Finally the humans are on the move again. But the cat has spooked, and is gone.

"Who'd it look like?"

"I think it's Booger," the girl says. "Same markings."

"I'll hang back then," the man says.

The girl nods and heads forward alone, towards the spot where you last saw the cat.

The man strokes your head while the girl shakes her container of treats, calling out Booger's name. She peers under the nearby fences, at one point even getting on her hands and knees. Finally she stands

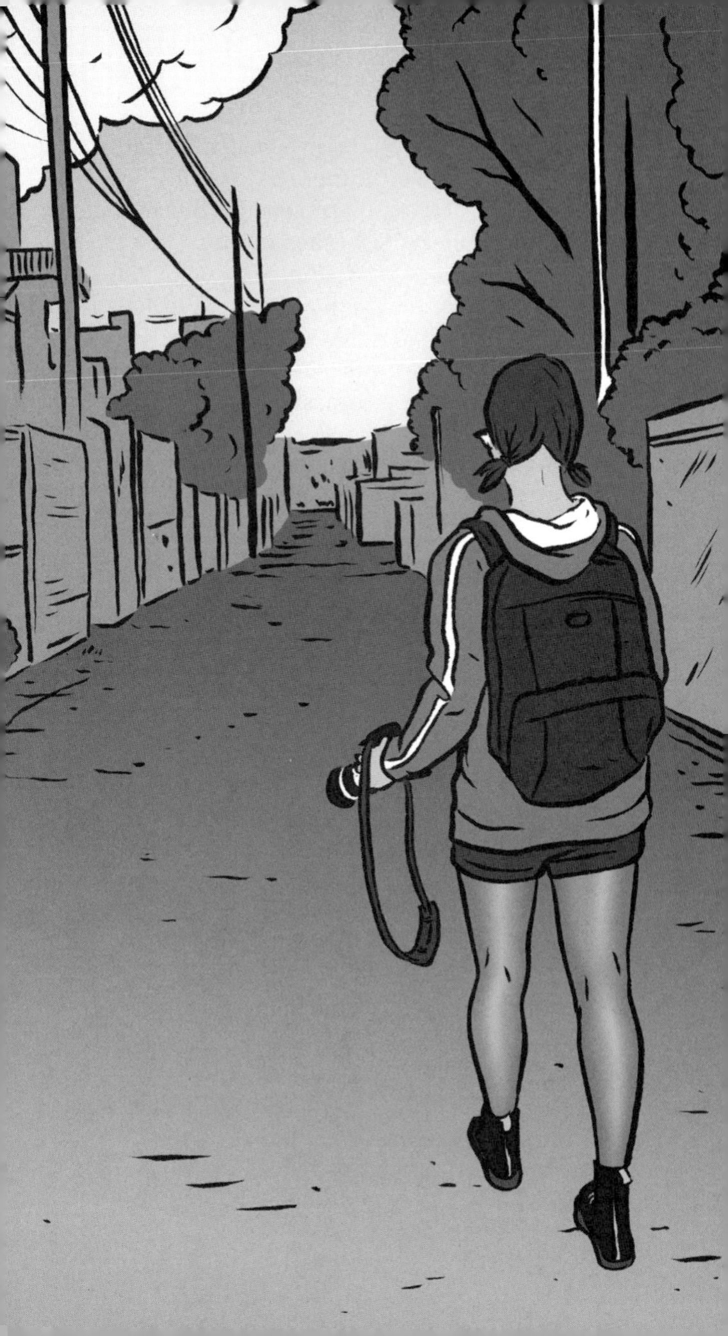

up, brushes herself off, looks at the man and says to him, "You think I should hop the fence?"

"God, no," the man says, walking toward her.

"I can make it," the girl protests. "It's not that high."

"It's not that. It's a safety thing. In the early days I used to crawl under decks, climb over fences — until I was confronted by a guy with a *gun* wondering what the *hell* I was doing trespassing on his private property."

"Jesus!"

"No, look," the man says, "at least we have a photo. We can get back and enhance it. Make a comparison. See if it's really him. We can at least let his owners know if he's alive or not."

The humans start walking again and you decide to take a nap since it's clear you're not getting any treats.

Turn to page 80.

This is your chance!

You've seen birds before, out in the world, flying in the sky, but they've always been very far away. Strange pinwheeling ciphers.

This is the closest you've ever come to an *actual* bird — other than the seagull that scared you half to death when you were stuck on the river in that flimsy white bag.

"You can do it!" the man calls to you, encouragingly.

You look up at the bird, whose tail flexes pleasingly. It shuffles along its stick.

The available perches stick out of the walls in a kind of random way. You wonder if you can jump up on to one and use it to climb higher.

Steadying yourself, your legs tense and your hindquarters wobble as you ready to launch yourself skyward.

Finally, when you can't take it anymore, you jump!

The bird takes off into the air, hovering in a panic near the ceiling, losing a couple of feathers in the process, which float down lazily to you.

You grab a perch, but it breaks off the wall, and clatters to the ground. The perches, you realize, are really flimsy.

After awhile, the bird, unable to stay aloft forever, drifts down onto another perch.

But now it has one fewer option.

This is a fun game. You leap again! You snag another perch, and once more the bird flutters like a maniac to the ceiling. It tires, then returns to a remaining perch.

Two sticks lie on the ground now, like bodies.

Now you're addicted. Over and over you leap into the air, bringing sticks down. Each time, the bird returns to another perch. Each time, its flight time is shorter than the last.

You're wearing it out. The bird is tired and weak. You're going to get it eventually!

"This is sick," the girl mutters.

"How else is he going to learn?"

"Why not just keep him indoors?"

"You know that's not much of a life for a cat."

"What about all of our clients?" the girl protests, "*Half* their cats are *indoor* cats!"

"*I* don't think it's much of a life."

Eventually, there are no perches left. The bird struggles to stay out of your grasp — even attempting to find purchase against the thin lip of the window ledge, but it slips off and is forced to flap its wings to survive.

You are hypnotized by the movement, and the anticipation of what comes next makes you salivate.

Flap by laboured flap, the bird gets bigger as it descends toward you. And when it's within reach, you don't wait — you make a final jump into the air and snag it!

Behind the door, the man cheers.

The bird doesn't fight you. Exhausted, it drops to the floor at your touch, almost welcoming you.

It's too big for you to fit completely in your mouth, so you go for its neck, where it's skinniest. Once your teeth dig into it, it struggles. You bat at it with your paw. It tries to escape again, but your rough tongue keeps it in place, and you press your paw against its stupid face.

It takes a long time for the bird to die, even af-

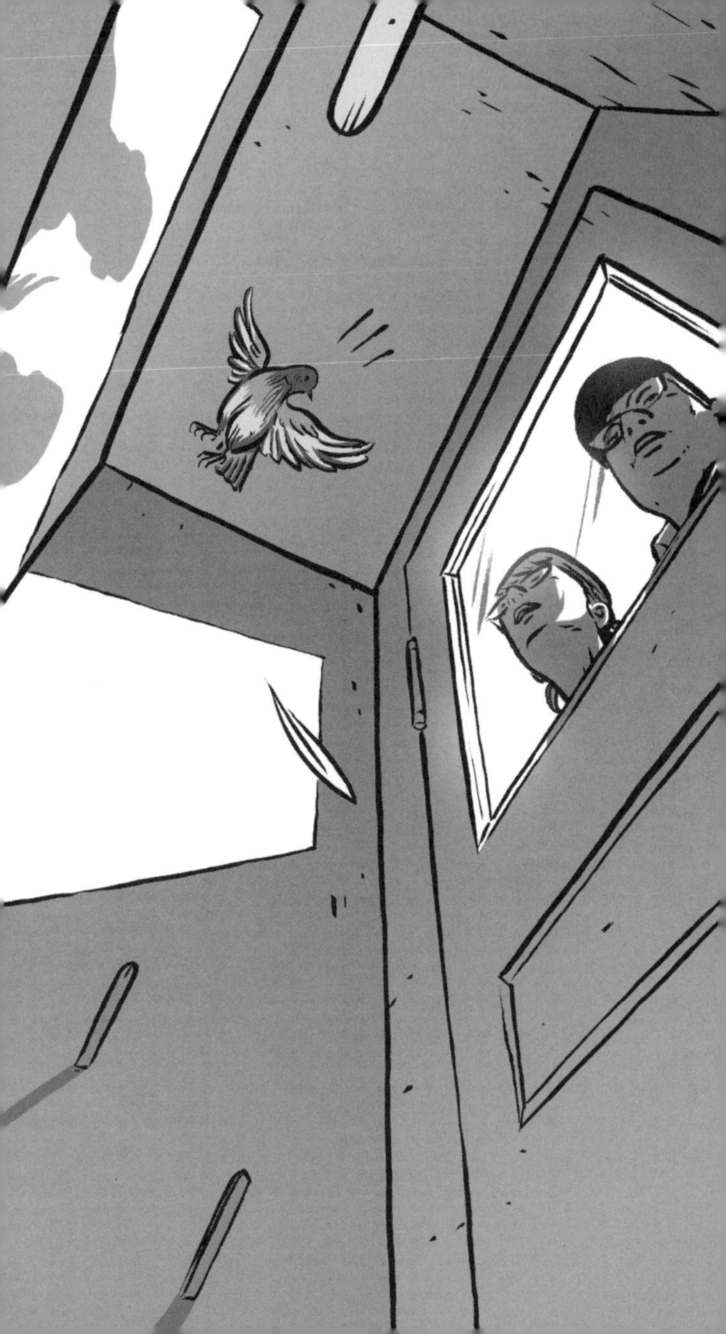

70

ter you rip into its neck. Then, after a final shudder, the bird is still. You knock it around the floor, leaving shiny smears of blood. You kind of don't want it to be dead yet, even though you are the one who killed it.

"This is fantastic," the man says. He opens the door behind you, and bends down to pat your back. "Outstanding! I better go buy more epoxy resin. You'll have your *own* trophy wall soon."

"Ugh," the girl says. "You know what? I don't know if I *feel* like patrolling today."

"Not today," the man agrees. "It's been a busy day. Tomorrow for sure."

You lick the blood off your mouth. It's tangy and tasty and warm.

"Can you take him into the other room while I clean up?" the man asks the girl.

The girl picks you up and takes you into the living room. "C'mon killer," she says.

Later, the man joins her and they talk late into the afternoon. After such a momentous day, the gentle murmur of their voices puts you to into an exhausted sleep.

Turn to page 37.

Still wary, you pad your way downstairs, then make your way up a cat tree, settling on the highest platform. If Sofia comes attacking, you want to be ready.

In the kitchen, the man leans up against the counter and the girl has her face pressed up against his. They are making eating sounds.

On the floor, one of the smelly drinks has fallen and the glass has shattered, resulting in a large purple puddle. The smell of the wine fills the room and it is both unpleasant and heady.

Sofia sits on the arm of the couch, staring at them.

Then the doorbell rings, startling everyone.

The girl and the man stop kissing for a second.

"I should get that," the man says.

"Let's go upstairs," the girl replies.

"I should clean this up," the man looks at the mess on the floor.

"Let's go upstairs," the girl repeats. She takes the man's hand and places it on the shaft of her costumed tail. Then she spins and starts making her way through the living room. The tail slides through the man's hands until near the tip, at which point he holds on and in this way they make their way upstairs.

Turn to page 143.

You sit at the bottom of the closet and don't move.

The man and the girl murmur to each other behind the door.

The bird has begun to release a smell — it's scared. Why are so many creatures scared when they're around you?

A sudden motion.

You look up and see the bird flutter up to a higher perch.

"What was this closet used for, anyway?" the girl asks.

"Before I got here?"

"Yeah."

"It was just storage. Aunt Sarah had her lawnmower in here."

They're silent for a moment, watching you.

"Have you given any more thought to the bloodhound?"

"Yeah," the man says, "but I don't know."

The girl sniggers. "You just hate dogs."

The man nods. "Yeah."

"But it could help us find cats!"

The man hangs his head. "I know." Then he turns to the girl. "But *you're* okay with dogs, right?"

"I grew up with both cats and dogs, so yeah."

"We'll see," the man says. "But it'll have to live with you. *If* it happens."

The humans go quiet again, as they watch you sitting, still as a rock.

"I don't think the kitten wants to," the girl says.

"No," the man replies in a small voice.

Suddenly, a hand reaches through the cat flap and pulls you back into the garage.

The girl takes you into the living room and holds

you in her arms, stroking you.

You purr, thankful the busy day is over. Later on, the man joins her, and their talking voices sing you to sleep.

Turn to page 37.

Above you looms Sofia's huge face, seething with anger.

Her lips drawn back in a grimace, she hisses, then cuffs you with her paw!

Quickly getting to your feet you run down the hall! Fortunately, the entire length of it is carpeted, so you get a lot of traction, but Sofia is bigger and faster than you are, and she chases after you, eventually pouncing on your back!

You scream, and scrabble at her. She yowls and holds you down. Her weight is just too much. You push with your hind legs, to try to get free, but can't.

Her mouth comes down, jaws snapping at your face and your eyes. You shake your head from side to side, trying to avoid her teeth.

"Sofia!" the man pounds down the hallway, which is suddenly bathed in light. "Fuck! Sofia!"

The cat lets out a shriek as the man yanks her off you. She struggles as he throws her into another room, slamming the door shut.

You don't wait around. You run to the end of the hallway and tear down some stairs. You don't know where you're going, but you need to get away from *her*.

At the bottom of the stairs, you realize you're back in the living room, and you hide under the couch. It's actually low enough that you think perhaps Sofia can't squeeze in underneath and get at you.

You are panting for breath and your heart pounds in your chest.

From upstairs, you hear the other cat yowling and running around in the room it's in, like a little cyclone.

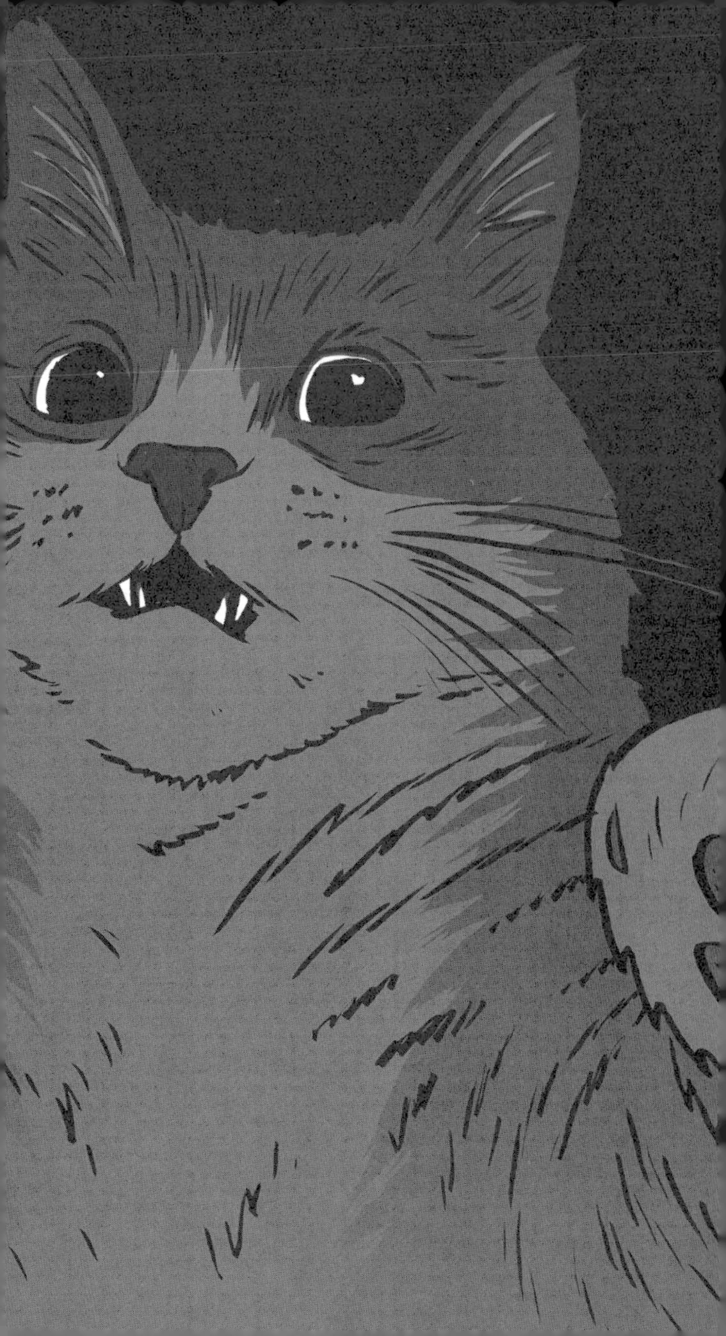

76

After a long time, the house finally quiets.

The man pads down the stairs and turns on the light in the living room.

"Kitten!" he calls softly. "Kitten!"

You watch him walk to the front window, draw back the drapes and look outside.

"Fuck," he mutters to himself. "What *time* is it? It's getting light."

You watch the man go into the kitchen and then return with a small saucer which he places on the floor in the middle of the living room. You can smell the milk and you finally feel safe enough to come out and lap at it.

After you're done, the man picks you up and settles on the couch. He starts to purr, and a little while later, you are purring too.

Turn to page 31.

"Joe, Joe," the girl kneels by the man. Her voice is strained and her bottom lip trembles in the light of the streetlamp.

You climb the man's chest and stare at him. The man's chest is strange. There are two padded lumps where you sometimes knead. The normal regular up and down of his breathing has stopped.

Oh no, wait. There it is.

The man's eyes flutter open, but then they close.

"Joe!" the girl screams. You have never heard her voice so distraught. "Joe, don't go. Stay awake! The ambulance is coming!"

The man is very still. He's not sleeping. You move over to his face and lick it.

Flashing lights catch your attention.

A loud squealing pierces the air and this enormous vehicle arrives on the scene.

You're scared by it, and you run to the sidewalk.

The girl says something to the two men who rush over. They touch him, ask the girl questions, put various things on him. Then they bring over a skinny bed and the girl helps them lift him onto it. Everyone gets into the back of the vehicle.

It quickly accelerates away.

Where did everyone go?

You want to stay outside, but are too scared. You need someplace warm and regular and familiar.

Even with the risk of Sofia, you head back to the house.

Turn to page 41.

You close your eyes. Maybe the other cat will leave you alone if you are sleeping.

You let your muscles relax and go slack.

But the fur on your back hasn't stopped standing up.

You swivel your ears, listening for the most tell-tale noise. The merest footfall.

Despite the quiet, the smell of the other cat is everywhere.

When she strikes, she is quick about it.

A low growl accompanies the huge maw that lifts you by the neck!

The cat shakes you! You can't breathe! Then she adjusts her bite and the worst pain you've ever felt shrieks through your body.

Immediately you notice that your chest is all wet.

You hate being wet.

But you get wetter and wetter as the other cat closes its jaws in a deathgrip and shakes you until you are dead, sodden with your own blood.

When the man finds you the next morning, he is very sad, but he understands why Sofia mauled you.

He takes your limp body to a taxidermist friend of his named Kate, who takes your paws and preserves them. Your limbs will sit in a drawer for a few years until the man takes up painting again. He uses your paws as paintbrushes to paint very special pointillist portraits of cats. Or as he likes to call them, "pawtillist" portraits. They go viral on the Internet for a couple of weeks.

THE END

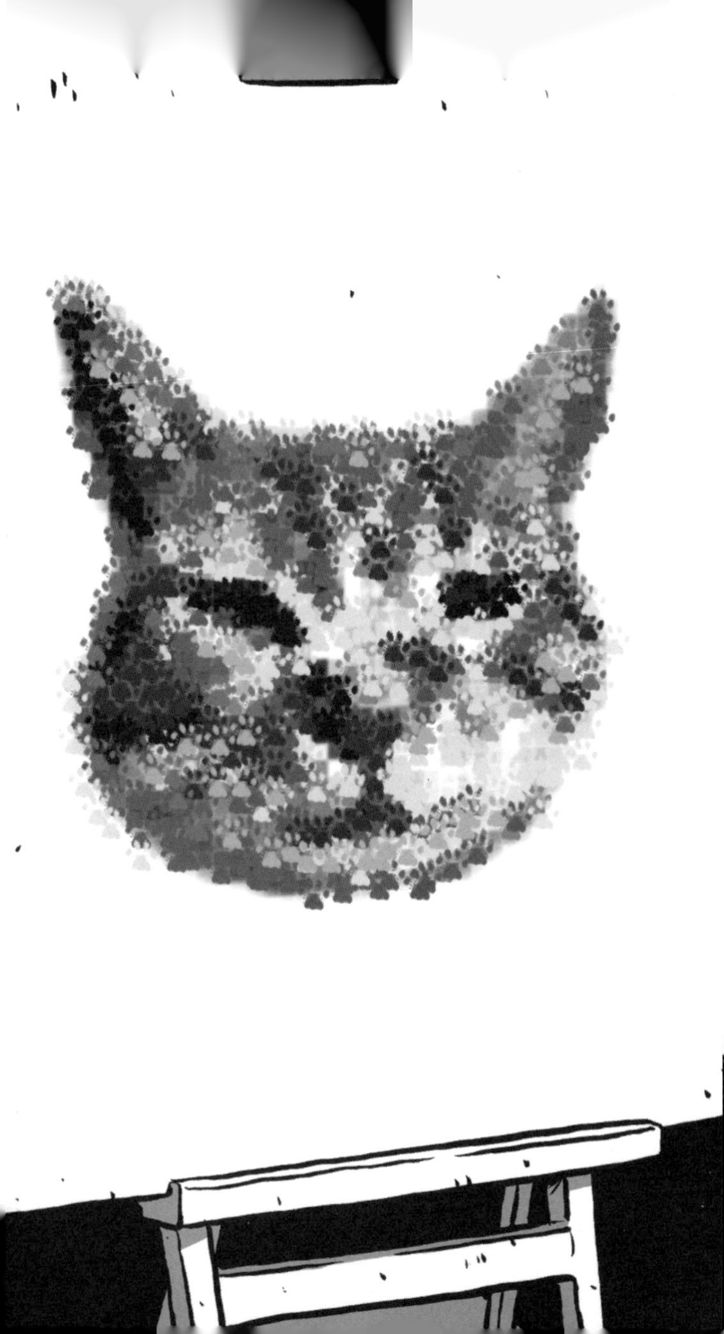

"Something I've been wondering..." the girl says.

"Yeah?"

The humans are almost back at the house. You recognize the smell here.

"I was telling a friend of mine about my job, and how — well, you call your company the Federal Bureau of Missing Cats, and she was wondering if you ever thought about starting a Bureau of Missing *Dogs*."

"I don't like dogs," the man explains. "I want them to *stay* missing."

The girl laughs. "I know that's a joke, but you shouldn't say that out *loud*."

"It's no joke," the man replies with a smile. "I'm a cat purrpremacist. Cats are simply superior to dogs."

"Like I said — *don't* say that out loud."

"In all seriousness, we *do* get the occasional call for a missing dog, but there's no work for us there. They just don't go missing as much."

The man unlocks his front door, and a breath of warm air blasts you in the face as you walk in.

Sofia is there, on the couch. She sees you and hisses.

"I'll go feed her," the girl says, and despite the angry catface, picks Sofia up and carries her into the kitchen. "She's probably hungry."

"I'll upload today's sightings," the man says, shrugging off his backpack. "Can I get the camera from your bag?"

"Sure," the girl calls over her shoulder. "Hey, what are you doing Saturday night?"

"Ah," the man tenses behind you. "Not sure. Why?"

"There's this burlesque show I'm going to. Wanna

come?"

"Oh," the man says uneasily. "I'm on the phone with my sister that night. She's better at business than I am, and I had some questions for her."

"Oh, okay," the girl says breezily. "Some other time then."

"*You* do that, right?" the man asks. "You mentioned it."

"What — you mean burlesque? I'm a performer, yeah."

"That's stripping, right?"

The girl laughs. "There's stripping *involved*, yeah."

"Whoa," the man says. "Are you stripping on Saturday?"

"Why don't you come out and see?" the girl says, winking.

When the man doesn't say anything, the girl laughs. "I'm kidding!" she says. "I'm not performing this Saturday. I'm just going out to see some of my friends' work. They've got new acts and I want to go see and support them. And you should come with."

The girl is in the kitchen and you hear her pouring kibble into a bowl. You struggle in the harness. You're hungry as hell, and if food is being distributed, you want some!

"Whoa, kitten!" the man says, dealing with your flailing limbs so close to his exposed neck. "Hold on! Lemme help you!"

The man lifts you up and out of the harness and drops you gently to the ground. It feels good to walk. You can contort your body into extraordinary positions for long periods of time, but it feels good to stretch and run. Which you do now into the kitchen.

82

"Kitten gets some kitten milk," the girl says primly, pouring another bowl, and placing it on the table.

The man picks you up and puts you beside the bowl. But before you can even take a sip, Sofia leaps up from the ground and thrusts her smelly bum in your face, blocking your way. Then *she* starts drinking your kitten milk!

"Ah!" the man sighs, exasperated. "Sofia!"

If you challenge Sofia for your milk,
turn to page 96.

If you decide to let her do what she wants, hoping
there'll be some left for you, turn to page 98.

If you run from the kitchen and hide, turn to 88.

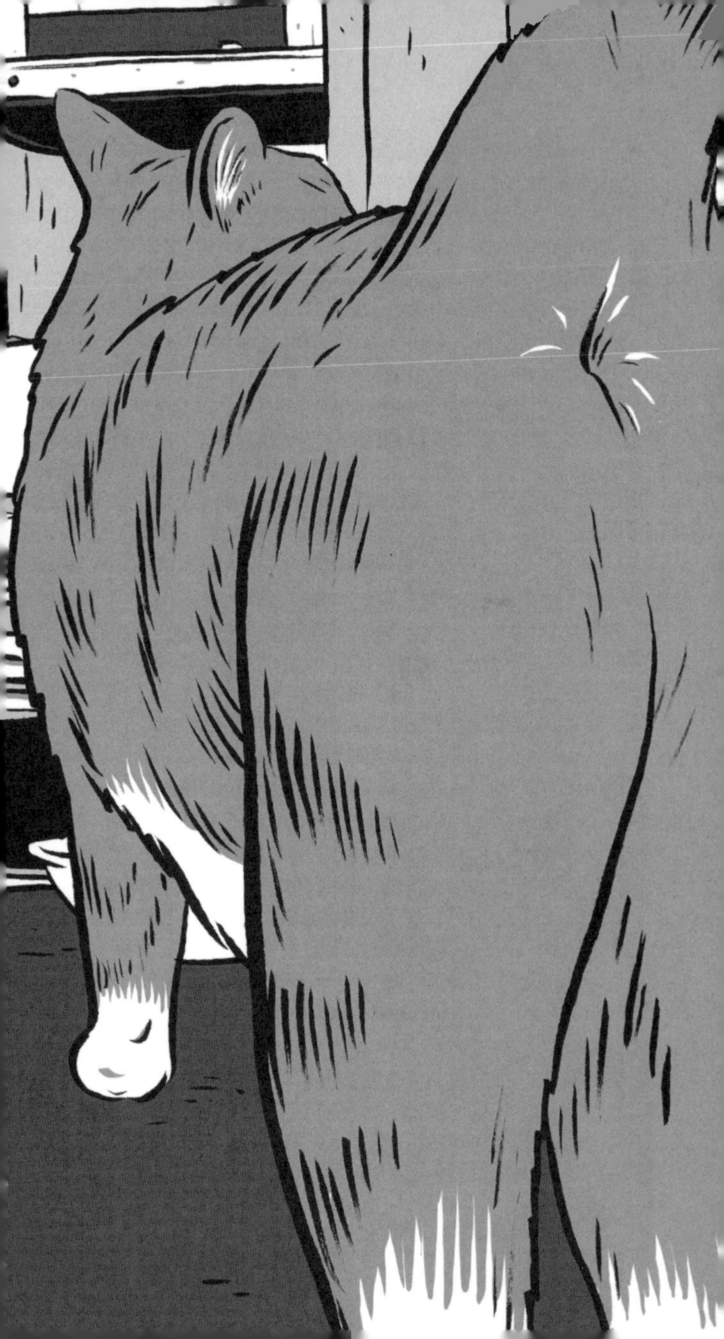

You drop down from the couch and look for a place to hide.

The living room is full of possibilities — lots of cat trees and little enclosures — but that is too easy. You need a place where Sofia can't find you *either*.

Finally, you spot a doorway with stairs leading down, and you decide to go for it. The steps themselves are quite high, and taller than you. Instead of hopping down each step, a more accurate description would be tumbling down. Even if you wanted to, it would be hard for you to go back.

The temperature drops palpably by a degree or two as you descend. It's dark down here, and dank.

At the bottom, you scan the room. There's not much here that you can reach. Shelves line one side of the room, while a large metal, rumbling behemoth sits on the other side. In between are two large white boxes.

Then you see it — where you'll hide.

In front of one of the white boxes, there's a mesh basket filled with blankets, and you climb easily up and over into it. Then, from here, you clamber into the white box through a half-closed door.

There, you make an interesting discovery.

Damp clothes and towels sit rumpled in a large round cylinder. They smell familiar. They reek of the canal water from the other day.

You snuggle inside the dryest part of an orange towel and fall asleep.

Later, you wake to the girl's high voice. She's upstairs.

"What happened?" she asks. "You look like shit."

"Sofia and the kitten fought," the man mumbles.

"Where's the kitten now?"

"Hiding. I don't know."

"Are we going to patrol today?"

"We have to. We've got too many open cases. Let me just get some laundry going, and then we'll put Sofia in my bedroom with some litter and some water. It's a little roomier than the bathroom, and it'll isolate her from the kitten for the time being. Everyone needs to just calm down a bit."

The man thuds down the stairs.

You stay very still. You are hiding, and determined never to come out.

The door squeaks open, and a large, soft bundle is dumped on top of where you're hiding.

You mewl in protest, but the sound of the door shutting masks it.

You like it in here. It's comforting and cozy.

Abruptly, the cylinder lurches into motion.

Whoa!

It speeds up and already you're feeling sick as the structure spins. You find yourself trapped in the blanket, being tossed around the box. Sometimes you land on other soft clothes, but more often than not you're slammed into the walls and set flying again.

To make things worse, it's getting crazy hot.

You don't like this!

You cry out, hoping the man hears you, but when you breathe back in, your throat is molten.

You need to escape. You claw at the clothes, whipping around you, trying to make your way to the door. But it's too hot. Your brain can't think.

Thankfully, you pass out. You are already unconscious as your body bakes to death.

THE END

You climb up the man's chest, steadying yourself on his collarbone, and jump up at his face. One claw snags on his cheek and cuts him as you tumble back onto his shoulder.

"Ah!" the man screams. He jumps up! You didn't anticipate that, but you jump off of him and onto the couch. The man clutches his face, then turns and glares at you. "Kitten!" he shakes his head. You can smell his disappointment. You watch him go upstairs.

He's gone for a long time. You curl up in a corner of the couch and fall asleep. You hope he's gotten the message.

Before she even arrives, you awake. A house is not a sealed egg — there are cracks everywhere. Around every door are thin gaps that allow air and wind and odours through. You smell her before she gets to the front door. When the sound rings through the house, you are already staring at the door.

Ding-dong!

The man comes down with a new shirt on, and something else. Black straps hang over his shoulders. He opens the door and the girl laughs.

"What are you wearing?"

"Kitten scratched me," he says, tapping his cheek. "Sofia tried to kill him last night."

The girl squints and examines the man's face. "Well, you can hardly see it. But you didn't answer my question."

"We'll have to bring the kitten along or Sofia will finish the job while we're out."

Turn to page 59.

You pull yourself free of the towel and lick yourself. Matted in some places, fluffy in others, your fur is in shambles. But you're dry — that's the main thing.

Quietly, you move down the man's body and jump onto the couch — which you immediately fall in love with.

With your claws extended, you move agilely and accurately across its entire surface.

This! Whatever this is! You like this!

Then suddenly, you see a shadow out of the corner of your eye.

You chase it! You grab it!

It's only after you are on your side and have it in your mouth that you realize it's your own tail. You lick the tip. You kind of knew it was your own tail, even before you grabbed it, but you had also sort of forgotten. Besides, sometimes it's fun to forget.

You love your tail. It keeps you balanced when you are walking along thin, precarious edges, but you are still getting used to it, too.

Now, what were you doing?

Before you can explore the house, a loud, high sound echoes through the entire house.

Ding-dong!

You bolt, jumping on the man's belly, then onto the floor. You scramble along the floor and run away.

"God!" the man groans. "Kitten, watch the belly."

From under a table, you watch as the man takes the towel off his stomach, pulls on some pants, then ambles to the front door, which he opens.

Turn to page 43.

You jump down from the kitchen table onto a chair, and then from there to the floor. You are shaking from anger and frustration, and you don't know what to do. You go where you feel safest — underneath the couch.

"Oh honey," the man comes after you. You hear Sofia's slurping all the way from the kitchen.

The man intercepts you just before you dart into safety and holds you in his arms. He settles into the couch and strokes you.

"How's the little one?" the girl comes out into the living room and sees your face. "Oh my god! He's so sad!"

The man shakes his head slowly. "I think I have to make a hard decision here."

"When?"

"Now. Any more of this is unfair to everyone."

The man puts you back in the harness, and lets the girl give you a kiss.

"Feel free to go home. I'll see you tomorrow," the man says. "I might be awhile."

Then you and the man go on a long walk. At the end of it, you end up at a strange grey building. Immediately, you are terrified. There are so many smells coming out of it — absolute chaos.

You are uneasy in the harness, but the man keeps stroking you, and cooing to you. You decide to reserve your panic until you absolutely need to unleash it.

A woman in a white coat sits at a large counter and she says something to the man.

He says something back. Everywhere, the smells of a million animals crowd in on you. Where are they coming from?

"Does he have a name?" the woman asks.

The panic inside you peaks, and you twist and turn in the harness, trying to get loose.

"Um, hold on—" the man mumbles, struggling to get you out.

"Holden?"

Finally you're free, but the man has a tight grip on you. When the woman opens a cat carrier for him, he drops you in, and she shuts the door.

At least *this* doesn't smell like anything. It smells like nothing. But there's also nothing in here.

"Can I say good-bye?" the man asks the woman.

"Take as long as you wish," she says, then turns back to some papers on the desk.

The man looks in the caged door and his glasses fog up. He takes them off and wipes his eyes. He is extremely sad. He swallows a few times, and sticks his finger through the bars, tickling your whiskers.

"Take care of yourself, kitten," he says. Water is running down his cheeks. "I know you're going to find a great home, and have a great life, and have crazy adventures, and I am so blessed to have been able to be part of that. So thank you."

At this, he turns away and marches, head hanging, out the front door.

Then you sit for a long time. So long, that you decide to take a nap.

Turn to page 246.

Ding-dong!

When the man lets the girl in, he also lets out a whistle.

"Whoa!" he exclaims. "What's this?"

The girl is furry, and in a yellow outfit underneath her hoodie.

"I'm Cheetah!" the girl grins, doing a spin. You watch as her tail spins too, and settles to a stop. You are filled with a desire to chase it, but by the time you think you actually might, it's no longer moving. "You know — from the comics? Legion of Doom? She's bad."

"She certainly *is,*" the man replies, staring. Then he catches himself, and blushes. "Sorry. I didn't mean to create an unsafe work environment."

The girl laughs. "That's more consideration than I get at some of the bars where I perform, so don't worry about it. Aren't *you* gonna dress up?"

"What? To patrol?"

"Today's Halloween! You *have* to! C'mon — weeks ago you told me you had a *costume.* And you're still coming with me to that party tonight, right?"

"Well, the costume is for tonight. To *patrol* I'm wearing the kitten bjorn."

"Uh oh," the girl says, suddenly serious. "Why? Sofia acting up again?"

The man nods. "Just a lot of noise." He picks you up and places you in the harness. "Hmm," he says. "It's a little snug. We may have to graduate to the cat bjorn soon."

These days, going out on patrol is rather a refreshing change from the endless war of the house. It's a little like flying — or at least, what you *imagine* flying to be. Effortless movement.

It's a long day. The humans leave the house just before the sun is fully up. They march up and down the alleys and streets. Then they take an extended break in the middle of the day. Sometimes they return to the house and the girl disappears, coming back only much later, as the sun is setting. Then they go out on patrol again. You like this because you can see better during those hours.

Today, late on patrol, the humans encounter a large, white cat. The girl bends down and it comes to her, purring into her hand.

"That was easy," the girl says, clipping a line to its collar. The cat is a little uneasy about this, but the girl strokes it. "Easy, easy," she says soothingly. "We'll let you go if you're not one of ours." The line is connected to her backpack, and is pre-emptive, in case the cat bolts.

"Maybe it's your outfit," the man jokes. "He thinks you're mom."

The girl examines the cat's tag.

"Oh god," she exclaims. "It's Tiramisu."

"Tiramisu!" the man grins. "He's been missing for two weeks!"

The girl pulls her notebook out of her backpack, and flips through it. "Owner's over on Duluth. Can you call them if I give you their number?"

"Gladly," the man says. He retrieves his own wafer from his pocket and punches in the numbers.

Both the man and the girl have rectangular wafers. You notice they spend a lot of time staring into them. The man stares at his for hours in the evening, even as the room darkens around him. You think you know why. The light from it bathes his face — it's basically a portable sunbeam that he carries around with him. You know how *you* feel when you're in a sunbeam. But you're dependant on its movements and timeframe. The man and the girl have the sunbeams whenever they want. Sometimes you'll nuzzle your head in between the man and his sunbeam, trying to enjoy it too, but it doesn't have the same feeling as an actual sunbeam. You don't know why. It must be something only the man can feel.

"Mrs. Odenkirk?" the man says into his wafer. "Yes. Hi. It's Joe, from the Bureau of Missing Cats. Well, yes, there's a reason I'm calling — we found Tiramisu!"

He aims the wafer at the girl, who's since picked up the black cat and is holding it in her arms. A tinny cheer comes from the wafer speaker and the girl laughs.

The man puts the wafer back on his ear and continues, "So, are you home right now to receive him? We're like, ah, fifteen minutes away."

Shortly, the humans are walking down the alley in a jaunty mood. The girl is carrying the white cat.

"What is a tiramisu, anyway?" the man asks. "Is it Japanese?"

The girl frowns. "I *think* it's a Japanese mountain?" She sounds uncertain.

"I guess we could Google it."

"Hey, the other day," the girl smiles, "my friend told me about this cat named Ali. And I was like, is that a Persian name? And she was like, no, it's a pun. Ali is just a different pronunciation of *alley*. As in, 'alley cat.'"

"Aw, that's very charming. I guess we should probably name *this* one at some point," he says, patting your belly. You lean back and rub your nose against his chin. "We've been calling you Kitten, but you're not such a kitten anymore."

Pretty soon, the humans are walking up toward this house with its lights all aglow. A large woman is standing there at the doorway and she runs down the steps toward the girl, taking the white cat into her arms.

"Oh god!" she holds it tight. The cat rests its arms on her shoulders and pushes its head against her ear. You can hear its purr rumbling in the night air. "My baby! Oh my baby. Oh my Misu."

The man and the girl grin like fools.

The woman blinks away tears and looks at the man and the girl. "Oh," she says, "sorry you've gotten hair all over your costume."

The girl looks down and brushes some of Tiramisu's white fur off. "Oh, it's okay. It's worth it!"

They talk a little more in the dusk, and then the woman gives them both a kiss.

"How do I thank you?" she asks.

"We'll send an invoice," the man smiles.

"Make sure you do! You guys are the best!" the woman turns and heads back into the house.

On the way home, little gangs of children run by you on the sidewalk. You are terrified of them. They are clad in long capes and masks. Some of them point at you with sticks that light up. Others just point. What neighbourhood is this? You need to remember its smells so you can avoid it.

"Well that was great!" the girl crows. She is practically skipping along the street.

"How long's it been since we did a Reunion?" the man asks. "At *least* three weeks. This is why we do it. Long slogs through smelly alleys are no fun, but

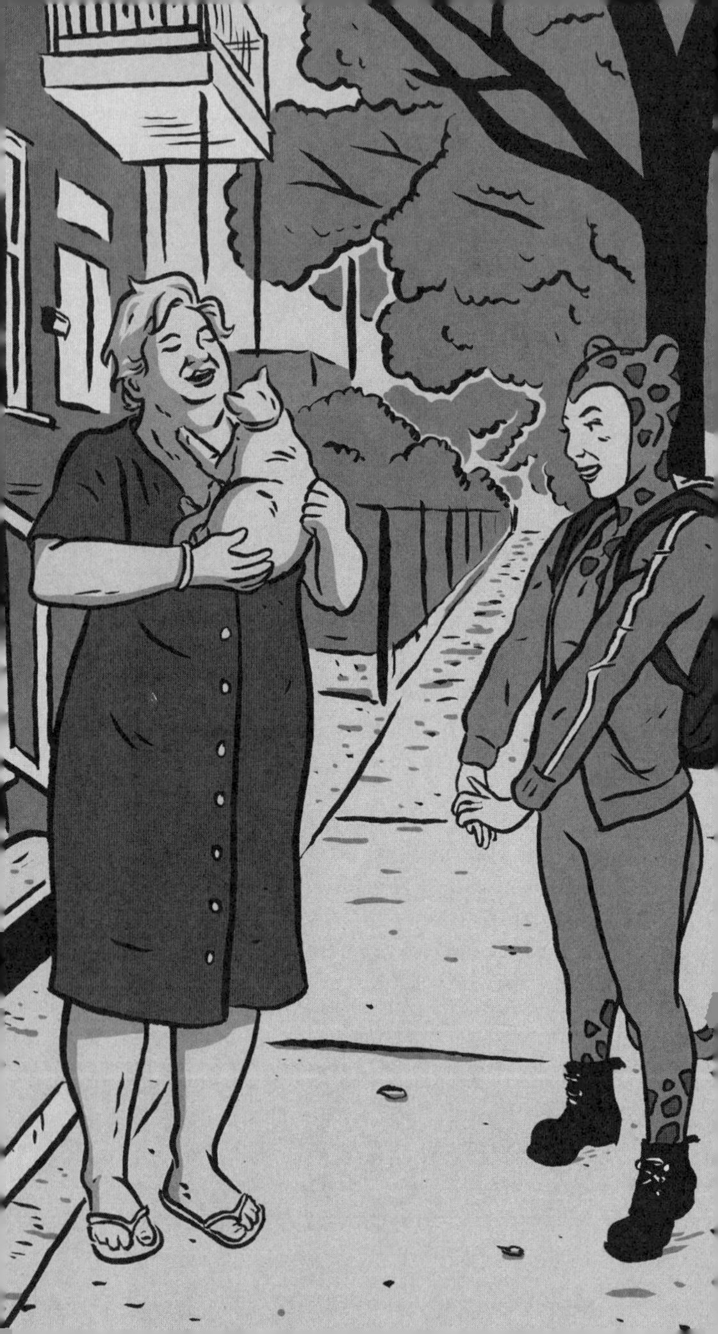

sometimes it really pays off. Times like this make it all worth it."

The girl dances and twirls her tail, spinning it.

"We rock, we rock," she chants. "We rock this fucking block."

Finally, after passing more bands of costumed raving lunatic children, you get home.

Turn to page 100.

You move so Sofia can see you clearly and you hiss at her! This is your food! She has her own bowl! This needs to stop!

Sofia barely turns her head to glare at you.

Then — like lightning, with a raised paw she cuffs you!

You're stunned. Not only by the blow, which shakes your little brain in your little head, but by the fact that she does it almost immediately *again!*

Bam!

"Should we —?" the girl ventures.

The man shakes his head.

Finally you back off, and Sofia returns to slurping your milk.

The man picks you up, and pours another bowl of milk for you on top of the fridge.

"Will that be okay?" the girl asks.

"Sofia knows about the top of the fridge," the man says. "It's a no-go zone for her. She knows what will happen if she tries anything."

While you drink, you look up constantly to make sure Sofia is still on the table, and not about to steal *this* bowl as well.

Over time, the house settles into an uneasy truce. You're fed on top of the fridge, which Sofia stays away from, and at night, you both sleep in separate rooms. She's claimed the couch, and you find a spot upstairs on the guest room bed. Ever since the hallway incident, you're paranoid about sleeping someplace so open to attack, but also paranoid about sleeping where you don't have an escape route.

The guest room bed solves this, as you can see her coming, and if she attacks, you can escape off any side of the bed — you'll never be trapped into a corner, and it's that sense of security that actually allows you to get to sleep.

Occasionally, on certain bad days when Sofia's seething anger reaches a boil, the man will take you out on patrol with the girl. But that's largely stopped when you and Sofia prove that you can finally be in the house together without constant conflict.

You've also started leaving the house on your own through the kitchen's cat flap. You try your paw at hunting, occasionally netting small mice and flies. You bring them home sometimes. When the man discovers them, he is more than proud, and lavishes you with love. He keeps every prize, and when he has time, preserves them in lucite. The garage always stinks of chemicals for a few days before he unveils your new trophy to you.

What's also amazing is that you are growing day by day, and getting larger. The added size helps when you're standing your ground against Sofia, who has been more ornery for some inexplicable reason the last few days.

Turn to page 90.

You watch with a terrible dread as Sofia drinks your milk. She makes a point of drinking it all, licking her lips when she's finished, and cleaning her face with her forepaws. Then she drops down gently from the table and continues munching on her own food.

The man strokes you on the table while you wait. Finally, only after Sofia stalks off somewhere to rest and digest, do you drop down to the floor and move to her food bowl. There is still some kibble in it. You want to munch on it, even if it'll hurt your nascent teeth, because you are so hungry. But you don't dare. If she smells you on her food, the consequences will be worse. So you hang your head and feel terrible.

"It's okay, kitten," the man says. He picks you up again and places you on the kitchen table. He refills your bowl with milk, and you slurp away gratefully. "Not all cats can be alphas. Most of us are betas. Every house has an alpha and a beta. Being beta just means you're a regular person, trying to get by."

Over time, the house settles into a rhythm. Since you backed off, Sofia isn't so hard on you, but she cuffs you once in a while, to put you in your place. Sometimes she messes with you, just because she can, because it *amuses* her.

Every day she'll do *some*thing — whether it's blocking your way when you're going someplace, cuffing your head while you're playing, pushing you off a bed, or edging you out of the sunbeam.

Just because she can.

Occasionally she'll make her way to where you are and stare.

Just stare.

You are miserable. You spend more of your time

in the far corners and back rooms of the house, where Sofia doesn't frequent. Or you go outside through the cat flap, but you have to travel a long distance to get out of her territory, and you are still a bit afraid of the larger world, despite the introduction you had to it from the vantage point of the man's harness.

He still occasionally takes you out on patrol, especially on days when the conflict between you two cats can't seem to cease.

But over time, you grow bigger, and you can tell that your increasing size troubles Sofia. She still bullies you, but she is less aggressive. You're grateful for this, as she has been more ornery the past day for some inexplicable reason.

Turn to page 90.

Inside, the man lifts you out of the harness and drops you on the couch. Thankfully Sofia's not on it, or she would have had a fit. Still, you get off the couch as soon as you can, to leave as little of your scent on it as possible.

"Hey," the girl says with a smile, pulling a tall bottle out of her bag. "I got us something to celebrate."

The man looks puzzled. "Celebrate? For finding Tiramisu? But how did you know we'd find him today?"

The girl laughs. "My powers of deduction *are* pretty good, but no, not for that. Guess again."

"For Halloween?"

The girl shakes her head.

"One last guess."

The man opens his mouth as if to say something, then closes it. He shakes his head, dumbfounded.

"One year ago you *hired* me! Remember?"

The man laughs. "Oh, that's right! It's been a year already? I should be buying *you* the drink!"

"Well," the girl says, looking to the side and arching an eyebrow, "I *could* use a raise."

"Ah," the man says. "Lemme think about it."

"Kidding!" the girl says. "I'm just kidding, kinda." She hands the man the bottle and walks to the kitchen. "I'm gonna get us some glasses. We should toast Tiramisu's homecoming as well!"

You're terribly hungry, and you follow the girl into the kitchen, staying close to her ankles. You need food! Where's the food? You meow at her.

She looks down at you while she rummages through the cupboard. "Kitten's hungry!" she calls to the man, who joins her in the kitchen. He reaches down and sweeps you off your feet and up onto the fridge top. Immediately you start in on your kibble, crunching away.

"Not such a kitten anymore," the man says, watching you eat. "We can't call him kitten forever."

"I was talking with my uncle the other day," the girl says, opening the wine, and pouring it into two delicate glasses, "and he was going on and on about how he hated it when animals had human names."

"What do you mean? Like Sofia?"

"Yeah, or like Michael, or whatever. He thought it was inappropriate somehow. He liked it when cats had names that were obviously not human ones."

"Huh," the man said. "Well, when your uncle adopts a cat, he can name it whatever he wants."

The girl hands the man a glass and they clink them.

"To your first year as a missing cat investigator," the man says, "and to hopefully many more!"

"Cheers!" the girl smiles, and the humans both take long swallows of their drink.

You look up when they clink the glasses, and take a moment to look for Sofia. She might be out. But she might be at home. It's hard to tell. Her smell is so pervasive. Still, you are grateful because the fridge top is one of the few places she can readily access.

"I once met a cat named Mammal," the man says, sitting down at the kitchen table. The girl joins him.

"Oh, that's a cool name. Like, that's its scientific designation, I guess. That's like if we named a person *Human*."

The man chuckles. "How about if we named a *cat* Human? Where would that fit in the list of names that pissed your uncle off?"

The girl shakes her head. "I honestly have no

idea."

"Hey kitten," the man looks over at you and raises his glass. "How about we name you Human?" Do you like that name?"

You look over at him. The smell of the wine drifts over to you. Every time he drinks stuff that smells like that he gets very clumsy and he starts mumbling after awhile. Usually he drinks alone though. You bend your head to continue eating.

"Hey," the girl says, refilling her glass, "I was wondering — you're someone who seems to like cat puns so much. Why did you name it, The Federal Bureau of Missing Cats? Why not the Federal Bureau of Missing *Purr*sons? Wouldn't that be cooler?"

The man stares at her for a moment, then puts his hands over his eyes and moans. "That's brilliant," he says. "I never even thought of that. That's what it should have been all *along*."

"I'll take that raise now," the girl says.

"You'll have it." The man downs the rest of his glass and the girl refills it. "I guess I just wanted to be clear about what it was we did to the general public. But Missing *Purr*sons is both clear *and* clever."

"Awright," the girl says. "No more stalling — get your costume on. We've still got a party to go to."

"I guess I do kind of stall," the man concedes, "especially when it involves going out."

"I know! I've been trying to get you to come out with me for weeks!"

"I guess I'm a bit of an introvert."

"That's an understatement," the girl laughs, "you're a hermit."

"Sometimes I get very stressed out by them — parties I mean — especially if like, everyone's white."

The girl is silent for a moment.

"It's just tough to be the only person of colour in a room full of white people."

The girl nods. "A lot of my friends *are* white," she admits. "But if you come to this party, I'll stick by your side all evening."

The man sighs, then takes a deep breath and downs the rest of his glass.

"I really want you to come with me!" the girl chirps.

The man smiles, nods, and goes upstairs to change.

Finishing your kibble, you lap up some water then meow to the girl to be brought down. She comes over, cheeks flushed and picks you up. She reeks of her stinky drink and you turn your head to the side when she goes to kiss you. "Oh, kitten," she says, rubbing her cheek against yours. "Oh, Human."

She brings you to the living room and drops you on the floor.

You jump up onto the computer desk chair. You like it there because Sofia hasn't claimed it, and it's usually tucked in under the desk, so no one can attack you from above, and you can see whatever comes from below. It makes you feel safe.

The girl walks over to a mirror on the wall and adjusts the cowl on the head, then adjusts her breasts. Finally, she pulls a thin metal tube out of her pocket and draws it across her lips. "He doesn't know it yet," she mutters to herself, "but I'm about to make this a decidedly *unsafe* work environment tonight."

The girl walks around the living room nervously. She grabs her tail and swings it. You watch it spin. You have half a mind to catch it, but you just ate and

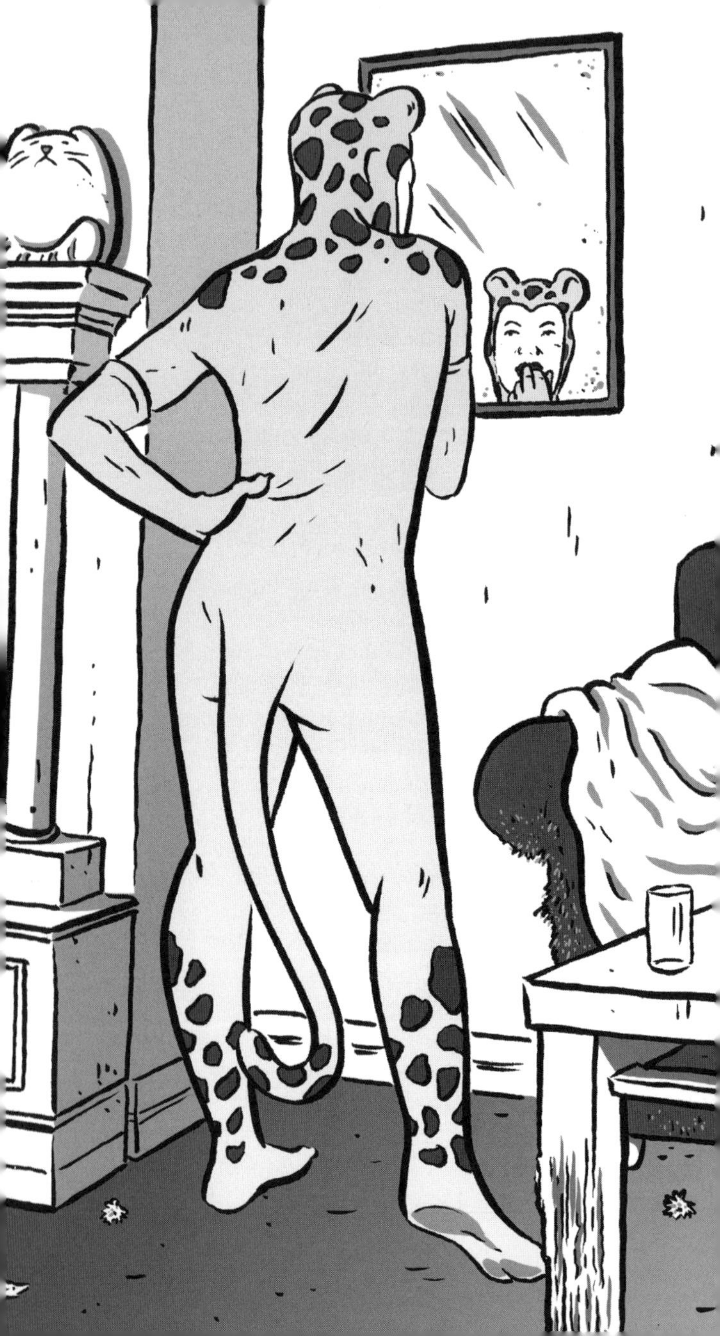

are too comfortable where you are. Drowsy, you think you might nap.

"Whoa!" the girl turns at the sound of the man coming down the stairs. She breaks out into a grin.

The man comes down into the living room in his shiny black outfit. It's skintight. You've seen him wear it before by himself. He lounges around in it.

"That's old school Catwoman! Like from the 60s!" the girl says.

"Yeah," the man says, smiling. "I watched a lot of those old Adam West *Batmans*. This is outfit is certifiably Julie Newmar-era."

"Well you like great. You've got curves and everything!"

"D'aww, well, everything's fake," the man says, brushing the hair of his wig back.

"You'll be a *hit* at the party."

Suddenly, Sofia strides into the living room from the kitchen. She spots you and fixes you with her gaze for a half-second, then she jumps up onto the couch, ignoring the humans. She extends her legs and starts licking the fur on her thighs and chest.

Ding-dong!

"Aw jeez!" the man says, moving quickly into the kitchen in his high heels, "that'll be trick or treaters. Dash — can you get that? I'll get the candy."

"Whatever you say, Catwoman," the girl grins and heads to the door.

Abruptly, Sofia stops licking herself and drops down to the ground. She makes a beeline for you, and you tense. What does she want?

A few feet from your chair, she pauses. From her stance, you know she's going to jump up onto the chair with you. But there's no room for the both of

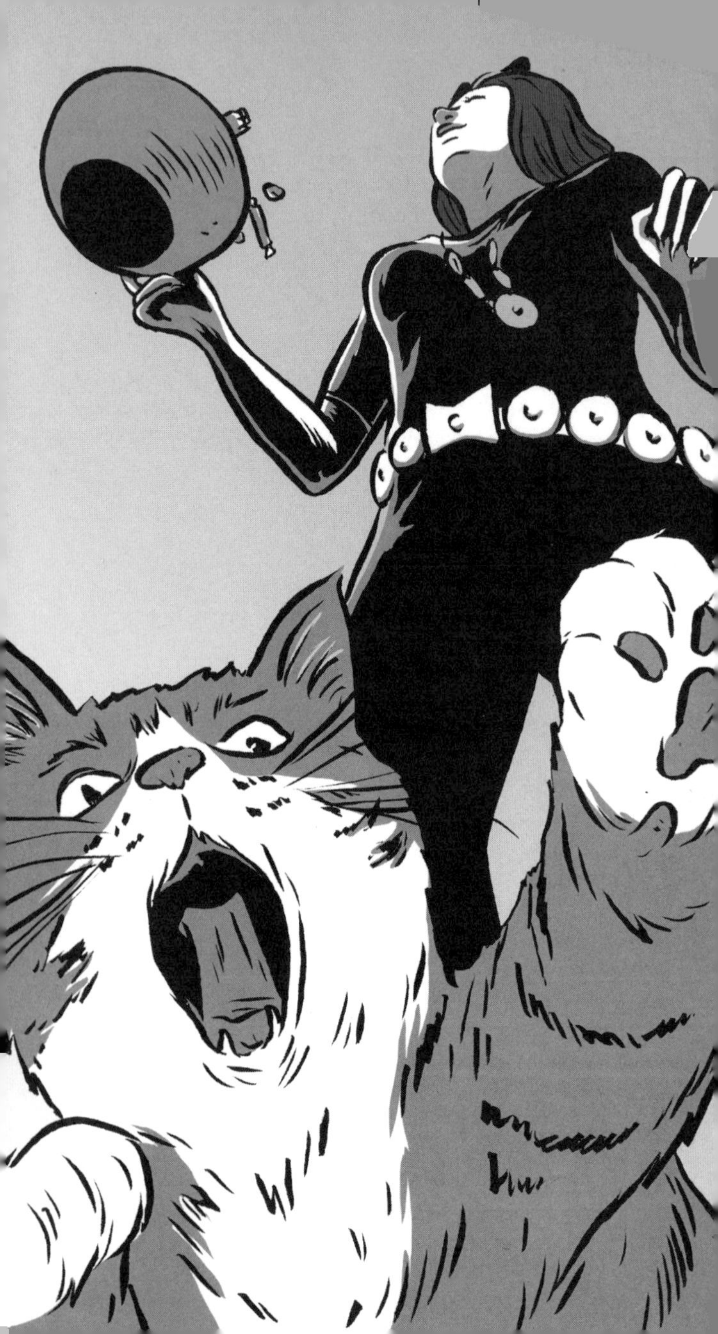

you. She waits, daring you to stay.

You give in. You're too tired for this. You drop down from the chair and cede your place. But instead of taking it, she raises a paw as if to cuff you!

A chorus of kids cry "trick or treat!" from the front door as the girl opens it. She turns to see the man coming across the living room with a bowl.

"Candy's coming kids!" the man shouts to them.

Sofia's picking a fight with you! But you just ate, and aren't at your best. What will you do?!

If you dash for the open front door,
turn to page 108.

If you decide to rush upstairs, turn to page 112.

If, despite your drowsiness, you decide
to fight Sofia, turn to page 111.

You run at the open front door, the little legs of children and the swish of capes greeting you. They stand there with pendulous pillowcase bags, and you deke expertly around them. But Sofia is undeterred and follows!

"Kitten! Sofia! No!" the man yells.

The cold air of the night smacks you in the face and gives you energy as you tear along the footpath to the sidewalk.

You can hear Sofia's claws scramble on the concrete path as she follows you. This time you're sure she intends to kill you.

You are so panicked and desperate to get away that you don't even notice the low rumble and sun-bright headlights bathing the street around you until it is nearly too late.

"Kitten!" you hear, and suddenly the man's strong hands are there, picking you up.

You have never been so grateful for the man and his hands in your life. You want him to hold on to you forever. Suddenly, you're safe.

But then the hands are gone.

You're thrown in a long arc, and you land on the other side of the street, on the grass beside the sidewalk. It's a soft landing. But everything behind you is chaos.

A shrieking *screech* and a thud. In your peripheral vision you see the man in his black outfit flying through the air like a bird. When he lands, it's awkwardly, his limbs limp.

The young man at the wheel has his eyes wide, lit, you think, by a wafer of some kind.

Then the girl is rushing outside, screaming.

The car that hit the man lurches into movement,

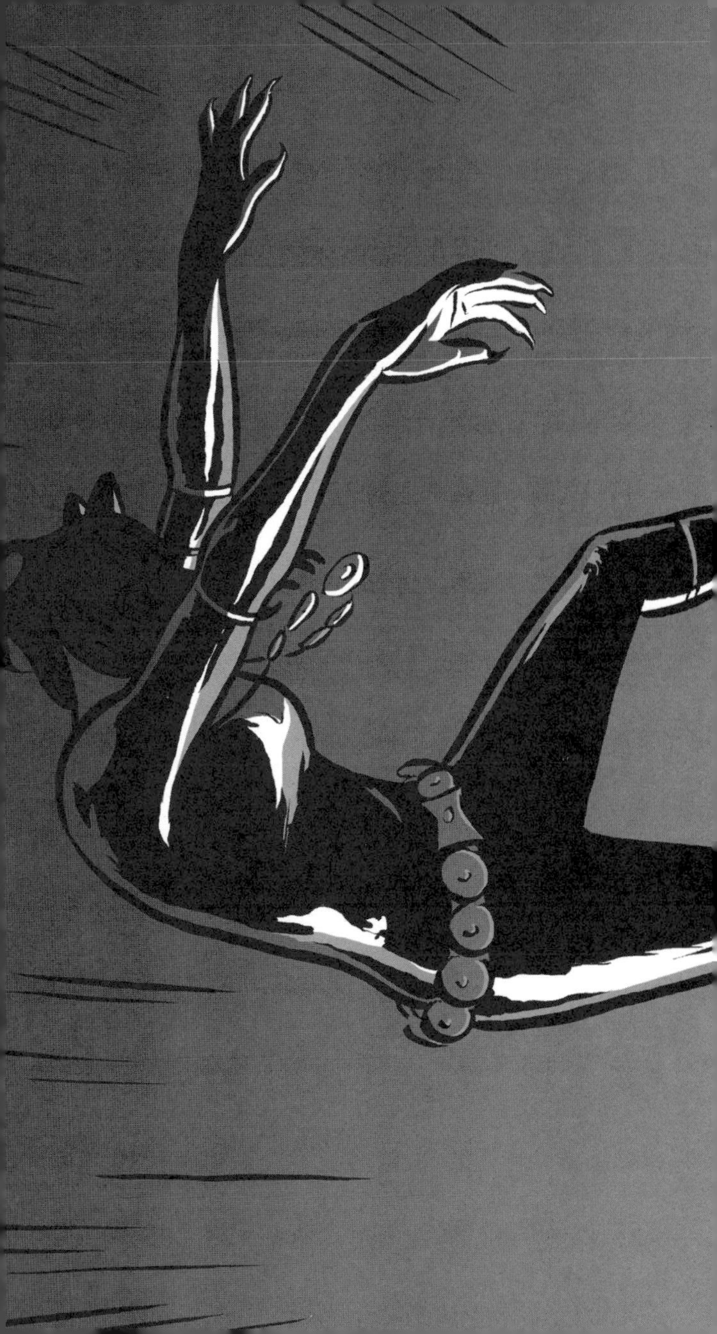

zooming down the quiet street. It even runs over the man again in its haste to get away. You hear the sickening thud and wonder if the man is okay.

You have watched other cars speeding along the street and have shied away, never wanting to get caught under one of them. Now it's happened to the man.

The girl runs into the street and stops mid-step when she sees the man's body. "Call an ambulance!" she screams at the children, and runs to the man, bending down at his side.

If you decide to go to the man, go now to page 77.

If you decide all this is too much, go back into the house on page 41.

If you don't want to go anywhere, and just want to hide under a bush and wait to see what happens, turn to page 114.

You're done with running, you decide, and you turn to fight Sofia.

But her sudden overwhelming ferocity surprises you, and you retreat, bounding up and onto her couch.

Oh no. That's *her* territory. That's going to make her even angrier.

She chases you onto the couch and jumps on your back, biting at your neck.

"Hey!" the man yells at the both of you, but in the panicked moment, his voice seems very far away.

You turn to face her, swiping claws at her face, desperate to get away. Her flurry has stunned you and you don't know how much longer you can fight her off.

You are so tired, and her rage seems limitless.

Finally the man yanks Sofia off. She is so pissed, she even takes a swipe at *him*.

"Hey!" the man shouts, dropping her.

You take this opportunity to escape, and dash for the open front door!

Turn to page 108.

112

You tear up the stairs, taking them two at a time. You have never taken them two at a time before, but the adrenaline lends you power. When you get to the top, you gallop down the hallway and pause outside the guestroom. You are worried about being cornered, but being out in the open gives you no comfort either.

Sofia rises like a demon from the stairs and slows. She stalks toward you, hissing the entire time. Then, before you can blink, she sprints, closing the distance in an instant and jumps on you! The two of you tussle, rolling into one wall, then the other, panting and furious.

Then, for the first time in your life, you manage to throw her off of you!

You both breathe noisily in the dim quiet of the hall.

Making the first move, you run into the guestroom and jump up on top of the bed, prepared to go another round.

But Sofia doesn't follow. She turns and goes back downstairs.

You wait. You listen. You even jump down and peer into the hallway, expecting an ambush.

But no Sofia.

Exhausted, you get back on the bed and catch your breath.

Downstairs, the doorbell rings again, startling you. More children yelling "trick or treat!" This happens all night. There is a period of time when the doorbell seems to ring incessantly.

Over time, the man and the girl's voices get louder and more raucous.

Then you hear a glass breaking. The man and the

girl laugh uproariously.
Then the voices quieten.

Maybe it's safe to go back downstairs?
Turn to page 71.

Turn to page 116 if you'd rather stay in here.
From the bed you can jump up on top
of the dresser, where it's safer.

All the excitement is too much for you and you enter a small front yard and duck underneath a leafy bush.

The girl talks to the man in a constant stream of dialogue. She rubs his chest and kisses his forehead, all the while rocking back and forth. Finally, flashing lights bounce off nearby houses and a giant white truck roars up to them.

The spinning lights on top of the truck hurts your eyes and you half-close them.

Two men emerge from the truck and go to the girl and the man.

As a couple with a dog walk by and slow to watch the proceedings, the dog smells you and looks in your direction. But when he starts barking, his owners tug on his leash and they move along.

Across the street, you spot Sofia, sitting beside the front yard fencepost. She is also staring at the man.

All the humans get into the large white vehicle, and it roars off, lights flashing and siren squealing.

Then the street is calm.

You sit there for a long time. You are so tired, you think you might nap, but it's too cold to nap.

The sight of the still man flashes in your head. He has never been that still. The only time you've seen anything that still is if you *killed* it.

Finally, you go inside. Since the front door is closed, you enter through the kitchen cat flap. Warily, you check for Sofia, but she's disappeared.

Upset at her, you munch on her food and drink from her water. You understand that that will bring reprisal but you don't care.

Then you go to the living room and jump up onto the computer desk chair.

Finally you manage to drift off.

Hours later, when you awake, the morning sunbeam is streaming through the front windows.

Turn to page 133.

116

You stay right where you are and make your way to the top of the dresser. The man knows you like to hang out there so he placed a cardboard box on it for you. You fill it quite amply, and rest your cheek against its pliable edge. Over time, its walls have spread out, but then you have grown to fill it. It is a good box. You like this box.

Feeling safe, you nap. But you're woken later on.

The man pokes his head into the room and flicks a switch on the wall. A small lamp beside the guest-room bed comes on, illuminating his face.

"C'mon," the girl says, insistently, from the hall.

"Hold on," the man says, "I want to check to make sure the kitten is okay."

He sees you and strokes your ears. You press your cheek up against his knuckle and rub away.

The girl comes up behind him and cups his chest.

He looks down at her hands and chuckles. "Do you like my fake tits?"

The girl removes her hands and unzips her costume beginning at her neck.

"Do you like my real ones?"

At this, the man abruptly turns around.

Hey? What happened to the affection?

The man and the girl go to the bed. They are all over each other. You have never seen them all over each other like this before. It almost looks like they're fighting. But the smell is all wrong. The smell they're generating is unsettling.

At the doorway to the guestroom, you notice Sofia. She stares at them, then looks up and sees you. A moment later, she's gone.

The man and the girl start taking their costumes off in between bouts of kissing.

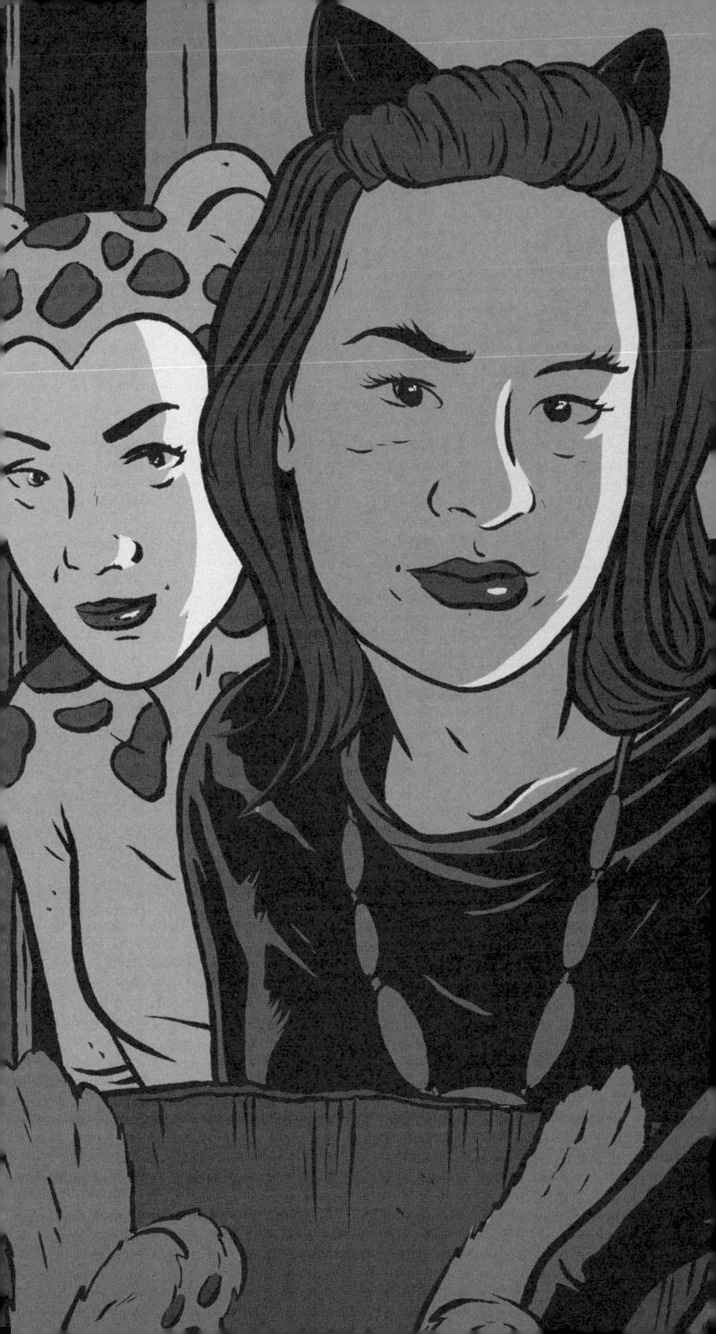

118

"Keep the ears on," the girl whispers.

"Are you sure this is a good idea?" the man asks, a note of hesitancy in his voice.

"Do you have a *better* idea?" the girl smiles.

"I mean — I'm your employer."

"So, employ. Employ those hands. Employ that mouth."

You try to go back to sleep, but their increasingly frantic noises alarm you, keeping you up. Eventually you head into the hallway and doze off at the top of the stairs.

Turn to page 143.

You raise your puny paws and try to slash at him, but the man grabs you by the armpits and lifts you up, keeping your claws just out of reach. He's puzzled by something, though.

"I thought you were smaller," he mutters to himself.

Suddenly, the door to the lab bursts open and a person in a ski-mask stands there.

"What?" the man turns his head. "You can't be in here — "

Though your paws can't reach him, you kick your hindlegs powerfully at the man, hitting him in the chest, and he stumbles, dropping you in the process. The man hits the back of his head on a table ledge and falls to the floor.

The ski-masked person runs to him.

"Hey, hey!" she says, shaking him.

Two more people appear at the doorway. They are wearing bandanas over their faces, below their eyes.

"Emily, what the fuck?!" one of them says. "This was supposed to be *non-violent*."

"I didn't do this!" she says.

"Well, whatever," the other one says. "Too late now. Let's get these animals out of their prisons."

You take this opportunity to rush out the door they are holding open! Run to page 187.

You jump to the ground, and start for the open door. Satisfyingly, you hear Sofia drop to the floor too, following you outside.

It's a brave new world! New adventures! What will happen?

Venturing out into the front yard, suddenly your bravery leaves you. When you reach the sidewalk, you remember the car from the other night, hitting the man. And the man lying there, absolutely still.

You stop there on the sidewalk, reliving the moment.

You smell her before you see her. Rushing back along the sidewalk, the girl stops and catches her breath when she sees the both of you.

"What? What are you two doing out here without your collars?"

She looks back at the house, her lips tightening grimly. Then she turns back to you.

"I couldn't leave you kids," she says. Then she picks up Sofia under one arm and you under the other and she walks calmly and deliberately to her place. It takes a long time, and you squirm, but you are so grateful to have a familiar face and smell taking care of you.

The girl lives in a basement apartment. There are no sunbeams, and it's a tight fit for Sofia and yourself. Neither of you are very happy about this, and there is no easy cat flap to allow either one of you to venture outside. The girl has to be there to open the back door to let you out. But once outside, you have access to all the sunbeams you can absorb.

Over time, you come to understand that the man is gone. And that this is your new life. But before you can really settle into a rhythm, something hap-

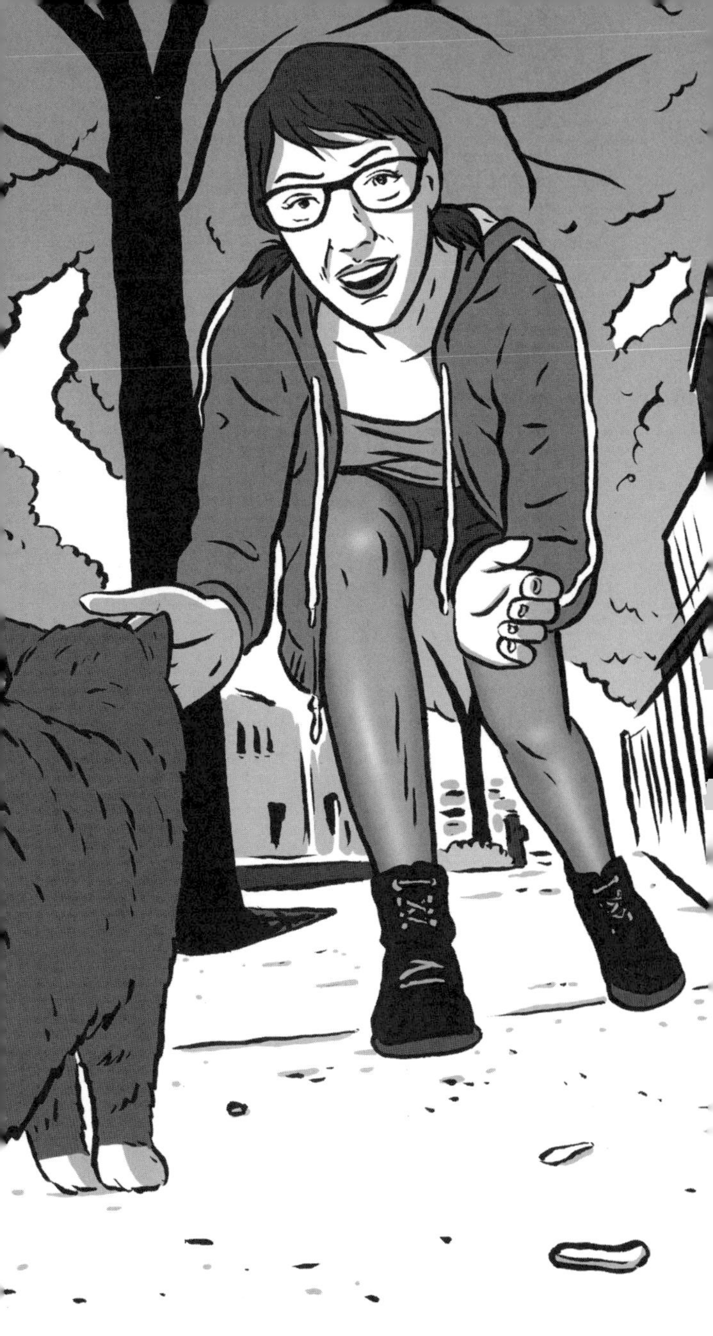

pens with Sofia. One day she stops eating, and she's no longer interested in bullying you, or asserting her dominance. She just lies there and sleeps and doesn't eat. She's even begun to *smell* different.

Alarmed, you actually go over to her, give her licks, but she remains inconsolable.

The girl notices this, and takes her away one afternoon.

Later that evening, she comes back, but without Sofia, and in tears.

"I'm sorry, kitten. Sofia never really recovered from the change, I guess. Her kidneys just started to fail. There's an operation, but I can't afford it. So I thought the best thing would be to — " The girl can't continue. She just collapses into sobs.

It takes you a few days to really realize that Sofia is gone, but when you do, it's quite nice. You're no longer afraid to be attacked at home. You don't know where she went, but you're glad she did.

But once again, this doesn't last long.

Soon the girl is packing her things.

Why are all her things going into various boxes?

You can sense more changes are coming, which are the things you hate the most.

Finally, one day, a bearded man comes into the apartment. He sits at the table and has a drink with the girl, but he is not interested in her. He is interested in you.

He gets down on the floor and plays with you a little bit, and you sit in his lap.

"What's his name?" the bearded man asks.

"Human."

"Human?"

"Yeah."

"He's nice, I like him. I think my kids will too."

The girl nods and smiles. Later, she gives you the longest hug she's ever given you, and certainly the longest hug any human has given to you, then the man carries you out into his car and places you on the passenger seat, before closing the door.

"Good luck with school!" he calls to the girl, and she waves at you.

You drive for a while. It is an exhilarating ride. You spend the whole time with your paws on the window, watching the world rush by.

"So your name's Human, huh?" the man says to you. Even though his voice is quite low in register, and harder to pick up, it's very soothing, like a rumbly purr, and it comforts you. "Human's a *stupid* name. I'm not gonna call you *that*."

Finally the man pulls up to a house at the end of a smooth road. He picks you up and brings you inside.

"But we need a name that you're going to respond to — so maybe... Holden? That *sounds* like Human. We'll call you Holden."

Turn to page 264.

You blink blearily at the bright morning. Your eyes are encrusted with dried stuff and you rub it away with the backs of your paws. You're pretty cozy here in the stadium. You stretch your feet out and they stick out over the lip.

You rub your back against the seats on one side, feeling them break under your weight.

Wait — there is a man! Is it a man? He is so tiny. Maybe he is an ant.

He stands just outside a small tunnel leading out to the field you're resting on.

Idly, you try to grab him, but he runs back inside. You poke your paw into the tunnel after him, but it won't fit.

You lick yourself for a while, washing the night off of you. You grab your tail and suck on it. You miss your mom! You miss the total warmth of the kitten-pile!

Very soon you hear a small buzzing.

It is something small, like a fly.

You focus on the airspace around the stadium and spot a few!

If you decide to swat at them, turn to page 254.

If you keep cleaning yourself and ignore them, turn to page 258.

When neither you nor Sofia move, the woman sighs and shuts the door.

"What are you going to do?" the man asks her.

She shakes her head. "I suppose I'll have to take them to the shelter."

The two humans spend another couple hours looking through the house, checking out the kitchen and filling bags of stuff.

It's very upsetting to you to have these strangers pawing through everything like this. They leave their strange scent on everything.

Later that afternoon, the man leaves with most of the bags. Then the woman pulls out her wafer and talks into it.

"Hi. Yeah," the woman says. "I had a question — my brother died and I have his two cats. I was wondering when it would be good to drop them off today."

All afternoon you have been hoping the sunbeam would come out, but the sky is a dull, desultory grey.

"Uh. I don't know anything about them. Their health or anything. They seem okay. I mean, they seem fine."

The woman paces along the length of the room, moving from the kitchen to the front door and back.

"One is a lot older than the other. Old. I mean, she's an old cat. He had her for a long time. But she's still active. She gets around."

There is more talking into the wafer, and it bores you.

You drop down from your chair and go to take a shit. You could go out, you suppose, but you are wondering where the man is. When is he coming home?

He was so *still*.

You poke your head back into the living room to

find the woman talking to Sofia.

"Sorry grandma," she says. "They don't want you. They're full-up. They'll take the other one because everyone wants kittens, but they don't want you when you're old." She glances in the living room mirror and catches her reflection. "Isn't that always the way."

She slumps down on the couch. "And they say that you'll probably be there long enough that they'll finally *have* to euthanize you. So it's best that I find you a home on my own. But I don't have *time* for this. The estate sale manager comes *tomorrow* and my flight is the day *after*."

The woman sighs, then pinches the flesh between her eyes, frowning.

"Why me?" she mutters, and scratches her neck.

This is one of the rare moments that the woman is sitting down. Despite her unsettling energy, you look at her warm lap. Maybe if you made your way over to it, you could find some comfort there.

The woman sits and thinks for a bit, then suddenly sits up. She leaves the house and doesn't come back for an hour.

But when she does, she brings treats!

You and Sofia are immediately on your feet, recognizing the crinkle of the bag, and the woman generously drops treats in a ragged line. She leads you out into the garage and into her car, where she pours the rest of the treats onto the back seat. You notice that everything is covered in newspaper. But you pay it no mind, you're so busy eating the treats.

The woman shuts the doors and gets in the front. She starts the engine and the vehicle begins purring.

Then she leaves the garage.

Very soon, you feel very drowsy.

It's difficult to keep your head up, so you don't.

Sofia comes stumbling toward you. But not in an aggressive way. She's puzzled by something, and she lies down next to you on the back seat trying to figure it out

When the woman returns an hour later, she first opens the garage door to air everything out. Then she drives you in the rental car to a nearby Wal-Mart, where she gathers you and Sofia up in the newspaper, and tosses you in a dumpster.

THE END

You have just used up one of your lives. You have eight more! Feel free to reincarnate on page 1 and make different choices! See another ending!
Pick another plot!

Pouncing on the car, you get your paws around it. You hear screams from inside as you crunch down on the roof. You roll onto your back and scrabble at it with your hind legs, biting the back bumper.

Then you notice that the whole area is beset with flashing lights. Blue and red lights oscillate on the buildings around you. A manic wailing siren hurts your ears, and thankfully it ceases when a small white car pulls up to the traffic jam all around you.

The lights are coming from the car's roof! You stare, mesmerized.

When two men get out of the car, you roll over and get to your feet, looking down at them, curiously.

"Holy," one of the men says. "What in the actual fuck is that?"

"I think it's a kitten," his partner responds. "But I've never seen one *that* big before."

Both men reach to their sides and lift small L-shaped machines from their waists.

A loud bang coupled with a bright spark greets you, and you feel a pinch in your shoulder.

You don't like the noise, and you scramble back away from them.

More bangs.

You run away, clambering up the side of a building, using window ledges as pawholds. Finally, from the top, you look down at the intersection.

If you decide to move along, and explore the roofs, turn to page 189.

If you'd rather play with the men making the loud bangs, go to 198.

In response to your cry, there is a sudden and unmistakable lurching.

The beast grabs the loops of the bag in its beak and with a powerful push of its wings, lifts you into the air!

The thin edges of the bag shiver. Wind whistles through its holes. You are not grateful to be freezing, but you are grateful that the water seems to be leaking out the way it arrived.

Miserable, unhappy and upset, you hate everything.

But then, a minor miracle — threading its way through the bag loops and beast's beak, a thin shaft of sunlight manages to slip in and alight on your nose. It warms your whiskers.

A moment later, it's gone. But it's enough to remind you of your mom, and the kittenpile, and the possibility of warmth in the world.

You don't know how long the flight is. You've lost track. It seems interminable, but then suddenly it's over.

The bird drops you!

You fall!

But not far.

You hit the ground with a thump. It's still enough to stun you, but you're grateful that *this* time you're not in the water.

You don't move for a long time.

Above you, the beast cries out. Long, sustained calls.

You hate it. You hate everything.

Finally the beast shuts up.

"Archie!" a male voice mutters, "shut the hell up."

You emerge from your bag and look around.

130

You're in a small round room, with soaring walls on all sides. Above them, a bearded man's face appears.

"What do you have for me? Hmm?" the man says. When he spots you, he frowns, then laughs. "That's amazing. You've really outdone yourself this time, Arch."

The beast squawks.

"Not your usual rodents, is it? I didn't think a seagull could *lift* a whole cat," the man says. Then he peers closer. "Or rather — a kitten. Still very impressive, mind you."

The man reaches in with one hand and strokes your head and back. You press against his warmth. It's welcome.

The man's other hand appears. It has something in it.

Ouch! It pricks you.

"What do you say, kitten? Want to help save the world?"

The bird squawks again, and that's the last thing you hear before passing out.

Turn to page 168.

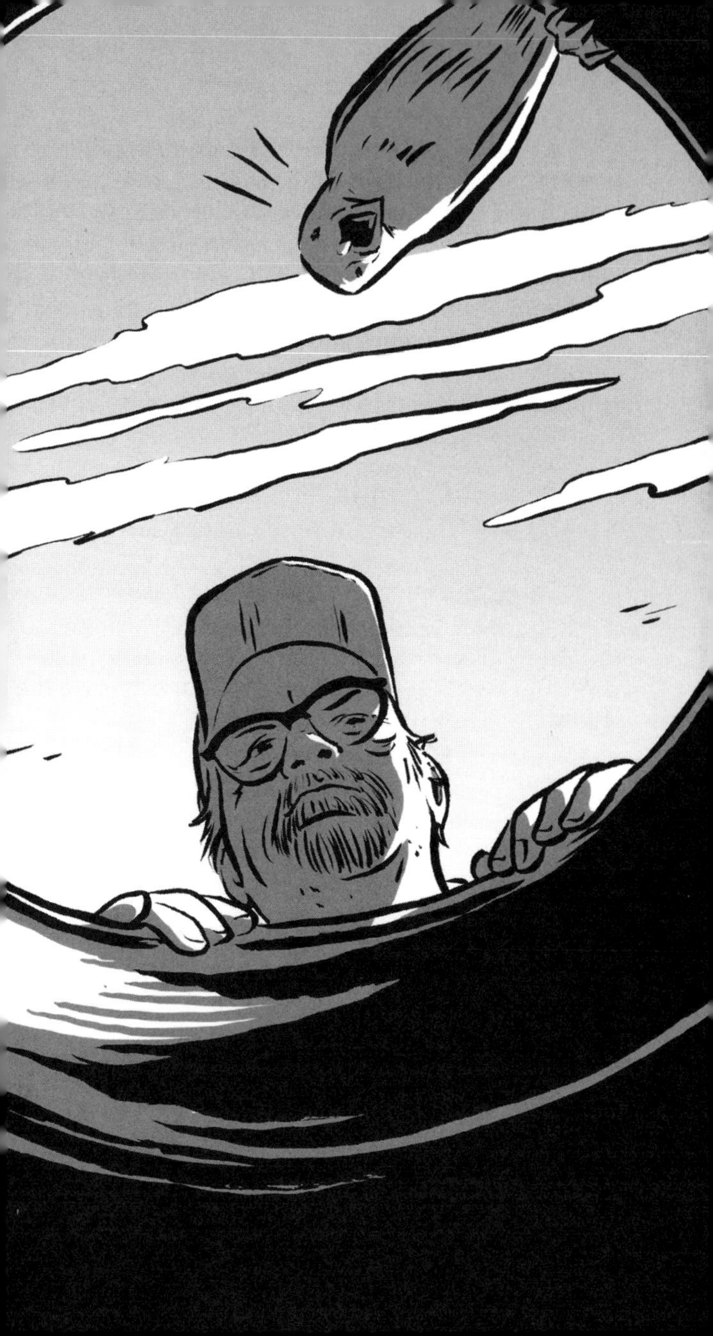

132

You watch the brunette. She keeps patting her lap and looking at you, "C'mere," she makes her voice go high. "C'mere."

You move closer.

"That's right," she urges. She keeps patting.

Finally, you get close enough that she just picks you up and places you in her lap!

At first, you're tense, but then the wide, warm expanse of her thighs calms you. The girl's hands stroke your head and back and you relax.

"That's right," she murmurs. "There you go. There you go."

And then, you begin to purr, gently, quietly, and sustained. At some point, you even fall asleep. It's been a long day.

But then a sudden noise wakes you! You tense. You stare at the screen. Loud flashes fill the room with a strobing light.

"It's okay, kitten," the brunette says.

More noises! What's going on?

"Hey, *claws!*" the brunette's voice takes on an edge. "Watch your claws!" The girl grabs you and lifts you off her lap's warmth and she drops you on the floor.

You are momentarily stunned. You see your tail and you lick it.

"Sorry kitten," the brunette bends down and strokes the top of your head with two fingers. "But no claws!"

There are still things to do! To explore the area near the front of the apartment, turn to page 190.

To explore the kitchen area more fully, turn to 166.

The girl lets herself in the front door and picks up the bowl and dropped candy bars from the floor. She doesn't acknowledge you or Sofia and goes into the kitchen. She spends a good amount of time cleaning everything up, almost in a daze. Then she flops down on the couch beside Sofia.

Sofia gets up and steps daintily into the girl's lap.

The girl doesn't even look at her, but her hand comes up and strokes Sofia's back.

Sofia starts purring.

The girl's odour is weird. Her expression is flat.

"Fuck," she finally mutters, "you guys are probably hungry."

She gets up and goes to the kitchen, pouring bowls full of kibble. She empties the water bowls and tops them off in the sink.

She lifts you up on top of the fridge then collapses into a chair, watching you and Sofia eat.

"So — " the girl says. It comes out as a choked sob. She tries again.

"So, I know you won't understand me. But Joe..."

The girl stops talking to inhale and exhale rapidly. You and Sofia both look at her, alarmed. What is wrong?

"Joe died. He's dead." The girl brings her hands up to her face and sobs.

You stop eating and jump down from the fridge. You go to the girl, leaping up onto her lap. She is in distress, and you need to go to her, just like your own mom came to comfort you when you were meowing over something or other.

The girl cries into your fur, leaving it wet. Normally you purr, but the girl is so tense, you don't feel like you can.

Finally the girl catches her breath and can talk again. "I'm going to come in for the next couple of days until his sister and her husband get here, but I don't know what's going to happen next."

Sofia sits by her food and looks at the girl. Neither of you know what's going on and it's scary. Where is the man? Normally he feeds you in the morning. You don't like this change in procedure.

"I don't know if I..." the girl starts, then stops talking. "If I can adopt you. I don't know what I'm going to do. Without this job, I might go back to school. I just don't know."

Then the girl gets up and lies down on the couch.

You follow her, settling down by her head and later, Sofia jumps up and sits by her ankles. For once, Sofia doesn't challenge your right to be there. You both doze with the girl.

Later, you wake to see her picking her nose with one hand while touching her wafer with the other. Deftly, she rolls her snot into a small ball, which she flicks onto the floor!

Scrambling, you chase it, jumping down from the couch. But you lose it along the way. You can't find it, though you scan the floor studiously.

The girl laughs at this, while Sofia watches you disdainfully.

"Thanks kitten," the girl says, "for giving me something to laugh about."

It is a quiet couple of days. The girl comes in to feed you, and she sits for a bit, giving you and Sofia affection, but she doesn't stay too long. She spends most of her time staring into her wafer, drinking in its sunbeam. At night, Sofia goes up to the man's bed and

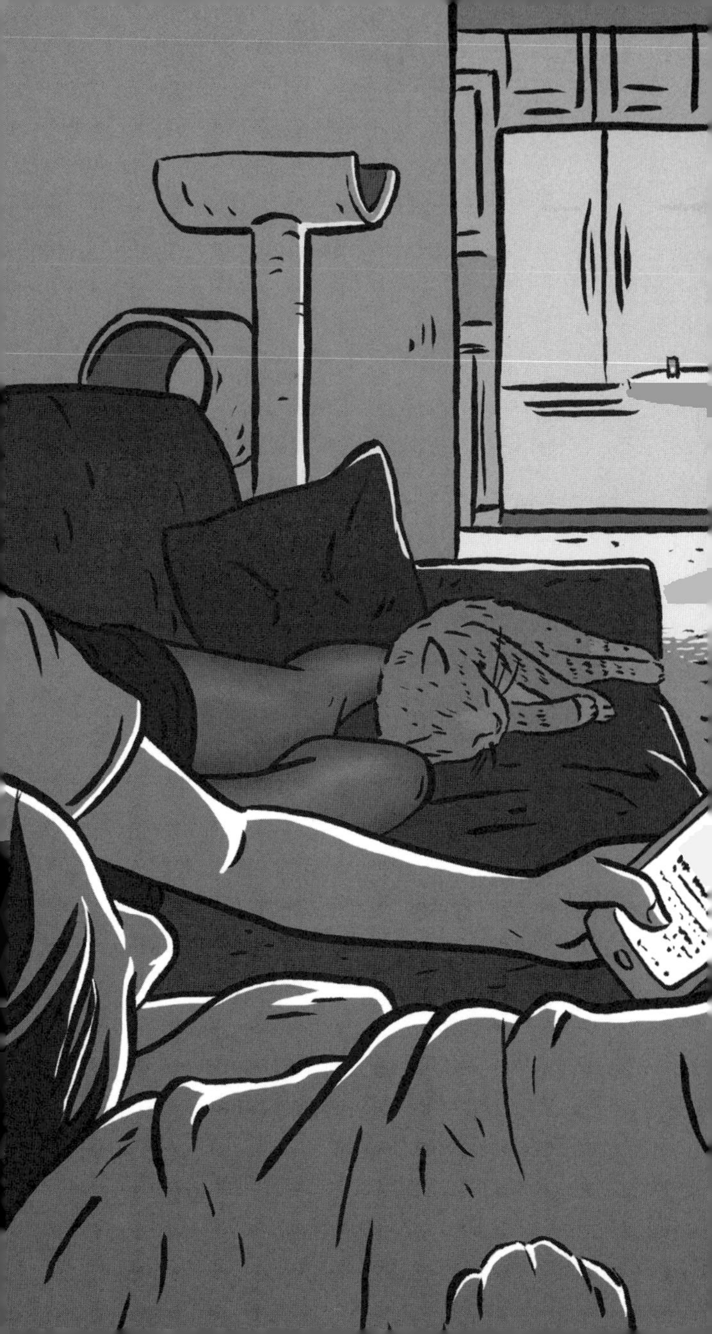

pees on it, mingling her scent with his.

Where is the man?

The next afternoon a woman and a man you have never met let themselves in the front door with a key.

She wears high-heeled shoes that clack on the wood floor and he smells strongly of something fake and fragrant. It makes you sneeze when he walks by you.

"Jesus," the woman exclaims when she walks in. "This whole place smells like *cats!* What the fuck did he do to it?"

"Calm down Jess," the fragrant man soothes her. "We can get a cleaner in here. A professional."

You are immediately on your guard. Who is this woman? Who is the man? Why does he reek?

"Look at all this cat shit," the woman declares, gesturing toward the cat trees, the pictures of cats on the walls. She jabs her finger at one photo of Sofia. "You see that one? He took his fucking cat to a Sears *portrait* studio. For a fucking *cat!*"

"Jess, don't stress," the fragrant man says, "I'll help you post this stuff online. We'll find buyers for all this stuff."

"There's just so *much* of it," the woman moans. "And not all of it is his. My Aunt Sarah was *also* a cat-loving loser. I think that's why she left the house to him. Can you believe that?" The woman stews for a moment then continues bitterly, "I could have done amazing *things* with this house. We could have renovated it, turned the house into *three* apartments and rented each *one* of them out."

"We still can," the man says.

The woman sighs and for the first time seems to

notice you and Sofia. "Well, here they are. The resident leeches." She points to Sofia and tells the man, "You wouldn't believe how much my brother spent on that one a few years back. Some stupid operation. Cost literally *thousands*. It's enough to make you cry."

The woman makes no move to approach you. Her energy is almost entirely contained. You have the feeling that like Sofia, she is unpredictable, and ready to explode. So you stay where you are.

"Awright," she says. "We should spread out. Look for whatever's still worth anything. Is there anything we can sell to help recover the equity of the house."

The woman heads upstairs while the smelly man goes downstairs.

You hear them rummaging around.

After a little while, they meet back in the living room. The woman carries the man's laptop. "Found this," she says, putting it on the computer desk.

The man places a small box on the table beside it.

"What the hell is that?" the woman asks.

"Remote-controlled mouse," the man replies. "Your brother really loved cats. The basement is full of this kind of thing. Abandoned toys. Bags of cat treats. Cat magazines. Trinkets. Lots of missing cat posters."

"Maybe we can get one of the shelters to come and take all of it. Save us a trip to the dump."

"Have you looked in the garage yet?" the man asks.

"Uh. No. Why?"

"Don't."

Abruptly, the front door opens and the girl walks in.

"Oh!" she says, "you surprised me."

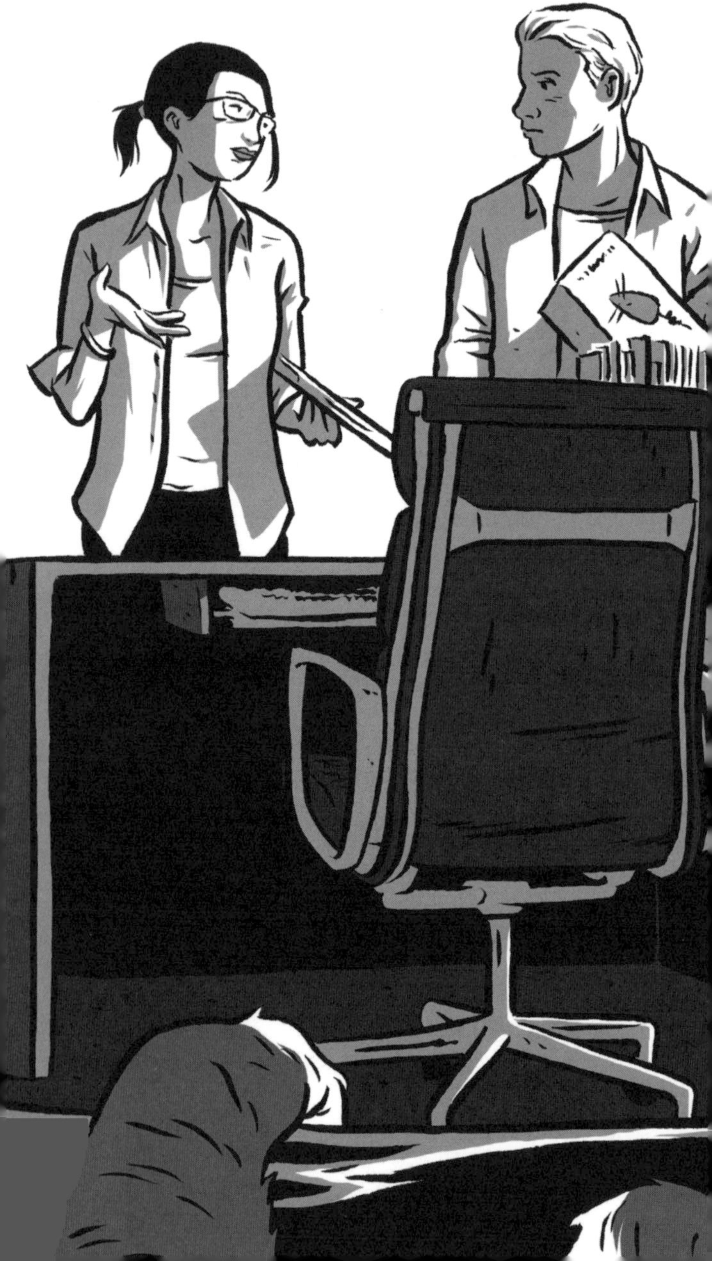

The woman walks over and shakes the girl's hand. "Hi. I'm Jess. Joe's sister. We talked on the phone? Are you Dashiell?"

The girl nods.

"Cool name."

"Thanks. Um. How was your flight?"

The humans make small talk while the girl moves between yourself and Sofia, petting you in turn.

Finally the girl asks, "When do you think the funeral might be?"

"Oh," the woman looks down, "We're not going to have a funeral."

"What?"

"We kind of don't have time. Me and Eric," she points at the man, "have got to get back to our firm. Joe would have wanted to be cremated anyway. So that's what we're going to do. And we're going to have a beautiful memorial on his Facebook page, so all his friends can chime in and remember him together."

The girl doesn't say anything. She's still taking it all in.

"Hey — do you want the cats?" the woman gestures at you and Sofia.

"Ah," the girl stammers. "I don't know if I can. I think I might go back to school, but that's up in the air. Also, they might — " The girl pauses for a moment and swallows. Then she continues, "They might remind me too much of Joe."

The woman nods, "No problem. We can take care of them."

"Uh. What do you mean?"

"We'll take them to the shelter. They'll find them new homes."

The girl nods, then spots the laptop and the box

on the desk.

"Oh don't mind us," the woman says. "We're just going over my brother's things."

"Are you taking the laptop?" the girl asks.

"Why?" the woman's eyes narrow. "Is it yours?"

"Oh, no," the girl replies quickly, "but we've just got so many open cases and they're all on it. I've got some, but he's got all the latest updates and sightings."

"Well," the woman says magnanimously, "why don't you look through it and copy whatever files you need."

Then the girl sighs, and looks close to tears. "But without Joe, I don't know if Federal Bureau of Missing Cats will continue. He was like, the heart of it. I was just his employee."

"You can have it if you want," the woman says. "It's yours."

"What?" the girl says, confused.

"You can continue the good work that I'm sure you and my brother did."

The girl is speechless.

"Normally," the woman continues, "when a business changes hands, you would buy it from us. But since it was a business in name only, we'll waive the fee."

"What do you mean — a business in 'name' only?"

The woman blinks. "It made no money," she explains. "Do the math — do you really think a reward of $300 one week, $400 the next is enough to pay the overhead on a home office like this? A full-time employee like yourself? The cost of printing posters. The website? My brother's 'business' was *hemorrhaging* money. He re-mortgaged the equity of this *house* to keep his 'business' running. In a few years, it would have been over. The bank would have taken it and the business would have died. So you can have the Bureau of Missing Cats. I'm sure it was a good thing what you two were doing. But it's not a business. It's a *hobby*. Its a pasttime. It's a joke."

The girl sits down on the couch and Sofia sidles up against her thigh.

"What we did wasn't a joke," she says, quietly.

"Oh no," the woman says, "sorry. I didn't mean it that way. Of course the work you did was very important. Good for the world. That's not what I meant."

The girl doesn't say anything.

"I'm just saying," the woman hastens to add, filling the uncomfortable silence, "that my brother should have opened up a cat café — or even, like he joked one time, a cat bar. *Those* are viable business models!"

"I have to go, I think," the girl says suddenly. She bends down and gives Sofia a kiss, then she comes over to you sitting on your chair and kisses you as well. "Thank you," she says to the woman, "for the offer of the business. But it was Joe's, and I couldn't do it justice."

Then the girl is gone, closing the front door behind her. You could sense, as she left, that she was a little like a wet towel, sodden with water. One squeeze and she would have burst.

"Well that's that," the woman says. She goes over to the front door and opens it again.

"What are you doing?" the man asks.

"Take those collars off those cats," she directs.

"Okay..." the man replies, going over to you. "But what are we doing?"

142

The man takes the collar off of you and the woman does the same to Sofia.

"We're hoping these cats run away on their own. Save us a trip to the shelter."

"Why take their collars off?"

"So whoever finds them doesn't *return* them to us!"

The man chuckles. "Oh, right."

Suddenly, your neck is free. You've had the collar on for so long, it seemed to have become a part of you. Now you feel a little naked, even though you are normally naked.

Sofia, normally unperturbed, seems as confused as you are.

A clean, cold wind blows in the front door.

"Get out of here, you leeches," the woman says. "You're letting the heat out."

If you run out the front door, turn to page 120.

If you decide to stay inside where it's warm, turn to page 125.

That night the girl stays over. She's stayed over exactly once before, months ago, when she and the man spent all evening out on an emergency patrol, looking for a newly-escaped cat. It'd been too late for her to go home, so she stayed in the guestroom, and the man slept in his bedroom.

But this night, the man and the girl sleep together.

They don't patrol the next day, though they do the day after.

Over time, the girl starts sleeping in the man's room, and she starts leaving things that smell strongly of her scent. The man seems happier, lighter. When he is alone, he sings to himself. Their smells begin to mingle.

A year later, the girl takes over the guestroom. One day there is a big move, where the front door is open all day and the man, the girl, and a few people you've never met before spend hours tramping up and down the stairs moving boxes and items.

You and Sofia stay out of the way, but later that evening everyone hangs out in the kitchen eating pizza and you taste a little bit. You like the cheese, though later that night you don't feel so good.

And then, one day, a few months later, Sofia stops eating. She just sleeps all day, licking herself. The man and the girl, concerned, take her away, but Sofia does not return.

Over the past year, the two of you'd come to an understanding. The moving-in of the girl had acted as a catalyst. You were both faced with this new change, and it somehow allied you. Or maybe it was the fact that you had grown to your full size and she couldn't just sit on you and beat you up anymore. Maybe it was her advanced age. Whatever the case, there came a kind of truce. And you are sad that she just disappeared like that.

Then one day, months later, she makes a weird sort of re-appearance.

The man brings home what looks like high-heeled shoes, only instead of heels, it's Sofia's forelegs supporting the shoe. He places them on a high shelf, so you can't reach them, but from the top of a cat tree you can get a good look, and they are definitely Sofia's.

Over time, something else changes — the girl. You can smell the changes before you start seeing them. Her belly is getting bigger and it won't stop. One night, when she is on the couch, you are resting on her belly when you feel it move! She laughs when you jump up and start looking for the creature.

As her belly gets larger, the girl stops going out on patrol — spending more time at the computer, and fielding calls.

Then one day, they bring a baby home. It doesn't smell like either of them. It has its own smell. The humans stop paying attention to you, and spend all their time focussing on the baby.

The baby gets its own room. Whole furniture is brought in for it. Everything begins to smell like it. And it howls. Sometimes for hours. All night. Sometimes you sleep in the basement, to get some relief.

And then one day the man feeds you wet food in the morning, then holds you for a long time on the couch. Normally he's out on patrol at this time, but today he's not. Something's wrong. The man has been quietly sobbing all morning.

The girl comes down, the baby asleep in her arms.

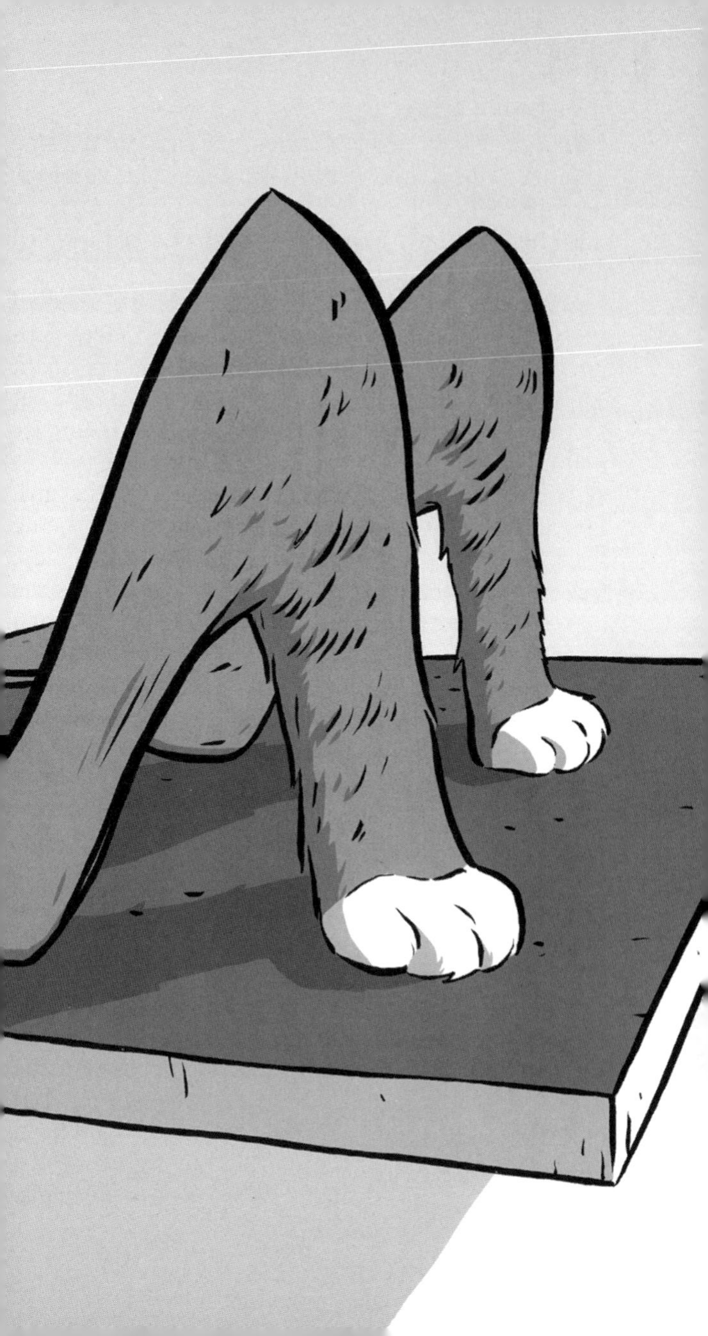

146

Last night, unusually, she spent a couple hours petting you, curled up against you, while the man took care of the baby. She was crying too. Why such sadness from your two favourite humans?

"Hon — how are you doing?" she asks.

"I know we've gotta do this," he says, rubbing your cheek. "Sarah's allergic, I know. It's gotta be done. But I'm just sad about it. Hugh's just been with us for a long time."

The doorbell rings, echoing throughout the house and the baby stirs. The girl heads back upstairs while the man gets the door.

A bearded stranger stands there. He lets you smell his hand. Then the man gives you a long hug, and brings you out into the bearded stranger's car.

"Goodbye, Hugh," the man says tearfully. "Have a good life."

You drive for a while. It is an exhilarating ride. You spend the whole time with your paws on the window, watching the world rush by.

"So your name's Human, huh?" the strange man talks to you. Even though his voice is quite low in register, and harder to pick up, it's very soothing, like a rumbly purr, and it comforts you. "Human's a stupid name. I'm not gonna call you *that*."

Finally the strange man pulls up to a house at the end of a smooth road. He picks you up and brings you inside.

"But we need a name that you're going to respond to — so maybe... Holden? That *sounds* like Human. We'll call you Holden."

Turn to page 264.

After a terrifying flight, you find yourself dropped on solid ground again. But the beast is not done with you — it peers in the bag, then starts pecking at you!

You cry out. You wave your puny paws at its beak. You don't know what to do!

The monstrous beak of the monster opens up and lets out a shriek that curls your earhair. Then, in the confusion of it flapping half in and half out of the bag, you manage to snag one of its wings! It doesn't like this at all, and it shakes you off frantically, leaving feathers flying.

Then it retreats, and is gone.

For the next few seconds you are panting, and angry, and scared. You tremble, filled with too much energy. Slowly, the plastic bag collapses around you. Slowly, breath by breath, you calm down.

Close by, you hear voices. Two girls.

"Did you see that?"

"Yeah, but what the fuck?!"

"Oh god! Look!"

Suddenly, the beast is back! It screams at you, then aims its sharp beak at your eyes! You bat at its head ineffectually.

"What a crazy bird!" one of the girls yells.

"Kick it!"

"Kick it?! I'm not gonna kick a bird!"

Then the bird is gone, a half-choked bleat and a feather's all that's left before you.

"Holy shit."

"I can't believe you kicked it!"

"Well — me *neither!*"

Two faces peer in the bag. One girl is blonde. The other brunette.

"Oh my god," the brunette says, a half-smile on

her face, "This is like, our prayers answered."

"Exactly what we were looking for. I can't believe it," the blonde responds.

The blonde reaches in to touch you but you are too keyed up and you back away.

"Here, gimme your hat." The blonde fishes a dark black woolen hat from the brunette's bag, then engulfs you with it.

You are too shocked to do anything as she traps you.

"Quick!" she orders. "Open my backpack."

You are unceremoniously dumped in the bag. It's not a long fall, but it's very disconcerting.

The last light disappears as the backpack zips closed.

Well, there's not much you can do now. At least it's warm in here.

"This one is younger than I'd like," the blonde says, "but I think we can use him."

They start walking, and the steady rhythmic pace puts you to sleep.

Turn to page 157.

Out in the yard, you crawl through the grass. It tickles your nose, and once or twice you sneeze. You are surprised by the sneezing. By its suddenness and explosiveness. How you have no control over it, but also how good it feels afterwards. You are still getting used to them.

Wait, there's something — in the sky! It flutters down and lands on a fence. The noises it makes are pleasing chirps.

Almost without realizing it, you follow the little bird. You want it. You want to get close to it. But as you approach, it flies away!

You duck out back into a long alley. Now the bird is perched on the opposite fence.

This time you creep forward *slowly*. You don't want to startle it.

Despite your best efforts, it flies off again — this time into another backyard with tall trees overhead.

Trotting as fast as your tiny legs can carry you, eventually you find the right backyard and duck in.

You see the bird immediately. It chirps at you, sitting on a little branch connected to a tiny green house, fixed upon a high tree. You watch as the bird zips into a hole in the house. The hole is the perfect size for the bird, you realize, as if it were made for it.

More than anything you want to get to that hole, and jump on the bird when it comes out.

But the house is high up. Higher than you have ever climbed, or ever been.

And then you notice something else — at the base of the tree, there is another little house. This one is red, and larger than the bird house. This one has a hole in it too, but sized just for you!

Curious, you move closer. You smell something

great inside. You're pretty sure you've smelt it before
— wet food. You'd had it once or twice before at the
woman's house. She fed it to you and your siblings in
the playpen. You love it.

Do you go after the bird? Turn to page 162.

Do you go after the wet food? Turn to page 172.

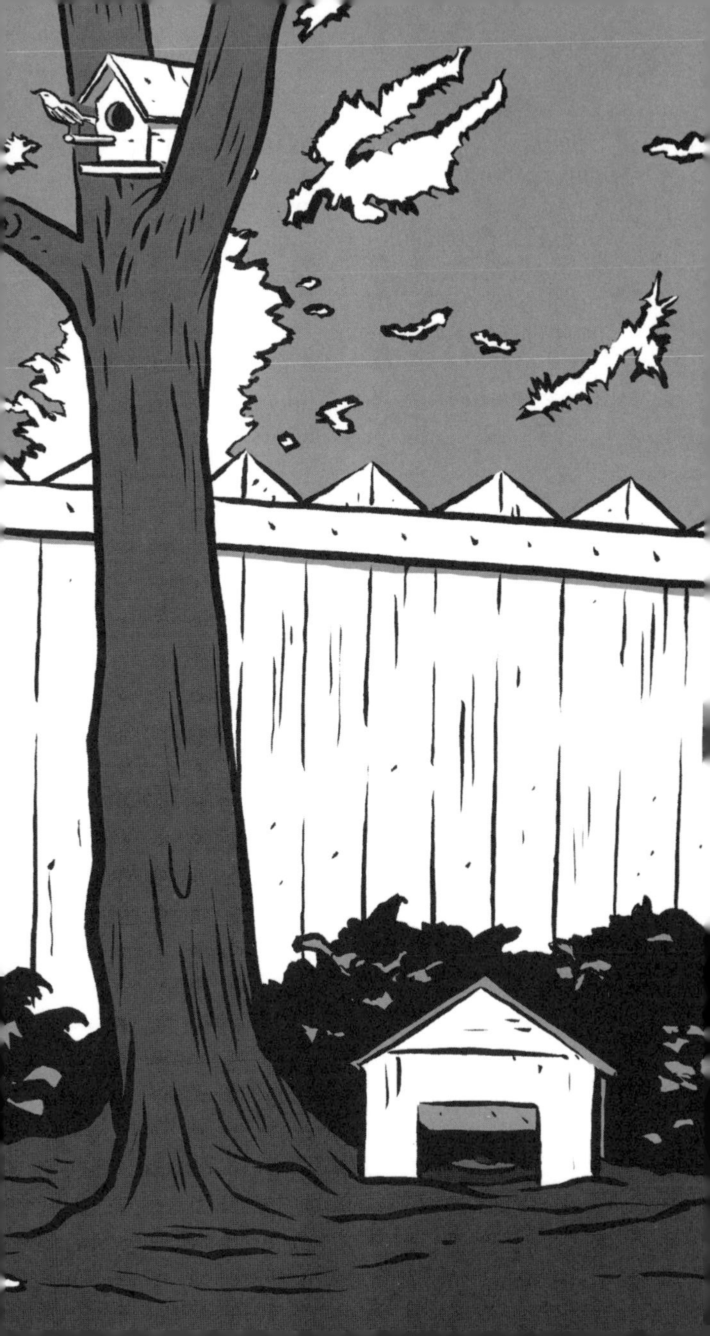

You bite down on the brunette's hand as it comes for you.

"Ah!" she hisses. "Fucking shit!"

You think she'll leave you alone now, but with her other hand, she grabs you by the scruff of your neck and tosses you into the open bag!

The blonde zips it up.

"You okay?"

"Not sure. Did it look like it had rabies?"

The blonde laughs. "I think you'll be okay." She slings you on her back and the two of them start walking. You search the bag desperately for a way out, but can't find anything. You meow at the girls repeatedly.

After awhile, the blonde stops.

"What?" the brunette asks. "What is it?"

"This cat."

"What about him?"

"It's a problem. It's unfriendly, and it's hostile."

"Uh...yeah? And...?"

"I don't think we can use him. No one's going to take him."

The brunette sighs. "What should we do? Let it go?"

"No," the blonde says. "You saw him. He's sooo young. The streets would eat him alive."

"Alright, alright," the brunette says, "I know what you're thinking. Let's just get it over with."

The girls start walking again and their steady pace lulls you to sleep.

You awake to hear the blonde talking.

"...found him near the railway tracks."

"Okay, what kind of cat is it? It's in the bag?" Another voice. An older woman.

"He's a tabby," the brunette supplies.

"Did it have a tag? Does he have a name?"

"He's kinda orange," the blonde says. "Golden."

"Holden?" the woman asks.

"Golden," the blonde repeats.

"Can I see him?"

The blonde unzips the bag and puts it on a counter. Blinking in the bright light, you poke your nose out of the opening, trying to get a sense of your surroundings. Without a word, two gloved hands surround you, then move you into another container.

You are sick of being moved! You are sick of containers! You struggle to free yourself, but the hands know what they're doing.

"Well thank you for bringing him in," the older woman tells the girls. "He's a young one. He should have no problem finding a new home. Kittens are always in high demand."

The girls turn to leave when the blonde stops and looks back at the woman.

"Hey," she asks tentatively, "is it possible that a white Turkish Angora cat was turned in about a month ago?"

"Anything's possible," the woman says. "We get a lot of cats. Was it chipped? Did it have a collar on?"

"No chip. And I don't know if she would have been turned in with a collar."

"We do our best to ID cats and return them to their owners, but with no chip and no collar, it might have gone to one of our animal rescue partners, who try to find fosters or permanent homes for the cats. Or..." and here the woman trails off.

"Or what?" the blonde asks, an edge to her voice.

"Or it might have been turned in to one of the private animal control contractors around the city."

"Really? How many are there?" the blonde asks.

"Well," the woman demurs, "you wouldn't find it there. Not if it was turned in a month ago."

"Why's that?" the brunette asks.

The older woman shakes her head. "They euthanize them. After a few days, if no one claims them, they're gone."

The blonde looks like she's close to crying.

"How can I find out? If they put my cat to sleep?"

"Well you can't," the woman explains. "They don't even advertise them. They don't keep any records. They don't make any attempt to contact the owner in any way. We've been trying for years to shut them down."

The blonde nods, and the brunette puts her hand on the girl's shoulder.

They walk out of the facility, leaving you there.

Turn to page 246.

Next morning, when the blonde finally opens the door, you are cranky.

You meow angrily at her.

"Oh yeah?" she taunts you. "Is that how it is?"

You didn't sleep well. You're hungry. And the backroom smelled strongly of another cat, so you've been unsettled the entire night.

"He's pissed," the blonde chuckles to the brunette, standing in the kitchen.

"I don't blame him," the brunette says. She is stirring something in a bowl, which she puts down on the floor in front of you. "He's probably starving."

Milk.

You start for it, but then you balk. It's different than your mom's milk. Its smells strange. But you're so hungry that you drink it anyway. It takes a little getting used to.

While you're drinking, the blonde puts the collar back on around your neck. You're so busy eating, you don't even fight it.

You lap at the milk for what seems like forever. You lick your lips. You bring your arms up to catch the wet on the side of your cheeks.

This morning, the whole process repeats. You're let out on the line in the front yard, and the girls go hide in the car. You're getting used to this. You like this yard. You're coming to think of it as *your* yard. This morning it's kind of quiet, so you chew experimentally on some grass. It's cool and wet, but not very tasty. It's a little bitter.

Hours pass. The only action is a mature black cat who wanders by on the sidewalk. He reminds you for a moment of Tupac. You can tell he has seen you, but he doesn't acknowledge your presence, and continues on his patrol of the neighbourhood.

Then a boy comes by, slowing as he passes. He takes a quick glance at you, then licks his lips as he keeps walking. For a while, you get distracted by a bird that's flying very far off, but then notice that the boy has returned.

This time, he has an open cloth bag in his hand. He stops at the fence, and looks around as he opens the gate. He makes a beeline for you, bending down to fiddle with the leash attached to your collar.

"67," he says to himself, "Cosgrove Crescent."

You're dumped immediately into the bag, and he closes the drawstring.

At first, you're upset, but then you make an amazing discovery — there are lots of *treats* in the bag!

They are so fragrant. You sniff excitedly at them. You know they will hurt your teeth and your gums, but they smell so good you are willing to risk it.

But you don't like the bag's swinging motion. The boy is moving too fast.

If you howl in protest, make some noise over on page 205.

If you eat the treats, turn to page 208.

If you decide to forgo the treats and do everything you can to escape the bag, turn to page 220.

When the backpack is unzipped, you are now reluctant to leave. It's cozy in here. Light spills in, but you don't move. Then, abruptly, the bag is upended, and you spill out awkwardly onto a table. You stand there, blinking, taking in your new surroundings.

"Aw, he's cute," the brunette chirps.

"He's crazy young, though," the blonde responds. "What can I feed him? Some milk?"

"I don't think cow's milk is good for him."

The blonde frowns. "I don't have any kitten milk. It's been a long time since I even *had* a kitten. This'll have to do for now."

The blonde girl goes over to the sink and grabs a bowl, filling it with water. Then she places it in front of you on the table.

"I can stop by the pet store on the way home tonight and pick some kitten milk up."

"Okay," the blonde says, "but don't get a large or anything. I'm hoping we won't have him that long."

You lap at the cold water. Ugh. You are tired of cold things. But you drink it anyway.

"Do you really think this'll work?" the brunette asks.

"What we need is proof," the blonde responds. "All we have now are suspicions. C'mon — get your camera out."

The brunette reaches into her shoulder bag and pulls out a small machine that she fits on her hand. She aims it at you, and a small red light appears in one corner. The brunette isn't looking at you, exactly, she's looking at her hand, but she's still following you around with the machine. It's unsettling.

While you're drinking, the blonde comes over and tries to fit something around your neck.

158

You back away from it, but she holds you still.

"Hold on," she mutters, as her fingers work on something you can't see, but which you can certainly feel. You don't like this at all. With every movement, something around your neck jingles.

"So," the blonde says to the brunette, who directs the camera at the both of you, "we're putting this collar on this cat we found. We're about to put him out in the yard. And we're going to see what happens."

You try to shrug your way out of the collar, but it's quite tight. You mewl in disapproval, but the girls don't seem to hear you. The blonde now clips a long lead to the collar. This is getting worse every second!

"C'mon kitten," the blonde says, lifting you up. She walks you through a couple of rooms and then out the front door into a yard. She clips the end of the lead to a post, then drops you on the grass.

The brunette follows, machine in her hand every step of the way.

"Can you just get a basic shot of the kitten's face?" the blonde asks. "We can use it for the posters."

"Sure," the brunette bends down and moves the machine closer.

Something's going on. You don't like it. Everything feels wrong. The glassy eye of the machine has a tiny reflection of movement in it. You want to look closer, but then the brunette is up and joining the blonde on the sidewalk.

You watch as they cross the street and get into a parked car. Inside, the brunette still aims her machine at you. They both stare at you.

There's not much to do out here. You explore the limits of your lead, and it allows you to go to the edges of the yard, but no farther. Every once in a while,

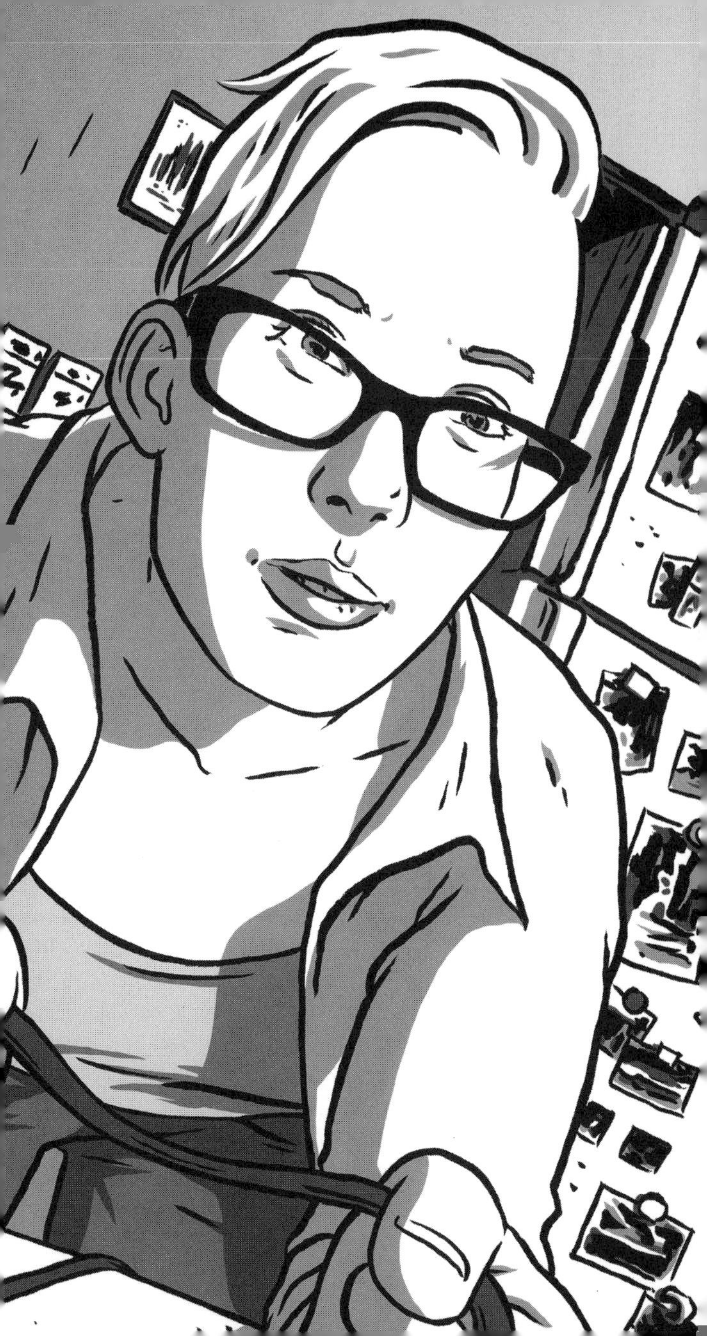

you take another look at the car, and the girls are still there. Sometimes they are watching you. Sometimes not. They talk. They look bored.

In the corner of the yard, there is a ratty wooden chair. You extend your claws and scratch it, digging deep. It's very satisfying, and you give it enough pulls to get a good start.

Throughout the day, a lot of cars move past. They are scary at first, but they never leave the road, and while you never really get used to the noise and their size and their movement — at least they are predictable.

Near the end of the day, a squirrel chatters in the tree above you. You have never seen such a magnificent creature. Its tail billows seductively. All you can imagine is jumping on that tail, clutching it in your arms. You watch the way it moves along the outer bark of the tree, sinewy and sure. You promise yourself that when you are bigger, you'll do everything you can to get closer to squirrels.

The girls reappear just as the sun is setting. It's too bad, because with the dusk, everything around you is coming into sharper focus.

They pick you up and take you inside, unbuckling the collar while they're at it.

"What do we do? Try again tomorrow?" the brunette asks.

"Can you come over?"

"Sure. I don't mind skipping class for another day."

"What do you want to do now? Are you hungry?"

"I could eat," the brunette replies.

You're really hungry. All you've had today was that water. You meow at the two girls, trying to get them to understand how unhappy and cranky you are. Then it occurs to you that you might have more luck appealing to just one of them.

Do you approach the blonde? Turn to page 177.

If you approach the brunette instead, turn to 170.

With trepidation you approach the tree. You find pretty good purchase with your claws, but it hurts if you hang on too long. But you go for it anyway. You want the bird in your mouth.

With your eye on the tiny house, you make a sudden effort, climbing a few feet up the tree trunk.

But you get nervous!

You are higher than you have ever climbed.

A terrified mewl escapes your mouth.

Perhaps this was a bad idea.

You try to get one paw free, but one of your claws is caught on some tree bark.

You get your other paw loose, and you start slipping, but the one claw is still caught!

You hang there like an idiot, the pain slowly increasing.

You decide you don't like pain.

Your hind legs scrabble on the tree, but can't seem to grip anything.

Suddenly, the pressure becomes too great and you fall! You tumble into a heap at the base of the tree. Something must have given way.

Thankfully the claw is still there. It aches, but it's okay. You flex it in and out of its sheath experimentally to make sure.

Above you, the bird reappears on the stick, chitters nervously, then disappears into its house, still out of reach. You are filled momentarily with a monstrous, immense rage.

So many things still so out of reach!

You pause by the base of the tree to lick your aching paw and gather your dignity. But then you hear something intriguing from the alley.

The gentle shaking of something in a container.

You know the sound because the woman used to call to your mom with it. And your mom always went running.

You are curious. But you are also curious about the house that you suspect has *wet* food in it.

If you explore the little kitten-sized house, turn to page 172.

If you decide to go to the alley, turn to 184.

164

The man chases you around the lab. You leap up onto a table, knocking over glassware, which rolls and shatters on the floor! But the man pays it no mind.

It smells bad, and the man is unwell. His scent betrays stress and anger. You need to get away from him.

You run into a darkened room and try to hide under a desk, but you don't quite fit. Instead, you jump up on top of it, ready to slash if you have to. But to your surprise, the man doesn't chase you — he simply closes the door on you. You're trapped! The man peers in through a window.

"You have shown unusual growth in a short time, my friend," he says. "This will yield some interesting data." Abruptly, the man turns, hearing something.

Three people appear behind him, their faces covered with masks or bandanas. They start opening cages, and coaxing other animals out.

"You can't do this!" the man shouts at them. He rushes to stop them, but two of the people grab him, and zip-tie his wrists behind him.

"'No animal experimentation,' right?" one of the intruders says. "How can we be freeing animals if they weren't supposed to *exist!*"

Finally, one of the people opens the door to your room, and you run out!

"Whoa, what is that? A cat?"

The scent of fresh air drifts in from the door one of the intruders holds open, and you dash for it.

Turn to page 187.

You trot down a side street and try to keep in the shadows. Finally you get to a large open area that's covered in grass, is poorly-lit, and dotted with trees.

You duck underneath one of these trees and rub your cheek against some of its bottom branches. But in doing so, you inadvertently disturb some birds! They fly out like a cluster of flies, scrambling in the air. You bat at them, but they are too fast.

You sharpen your claws on the tree trunk, one paw at a time.

Then you hear something behind you.

There is a small asphalt path on the ground some distance away, lit sporadically by streetlamps. A man and his dog pause underneath one. The dog sniffs at the lamp base, but then another scent catches its attention, and it looks over to stare at you. It barks twice, sharply cutting into the quiet night.

The man looks in your direction, blinks, and then jerks back.

"My god!" he shouts. "What is that?!"

Why doesn't everyone just leave you alone? What's with all the shouting?

If you try to silence the dog, turn to page 193.

If you'd rather steal off into the night, turn to 222.

166

As you make your way back to the kitchen, you discover a small room off the hallway. It's colder in here, more moist. What's more — there is the smell of another cat. For a moment, you are on your guard, but the smell is faint. The other cat has not been around for a long time.

On the wall, there is a small recess, and a round, white cylinder set inside it. A short tail of soft paper trails down invitingly. You move over to it and make a little jump!

Your extended claw snags it, and you manage to pull it further down. You jump again, and this time it's easier to yank.

Suddenly, the tail becomes a torrent, and the paper piles up at the bottom. It's very exciting! But then the stream stops.

You pull more — to get it going again. The paper unrolls fabulously, and gathers at the bottom. You love this, whatever this is.

But then, there comes a point where no more paper unravels. It seems to have stuck. You pull at the paper, but your claws only tear it. But that is delightful in its own way. Now you tear at everything!

The paper is so tearable. You roll around in the waves of warm paper. You fall on your side and gather it in your arms, your extended claws shredding it into thousands of floating pieces. There is so much paper in the air that you sneeze into it, and send it swirling anew. This place is fun, you decide. You want to see what else is out there.

Next, you decide to check out the compellingly smelly area near the front door on page 190.

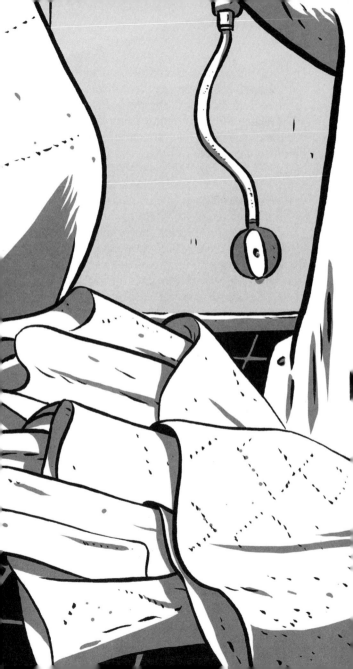

You wake up in a small cage. The only thing in it is a tiny, clear container of water in a corner, and you lap at it. The water doesn't taste like anything at all, which is unusual because most of the water you've ever had tastes like *something*. But this water is flat and flavourless.

"No, no, look— " a man says. He is facing away from you, by a desk, hand holding a rectangular wafer to his ear. "These activists don't understand. They have no concept of what we're doing here. Cancer is simply uncontrolled growth. That's all it is. It tries to turn everything *into* itself, until *itself* is all that there is. And we work to stem it. Animals are not used in our research, period. We are trying to cure *humans*."

You notice that your cage is just one of a long line of cages. There are creatures in each one, and this is your first time seeing them. One of them looks like a patterned rock, but you watch it for a few moments and it actually moves. But very slowly.

Farther down, you can smell a rat. Literally. You watch it scurry in its cage. Maybe it can smell you, too. And then there's a small sleeping dog. Past that is another creature you can't see.

"Well that's what these animal-rights activists are," the man spits, "a cancer on research that saves lives! You can quote me on that! And the sooner they stop these ridiculous protests, the sooner we can get back to trying to *help* people."

The man presses his wafer and drops it into the pocket of the white labcoat he's wearing. Then he walks down the line of cages and stops at yours. He bends down and smiles at you.

"Well hello there," he places his hand on top of the cage and you can smell meat of some kind, reeking. "Sorry about that. Didn't mean to wake you. Reporters have me all riled up today." Then he frowns. "Are you okay, kitty?"

For the last twenty seconds or so, you've been feeling weird, and swaying back and forth. The cage seems too small. You feel like it's closing in. You need to get out of it. You feel like you can't breathe all of a sudden. You throw your weight against the front of the cage, shifting it forward a few inches.

"Whoa, whoa!" the man shouts, but you throw yourself against the cage again and your momentum knocks it off the table!

When it crashes on the floor, the cage pops off its plastic base, and you are free!

The man comes at you, arms out as if to corral you.

He's going to grab you!

If you attack him, turn to page 119.

If you run, go to page 164.

You approach the brunette's feet and meow pointedly at her. She looks down, grins, and lifts you up.

"Whee!" she says, as she spins you around. "So cute!"

"I'm having a beer," the blonde says, opening the fridge. "Want one?"

"You got any wine?" the brunette asks. Then she puts you in the sink. You take a moment to assess your new surroundings — slick aluminum walls rise up on all sides. Plates and mugs inhabit the sink with you. There's food on them! You examine them very closely.

Behind a mug, there is a crumb and you eat it. You're not sure what it is, but it's edible. You keep following your nose, and you find more crumbs!

"No wine, sorry. But I've got juice? Pop? My mom has those coolers."

"Ugh," the brunette replies. "Okay. I'll have a beer."

The blonde checks on you in the sink.

"Thirsty kitten?" she says, and grabs a bowl from the pile in front of you. Then she reaches over you, and suddenly a huge torrent of water comes gushing out of this metal arm above you!

Whoa! You jump back in alarm.

But the fast-moving stream is *fascinating* to you — your paw reaches out and swings at it! You catch only water.

The blonde laughs, watching you.

And once it fills the bowl, the water stops.

You approach it cautiously. You look up at the metal arm, to make sure it doesn't just start gushing again. As you lap up the water, however, a single drop splashes on your nose! You lick at the moisture with your tongue.

"Here," the blonde says, turning away from you. You hear the clinking of glass on glass and then the brunette is peering down at you in the sink.

"C'mon kitten," she says. "Get out of there. You wanna watch a movie?"

She lifts you up, wipes you on her shirt, then carries you to the living room, where you're dropped on a couch.

Turn to page 182.

Eagerly, you creep into the little house. It's dark in here, and less exposed, and you like that. On a plate inside there *is* wet food. A small fly buzzes around it, which distracts you momentarily, but the smell of the food is incredible and you immediately begin licking it, taking huge bites.

All of a sudden, there is a loud bang! and the room goes dark.

You jump and run around in circles for a few seconds before you run out of breath and are forced to slow down.

Frozen, you stand in a corner and wait.

What's happening?! What's happening?!

Moments pass, but nothing happens.

Maybe that's all that was going to happen.

In time, the smell of the food brings you forward again, and you eat about half of the portion before you feel full.

Then you stumble into a corner and fall asleep.

It's bright when you awake.

You look up and the roof of the house is now a clear pane of glass. You're startled when you realize there's a boy's face staring at you through it.

"Hmm," he says to himself, "no fucking collar."

The glass slides away, and the boy reaches in with a gloved hand. He feels around the back of your neck, pressing the space between your shoulders.

"No chip, either."

He lifts you, then puts you into a carrier. You mewl in protest, but he shuts the cage door and you find yourself in another prison.

You watch as the boy lifts and examines the half-eaten plate of food you left behind, setting it back in-

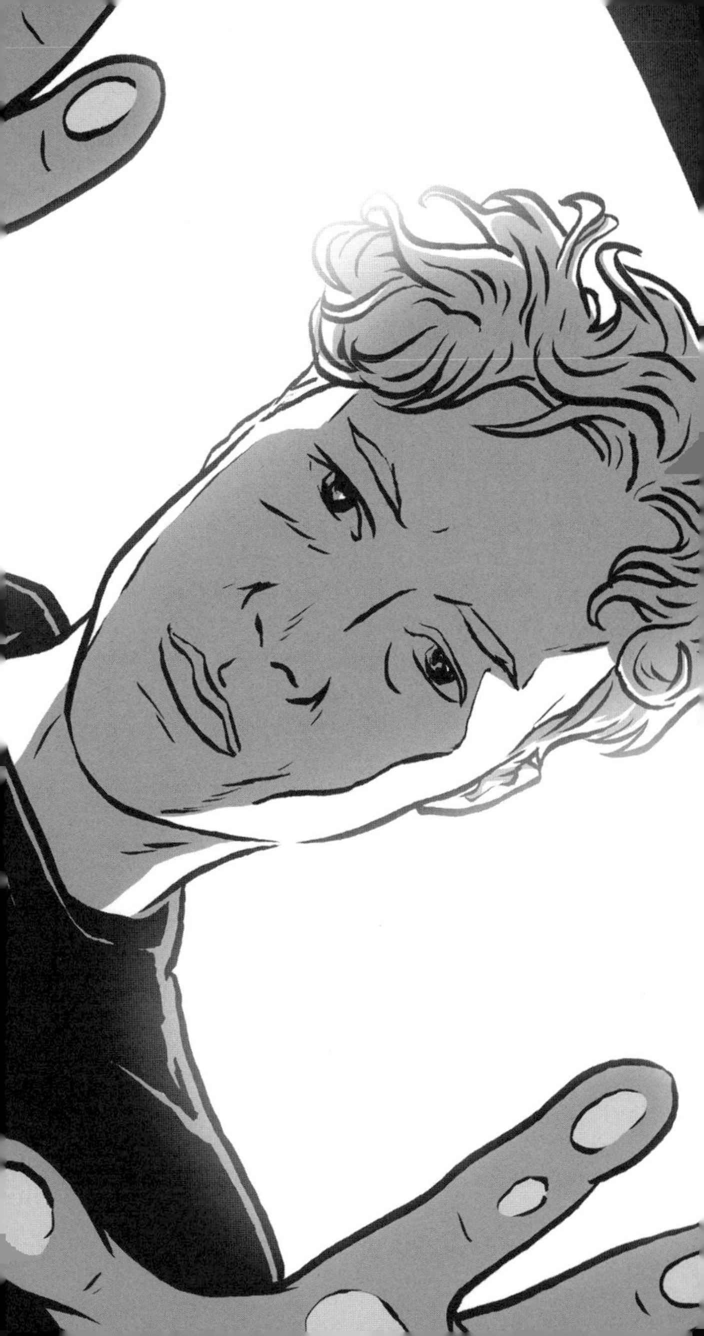

side the little house. He does something else you can't see, then moves the roof back into place.

Then he lifts the carrier, and walks you over to a locked shed in the other corner of the yard.

Once inside, you're placed on a shelf.

What's going to happen?

Before he leaves, the boy fills a shallow pan with litter, and shoves it into your cage. He also fills little cups with water and solid food and places them inside with you.

You meow at him in anger, but he pays you no mind.

There is another cat in the shed with you. It's very quiet, so you didn't notice it at first, but you could smell it. The whole shed smells like other animals in their panic and sadness. Almost overwhelmingly so.

The first day you called to the other cat, and it looked up at you once, but didn't pay you any more attention after that.

Finally, after two days of mindless boredom, the boy comes back.

"Well, Cleo," the boy says, bending down to open the other cat's cage, "you're going home. C'mere." You watch as the boy affixes a leash to the cat's collar, then lifts her out of the cage. She yowls in protest, but allows herself to be moved.

"Shut the fuck up, bitch," the boy says. "You're worth $250 to me. Don't make me hurt you."

Another two days goes by before you see the boy again.

This time, he puts you in a carrier on a bike, and you go on a terrifying and stomach-churning ride.

The whole time, you are crying. Finally, he stops, gets off the bike, and leans it against a wall.

"Shut up," he mutters at you, then pulls out a rectangular wafer.

Even though you've stopped moving, you can't stop crying. You hate this. You hate the boy. You hate everything.

"Yeah," the boy says into the wafer. "I'm here. It's a cat. It's a young one. Fifty, like we agreed."

Moments later, a man's bearded face appears in the doorway of the carrier.

"Well, Mr. Cotton," the man says, his shiny eyes taking you in, "this one'll do just fine."

The cage door opens, and the man reaches in with one hand to stroke you. You respond eagerly to this. The boy hadn't touched you for the past four days, and you missed the feeling of affection, of touch. Your purr starts almost as soon as you feel his hand's warmth.

Then the man's other hand comes into the cage. It has something in it.

You feel a sharp prick in your side!

The bearded man coos at you as you lose consciousness.

Turn to page 168.

You reach over and snag the girl's body with a claw, pulling her out. Then you bend your head down, using your tongue to work her into your mouth. You start chewing and feel her ribs crunch.

Suddenly, a bright light blinds you.

You freeze. You stop mid-chew with the girl's legs dangling out of your mouth. Looking for the source of light, you see a man standing just outside the back glass doors of the house. He drops the flashlight and grabs a long stick leaning against the side of the house.

"Let her go!" he yells, and runs at you.

You back off, turning and running.

"Come back!"

You jump over the fence and gallop through the back alleys. But you hardly even fit anymore, and you quickly make your way onto the comparatively more spacious roads. As you run, the girl's legs flap outside your mouth and smack your chin.

When you have a moment of quiet, you eat the rest of the girl, chewing her up enough to be swallowed. Then you consider your next move.

Far off, you hear sirens.

Some kind of commotion somewhere.

Maybe you've had enough of commotions.

Turn to page 224.

You approach the blonde as she's walking around the kitchen and meow at her pointedly.

She looks down, and nudges you with her foot.

"Good job today, kitten!" she says, opening the fridge. A gust of cold air slips out and you are momentarily shocked by the sudden change in climate. She grabs a bottle from inside then looks at the brunette. "I'm having a beer. You want one?"

The brunette chews on her lip. "I guess there's no wine?"

"No, sorry."

"Ahh...okay, then."

The blonde pulls another bottle out of the fridge and places them on the counter. The giant door closes and the cold slowly dissipates.

This time, you try to get the blonde's attention by climbing her pantleg. You figure if you can get in her face, get right in front of her, she'll understand how hungry you are.

"Aw, jeez!" the blonde yells. Her hands grab you, and try to pull you away. You try to hold on to the jeans. You don't want to be *ignored*.

"What's the matter?" the brunette asks.

"Fucking razor sharp goddamned claws is what's the matter," the blonde says through gritted teeth.

Finally she pulls you off her leg and places you on the counter.

This is better. Now you're closer to eye level. You smell the counter. There was food here recently. Fish? Tuna?

"Where's your mom?" the brunette asks.

"She's with my aunt for the weekend," the blonde says. She closes her hand over one of the bottles and you hear a *psssht!* sound. Then another. She drops the bottlecaps on the counter in front of you.

You sniff at them. They have a musky, murky smell.

"Hey kitten," the blonde says, picking one of the bottlecaps up, "wanna see something?"

Placing the cap on its edge with one forefinger, she flicks it with her other!

The cap is spinning!

Without thinking, you swipe at it and knock it off the counter and onto the floor where it bounces, rolls, then comes to a stop when it hits a wall.

You are filled with a crazy desire to jump after it, but you balk — you are so high up!

"Oh, he's scared!" the blonde puts a reassuring hand on your back. "Don't be scared, kitten. Want some liquid courage?"

She takes the other bottlecap and fills it with some of the liquid from the bottle.

"Hey, don't give him *that*," the brunette says. "That's so bad."

You sniff at the beer. It's earthy but sharp. You are so hungry, you give it a couple experimental licks.

"Hey, he's drinking it!" The blonde hands the other bottle to the brunette and they clink the bottles against each other.

You don't think you like this. It's very sharp. It makes your nose pulse. You back away from it, and then pawing the air in front of you... you sneeze!

Tchaa!

You have sneezed before. Not often. But often enough to understand that your face isn't breaking when you do it, and that nothing feels as good afterwards.

The girls laugh. One of them picks you up and

they march you into the living room where they drop
you on the couch.

Turn to page 182.

180

When the bag is finally loosened, and you spill out, you find yourself in a small cage on a high shelf.

There is a bright bulb hung from the ceiling, and it sets the whole room in a harsh light. It's not a large room, and a long table lines one side of the room, with shelves lining the other.

The bare lightbulb is like a little sun, but without the warmth of a sunbeam. You meow at the boy. You want out.

Across the room, from another cage, you hear a responding meow. Another cat sits in a cage. It looks at you for a moment, then looks away.

The boy is busy writing on a small yellow pad of paper.

"67 Cosgrove Crescent," he mumbles to himself, scratching away with a pen. Then he looks into the air. "Hmm. What's today's date?" He continues writing.

You meow again at the boy.

He peers closely at you. "Collar, with tag..." He writes more things down. When he's done, he peels a single page from the pad and fastens it to the shelf just below your cage.

"You're gonna be in there a few days, so get used to it."

Then the boy shuts off the light, and leaves.

In the sudden darkness, you can hear the other cat shuffling fitfully around its cage, quietly crying to itself.

Turn to page 194.

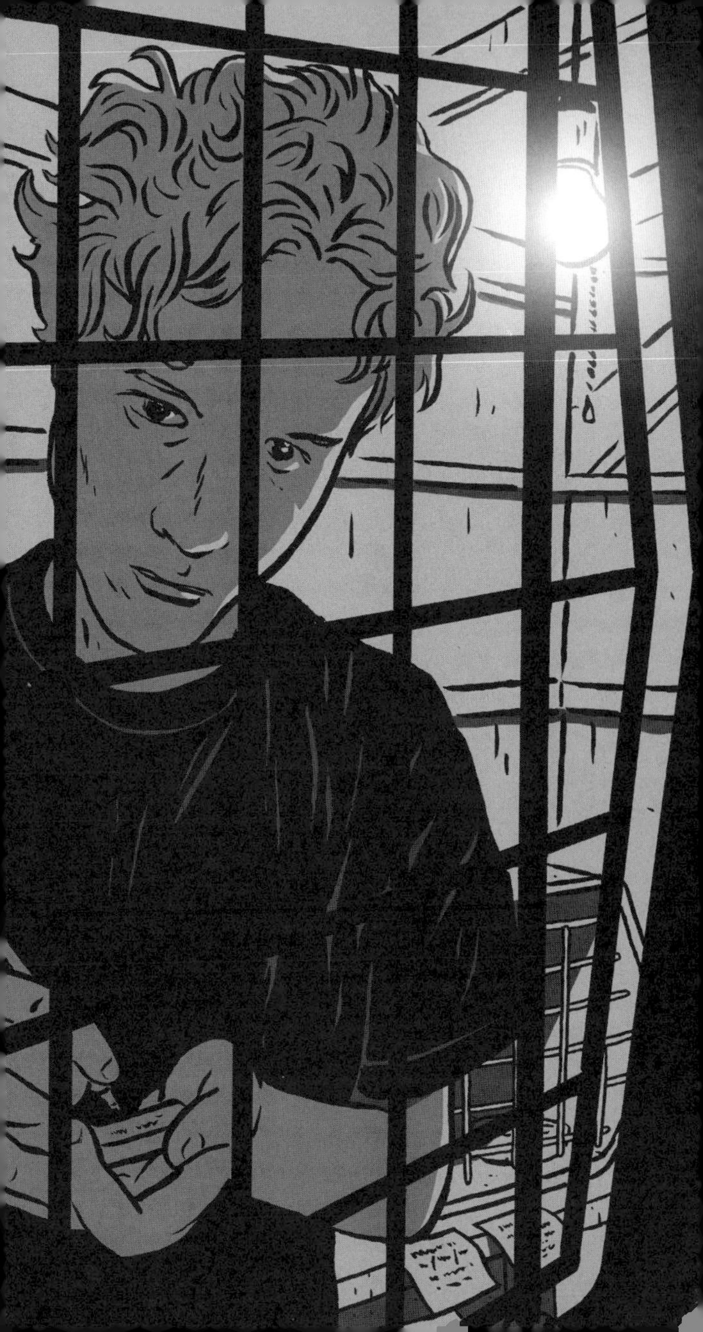

Once on the couch, you realize you really like it. It's like it was *made* for you. Your claws let you propel yourself around it like that squirrel on that tree.

The brunette flops down on one side while the blonde stands by a large black panel on the other side of the room.

"What do you wanna watch?" she asks, flipping through some discs. "We also have Netflix."

"Do you have *Gummo?*"

"What's that?"

"It's this weird movie. But it's great." The brunette watches you as you pretend to be the squirrel, moving on its tree. You roar your way to the top of the couch, run along the wall, then pounce down onto the cushions. "Let's just say," the brunette continues, "that it's singularly the most beautiful movie I've ever seen in my life, but it's also the weirdest."

"What about *The Matrix?*" the blonde asks.

"You *always* want to watch *The Matrix.*"

"That's because it's *always* good."

"Hey," the brunette says, "did you know one of the directors of it got a sex-change?"

"What?"

"Yeah," the brunette continues. "Larry Wachowski. Well, I guess he's Lana now. And I guess he's not a he anymore. But anyway, I saw a picture of him. He looks really good now. I mean — *she* looks really good now."

"What do you mean? As a chick?"

"Yeah. Like — happy. She's also got these pretty dreadlocks."

"Well that's good. So... you're cool with *The Matrix?*"

The brunette takes a drink of her beer. "Fuck it.

Sure. I could always use some mindless action."

"But that's the great thing about this movie," the blonde says, switching off the light, "it's mind*ful* action."

"Haha," the brunette laughs. "Right."

The blonde settles down on the couch as well, and the large black slate brightens.

After a moment, random things appear in the screen. Is it a window? Everything shifts so quickly however, it looks like the world is spinning outside. It's all very confusing.

You are half-curious about it, and where those things go, but the screen's speakers are blaring so loudly that you don't want to go near it.

The brunette catches your eye and pats her lap. "C'mere kitten. Sit with me."

*If you go explore the possibility of her lap,
turn to page 132.*

*To explore the apartment further,
especially the compellingly smelly area
near the front door, turn to page 190.*

To go back to the kitchen area, turn to 166.

You poke your head into the alley and see two girls. One has long, black hair and is shaking a container. The other has short, blonde hair, and she sees you first.

"Hey," the blonde whispers to the other, "look."

The brunette stops in her tracks. They both do.

Another shake of the container.

"Don't scare it off," the blonde says.

"I'm not! I'm trying to *attract* it."

Both girls get low, crouching down, and start calling to you.

You know that sound. It's familiar.

Little bits rattling around.

Your mom always left the playpen when she heard it, and came back awhile later, her mouth and tongue reeking of unusual aromas.

You know that sound means food.

The brunette places the container on the ground and pushes it toward you before backing away.

You're really hungry. You've gone a long time without feeding. You're not crazy about solid food, as it makes your teeth ache, but you're willing to give it a try.

You venture forward.

"He's doing it!" the brunette whispers to her friend.

"Don't blow it!"

"Is he what you're looking for?"

"Not really," the blonde says, "but we can use him. I mean, look at him. He's so cute. They're bound to take him."

You sniff at the container. You're not familiar with this type of food, but you start licking it. You get a couple pieces up into your mouth and start munch-

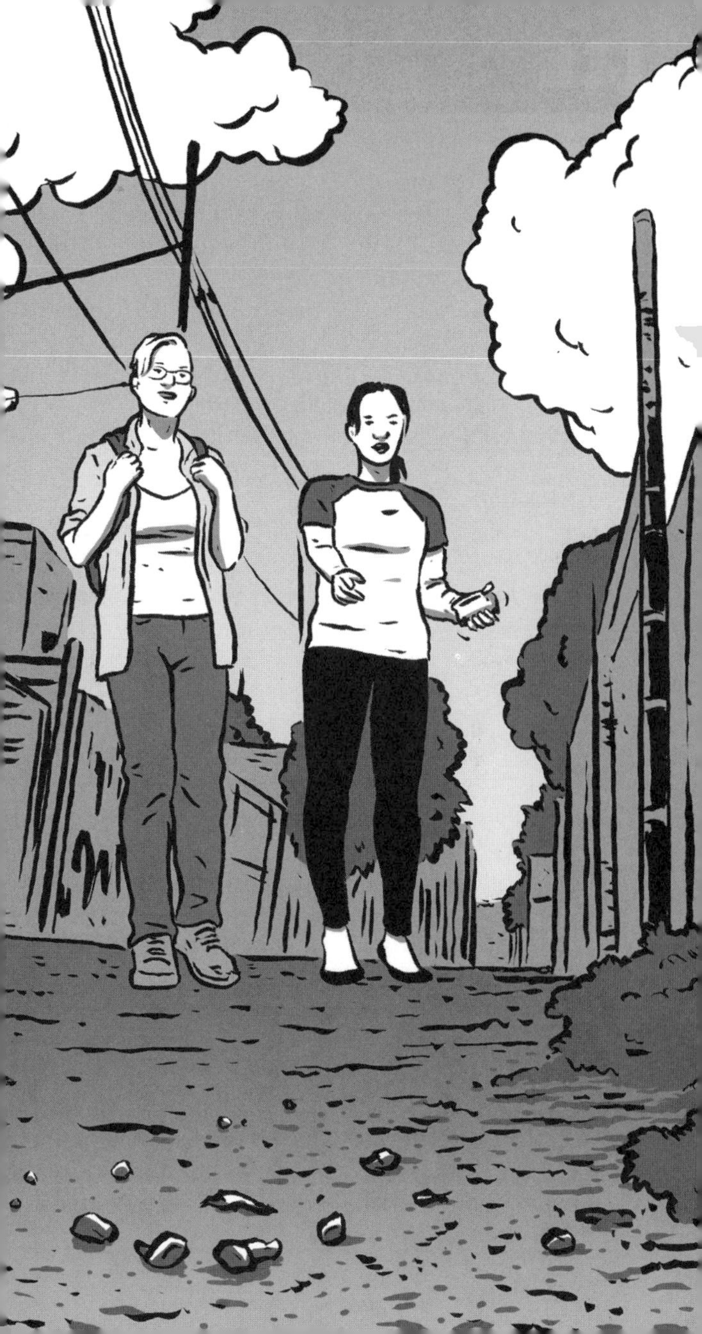

ing.

"I'll get the bag ready," the blonde says evenly. Between bites, you notice the girl take off her backpack and unzip it. Does she have more food in there? You are hoping for wet food.

"I'll grab him when you're ready," the brunette says.

The blonde nods, holding open her bag. "Do it."

Suddenly, in the middle of your meal, the brunette's hands come snaking toward you.

Do you bite them? Turn to page 152.

If you accept their embrace, turn to page 197.

You run down the hall until you encounter a propped-open door leading to a stairwell. The smell of fresh air drifts up from below. You trundle down the stairs, two at a time.

At the bottom, you escape the building through another propped-open door, and suddenly you are in a parking lot.

A cool gust of wind ruffles your fur, and you breathe in the night air. As good as it feels to be outside, you also feel very exposed.

You try to get underneath the parked cars, to find someplace to hide, but frustratingly, you don't seem to fit. You move out of the parking lot and into the street. Finally you find a tall truck, and you duck under its long payload and catch your breath.

Scared and hungry, you meow for your mom.

A couple strolling by stop at the noise.

"Did you hear that?" one of them says.

They turn to look at you, squinting in the darkness.

"I thought I heard a cat, but there's a *dog* there."

You meow again, stepping out toward them.

"Jesus! That's no dog!" the two of them back away, then start running.

Alarmed, you run away from them. You're not sure where you're going.

Suddenly you're blinded! Bright headlights flood the street around you and something slams into you! You roll from the impact, tumbling along the asphalt. It felt like when Tupac once threw himself at you, and knocked you to the ground. You're shocked, but not really hurt.

"What the hell was that?" someone inside the car says. "Did we hit a deer?"

188

Back in the playpen, you playfully jumped on Tupac and knocked *him* to the ground. Do you want to play with the car?

If you wrestle with the car, turn to page 128.

If you'd rather go someplace quieter, leave the street for page 165.

You step delicately across the rooftops. Stealing stealthily through this hidden landscape, it's much quieter up here. You prefer it — away from the ceaseless traffic moving about the maze of streets.

You stop in your tracks — the whiff of something delicious catches your nose. Stepping to the edge of the roof, you follow the smell. Looking down, you see an open window.

The smell comes from there.

You reach your paw down and claw inside.

A scream.

Something hot bangs against your paw, searing it!

You quickly withdraw your paw, and bring it back to your mouth, licking it. One of your pads is hot and it hurts.

You taste the barest tantalizing hint of it on your tongue — fish!

You consider reaching back inside, but the prospect of getting burnt again deters you.

A woman's voice from inside drifts out.

"Hello? 911? There's a monster out here. I need help."

You are frustrated by this.

You look up at the open sky and its speckling of glittering stars, hoping for an answer. Far off, you see the moon.

Turn to page 224.

In front of you, in piles, in bunches, and in pairs are the smelliest and most pungent objects you have encountered yet in your short time here.

This is what the people wear on their feet. They kick them off when they come inside. You sniff the soles and can smell the yard, and other, more mysterious things. Inside them is even better. The smells are so strong, they seem almost solid to your senses.

You examine one black shoe that is very fragrant. The skin of it is shiny in the low hallway light, and a long leather strap leads from it, like a tail. You gnaw on it. It's tasty. The leather is very pliable in your mouth.

You want to add your own scent to this rich bouquet of smells. You rub your cheek on the shoe, and spray a little.

Near the front door, you get a gust of air from outside, streaming through the thin crevices. It's the familiar scent of the yard, where you'd spent the whole day.

Then, before you see her, you hear her. The low thud of one girl walking.

The blonde steps into the hall, empty bottle in her hand. You freeze.

She sees you, then frowns, her nose wrinkling. She storms toward you. She is terrifying.

You take off, running past her feet, ducking into the living room and hiding under the couch.

"What is it?" you hear the brunette calling, above you.

The screen freezes, and the sound is blessedly gone.

"Kitten's peeing, I think." the blonde calls from the hallway. "Shit. It's my mom's nice shoes."

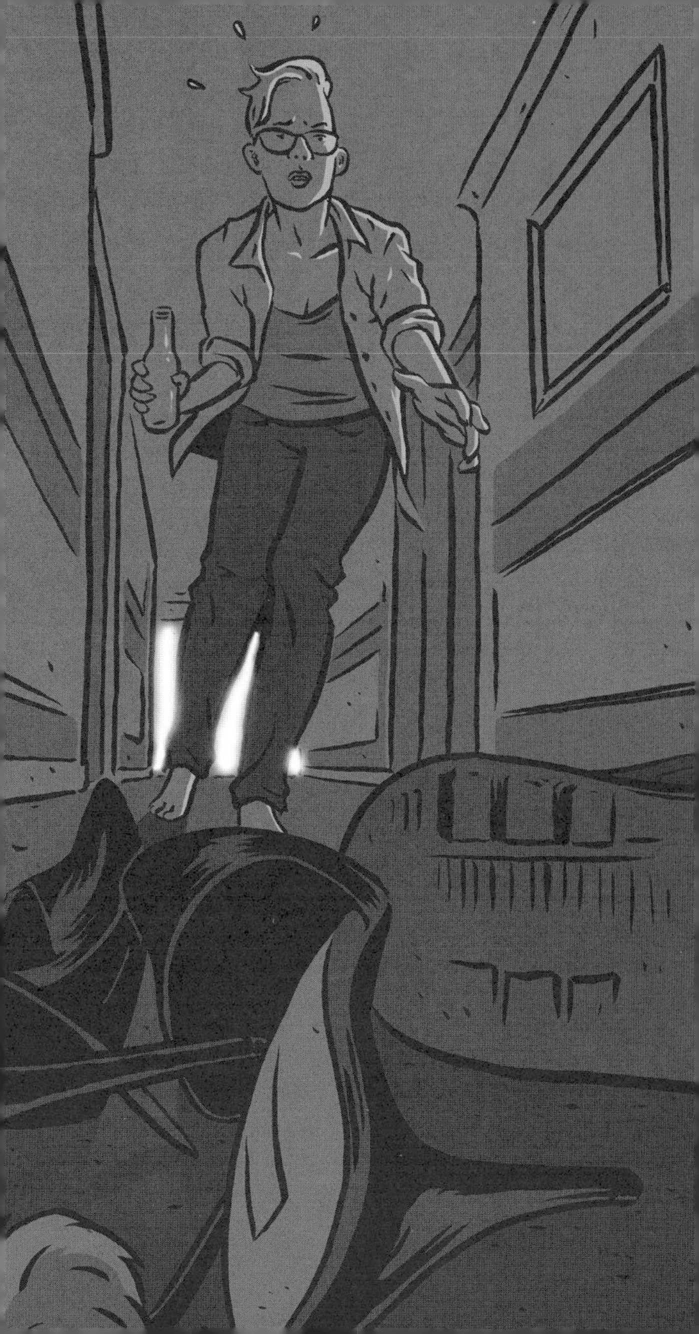

192

You stay under the couch. It's nice here. It's nice in the dark room. You feel safe under here.

The brunette's foot touches the ground, and you see her feet move into the hallway. The girls murmur amongst themselves and you look at the screen.

A blue sky looks back at you.

Is that outside? Nothing moves though.

Outside, *everything* moves.

"Alright. See you tomorrow then," the blonde says.

You hear a door close in the hallway, then the blonde comes back into the living room, turning on the main light, and shutting off the screen.

"Kitten? Where are you?" the blonde says. You see her walk around the room, then move into the hallway and the kitchen. She walks back toward you, and suddenly you see her face. She snorts.

"There you are. You've caused me a lot of trouble, little one." She reaches in gently with her hand, and you let her take you.

She walks you to the backroom, just off the kitchen. Inside, there's a small pan with litter in it, and a blanket.

"Sorry kitten, this is your room for the night. I'm going to bed." She drops you on the floor and closes the door behind her, shutting you in.

You hear her walk away.

You explore the room while you wait for her to come back, but she doesn't.

Finally, you fall asleep on the blanket, dreaming of your mom and your family.

Turn to page 155.

In a few bounds, you're on them. The man takes off running, and for a moment you consider chasing him, but the dog starts barking furiously, and you bat at it. You miss, but your claw gets caught on its leash, and you fling the dog around. One yelp, and the dog is silent.

Once you've worked your claw free, you push the dog around, trying to get it to play with you, but it's dead.

This is no fun.

With all of this action, however, you've worked up an appetite.

*If you decide to eat the dog,
munch away on page 201.*

If you'd rather keep moving, move on to page 222.

A minute later, you've finished exploring the entirety of your cage. A small tray of litter in the back corner, and tiny bowls of food and water, respectively. Other than that, the cage is empty.

You don't know what to do, so you're settling down to take a nap when you hear voices outside the shed door.

It's the girls!

"Where'd you learn how to pick locks?" It's the brunette talking. Her voice is muted, but you're sure it's her.

"When I was a kid," the blonde says, "I wanted to be James Bond. I learned to read lips, picks locks, I even took jiu-jitsu."

"Holy shit, that's badass. How come I didn't know this about you?"

You hear metallic scritching sounds from the door. What is that noise? You envision tiny rodents scurrying around.

Then the door opens.

"Ta-daa," the blonde sings.

Blinding light floods the room and you squint. You're happy to see the girls though. Standing up, you stretch and your tail rises in greeting.

The brunette marches in, camera in her hand, scanning the shelves. Immediately she spots you.

"This is proof!" she says, panning the camera around the shed, then focussing on you and the note stuck to the shelf. "Look at this. He writes down all the info, then uses it once the missing posters go up to claim the reward. He keeps all his captives in these ugly little cages." The brunette taps her finger on your cage and you go over to it and lick it.

"Awww," the brunette laughs, then unlatches the

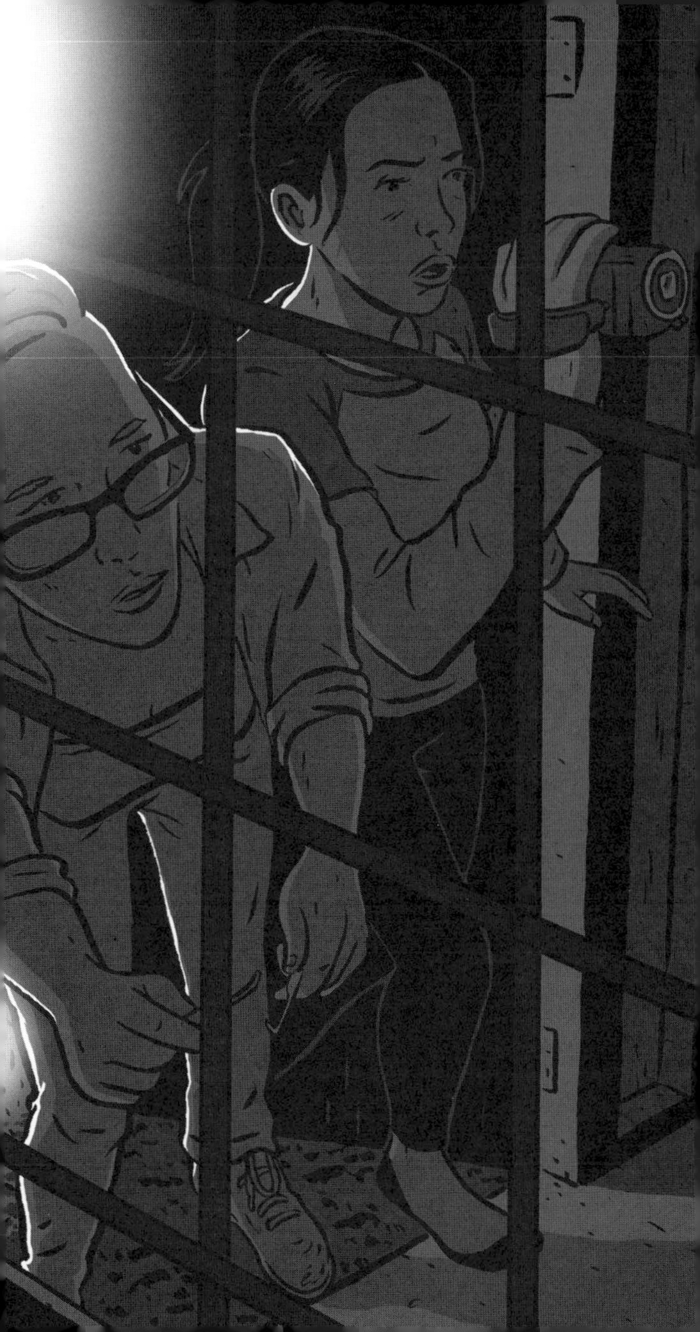

cage door. She reaches in and strokes your head and ears. You warm at her touch, and close your eyes in pleasure. You missed her.

"Hey," the blonde stands just outside the doorway of the shed. "Don't get too cozy. We can't take the cat back right now. We need to wait for the dude to show up for the reward."

Without warning, there is a shout from outside.

"Hey!" the boy yells. "Get out of there!"

"Fuck!" the brunette withdraws her hand and turns the camera outside.

"Whoa, whoa," the blonde raises her hands and circles away from the doorway. "The door was open. I was just looking around..."

"The hell it was!" the boy pulls a knife from his pocket and shakes it, threateningly.

Now's your chance! With the cage door open you have a few options.

If you jump on the brunette, and try to climb down her body, turn to page 238.

If you just jump off the shelf and hope for the best landing-wise, turn to page 225.

If you leave your cage, and just start yowling unhappily on the shelf, turn to page 214.

The brunette lifts you up without resistance, and she drops you gently into the blonde's open bag.

"Got him!" the blonde says, zipping closed your only way out.

"Well that was easy," the brunette says. You can hear her lifting the food container. You were hoping for an embrace, or some stroking. It feels like a long time since you've had any sustained, satisfying nuzzling.

"Well," the blond replies, "that was the easy *part*. Let's get him back to my place. We'll get him fed, get a collar on him, and then see who we can reel in."

At first, you scramble around the bag, looking for another exit, but pretty soon, the walking pace of the blonde girl lulls you to sleep.

Turn to 157.

As the blue and red lights swirl all around, you jump down onto the men, pouncing from above. One is knocked down and lies still, while the other one makes more loud bangs from his hand.

You swipe a paw at him, knocking him into the air. He cracks against a building, then falls to the ground.

No more loud bangs.

But more white vehicles with flashing lights arrive, and more people step out of them. More loud bangs from their hands!

You turn and run, feeling pinches on your body.

Galloping down the street, you quickly turn when the opportunity presents itself, and you head toward a tunnel. It's very bright, but once inside, you feel much safer. It curves down around you like a cave.

But people are everywhere. From in front and behind you, more vehicles screech to a stop. People step out and stare at you. Some point, some aim their wafers, others merely stare, mouths open.

You crouch in the tunnel, unsure which way to go to get away from the humans. You look out the direction you entered.

All of a sudden, you hear a loud buzzing, and a bright white spot of light appears in front of you. This draws everyone's attention, and the humans look up, pointing at something.

You retreat further into the tunnel. What's troubling is that it feels like the tunnel is getting tighter.

Suddenly, a man on a motorcycle appears and purrs to a halt in front of you. He takes off his helmet, dropping it on the ground, and grins. He waves at you.

"Hey pussy," he says, "wanna race?"

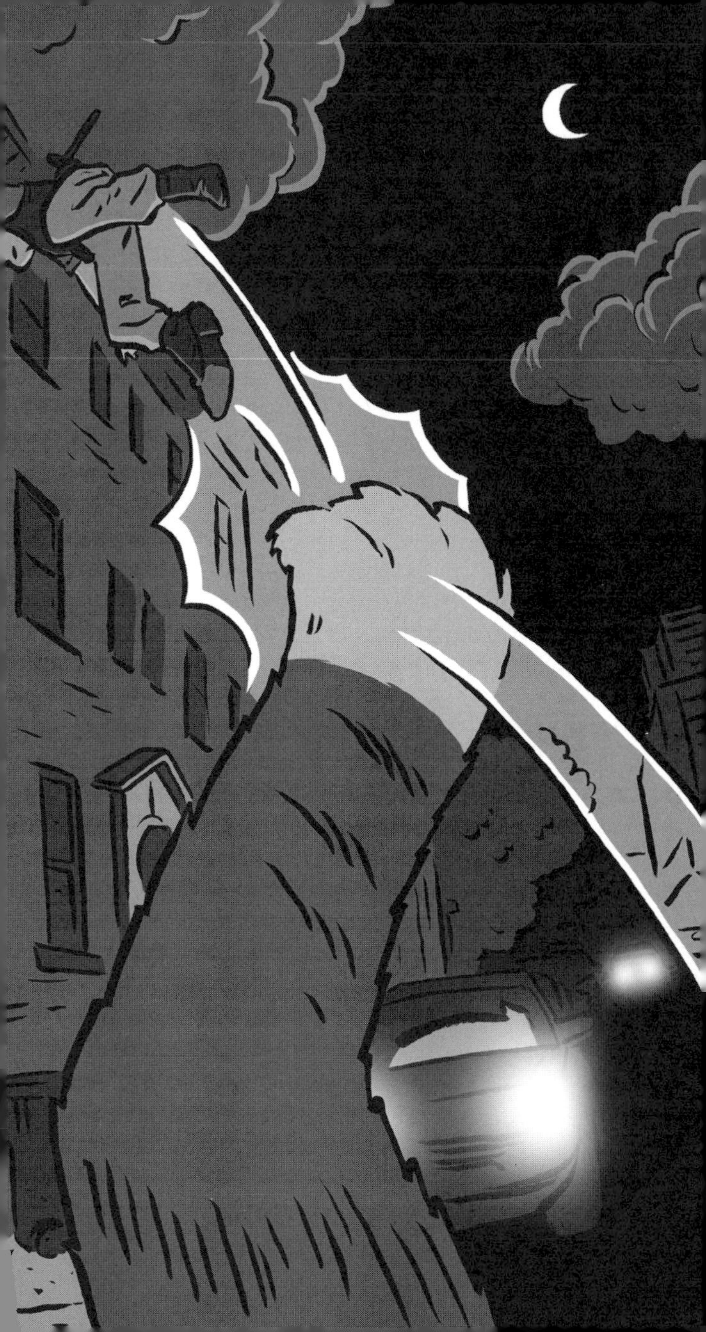

He revs the engine, then flashes his headlights in your face. You wince and half-close your eyes. Annoyed, you swipe at him, but he quickly zips away!

You turn to follow the man with your eyes.

Halfway down the tunnel, he skids to a stop, shouts, "C'mon bitch!" and revs his engine some more.

If you chase him, turn to page 244.

If you avoid him, and try to escape the tunnel the way you came, go to 235.

Bending down to the ground, you eat the dog. It's the first solid food you've had in a while. It tastes weird. Or maybe it's just because you've never *had* dog before.

You eat all of it, you're so hungry. You even swallow down the long leash attached to its neck.

When you're done, you wander farther into the dark park and make a wonderful discovery.

The comforting sound of running water from a giant fountain. You drink greedily, washing the dog taste out of your mouth. You avoid the leaves and branches that sit in it.

Now, with belly full, you really feel like finding somewhere quiet.

Just off the park, there is a long series of low buildings, which lead to an enormous parking lot, and a fenced-in structure.

You jump the fence easily, and move down a cramped tunnel to a large open field, surrounded on all sides by a sloping wall. You feel pretty safe here, and you bed down for the night.

Turn to page 124.

202

As she approaches, you back away from the girl Laughing, she chases you.

The sudden movement makes you nervous, and you bat at her.

With a squeak, she flies through the air and lands with a splash in the water bowl!

Ripples radiate from her still body as she bobs face down, hair fanning out. You poke at her, but she doesn't move.

You notice another light come on in the house More lights, you have discovered, is never a good por tent.

You're very hungry, though.

If you eat the girl, despite her soggyness turn to page 176

If you decide to leave before more peopl discover you, turn to 213

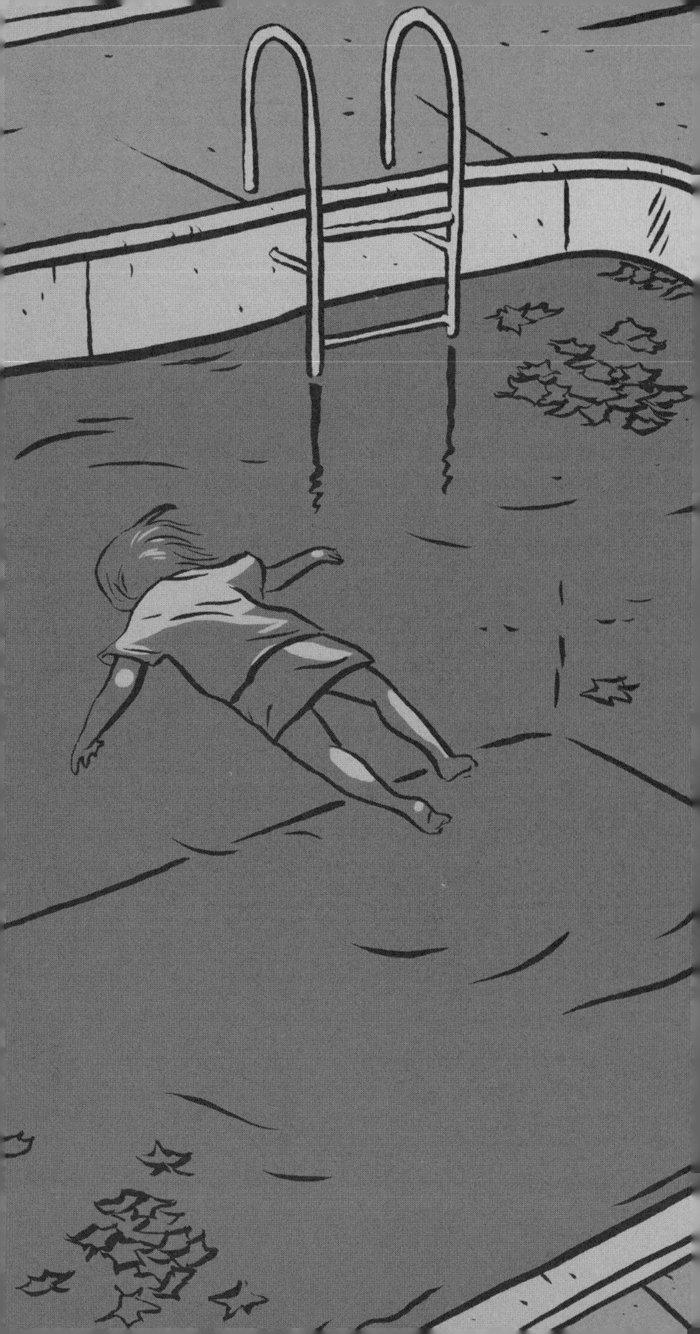

Getting to your feet, you scan the skies for the arrows.

One sneaks out of the fluffy whiteness and you bat at it, knocking it away into a flatspin.

Then you wait again, patient.

You don't have to wait long — *more* pain on your back. Something is hitting you! It's burning. You spin, paranoid, but can't find it.

You want a neck to grapple with, an ear to bite. But this enemy offers you nothing.

More pain. You drop onto your back, rolling again, trying to put the fire out, but as you do, something explodes on your belly and as you turn again to put that out more explosions come.

This enemy you can't reach and can't fight.

You turtle up, screaming at the world. The impacts continue and you can't avoid them.

The pain is immense and overwhelming, but the next blow hits your forehead, and soon you can't feel anything anymore.

THE END

You have just used up one of your lives. You have eight more! Feel free to reincarnate on page 1 and make different choices! See another ending! Pick another plot!

Though your voice is small, you yowl like an injured beast inside the bag.

"Hey!" the boy barks at you. "Shut up!"

You hope the whole neighbourhood can hear you and you keep crying.

"Shut up!" the boy says again, and he slams you to the ground!

The ferocious impact shocks you into silence. You're not sure if anything's broken, but you can't, for the moment, move, stunned as you are.

You try to cry again, but can only pathetically mewl.

After a long walk where the boy changes directions multiple times, he stops for a moment to fiddle with something, then the bag is in shadow and the world is quiet.

You are somewhere inside.

Turn to 180.

You move over the grass to the unconscious boy. You don't like his odour, but his hands smell of treats. Maybe there's a chance you'll get more.

You lick his hand and climb on top of his back.

After a moment, his eyes flutter open.

"Fuck," he breathes. "What happened?" He tries to get up, but stops. Still, the sudden movement prompts you to jump off onto the grass and get some distance. You watch him warily.

He clutches his ribs. "Oh, those girls." He rolls over, then looks over at you. "Fucking thieving bitches. What did they hope to find anyway?"

Then the boy's eyes blink in panic, and despite his pain, he gets up, moaning. He stumbles into the shed and starts kicking things around.

"They took my book!" the boy yells. "Fucking cunts! They took my book!"

He stands in the doorway of his shed, hands up to his face. For a long time, he doesn't move or speak.

When he talks next, it's in a whisper. "I gotta get some money. I gotta leave town."

The next couple minutes are a blur as the boy captures you — *again!* In your defense, he pulled out a crinkly bag of treats and lured you over, dumping you in the same bag as the one you'd been in earlier.

At least he poured the treats in after you.

It is a long walk for the boy. He grunts in pain with almost every step.

Finally, you hear him speak to someone.

"You can have the bag," he says. "Cat's inside."

"Thank you, Mr. Cotton," another male voice responds. "Here is your payment."

You hear retreating footsteps and then you're brought somewhere inside. Finally, you're hung up.

You feel a cool wall pressing up against your side through the bag.

Then, from outside, you feel a hand pressing against you. The probing fingers find your head, then your body. It feels for your legs.

There is a sharp pinch in your side!

Then the pain is gone, leaving only a dull, throbbing ache.

Moments later, you lose consciousness.

Turn to page 168.

At the bottom of the bag, you scoop the treats into your mouth using both paws. Greedily, you chew on the soft, tasty nuggets.

Each one springs a tiny bit of happiness into your mouth. You can't stop eating them. They are the most flavourful things you have ever tasted.

And there sure are a lot of them. Slowly, you make your way through the pile. And when they're finally gone, you want more of them. Even though you couldn't possibly eat any more.

You feel a little sick.

Abruptly, the boy changes walking direction. Outside, you hear him fiddle with something, and then the bag is drawn into shadow, and the world goes quiet.

He's taken you someplace inside.

Turn to page 180.

You chase after the girls down the alley. They're moving at a brisk clip, and you need to rush to keep up, but it's been a while since you've had free reign of movement, and you relish the freedom to move as fast or as slow as you want.

Then, without warning, the hairs on the back of your neck rise.

You stop, and look behind you.

Oh!

It's her — the other cat that was held captive. She's following *you*.

Perhaps she doesn't have anyone to take care of her *either*.

You let your tail rise in greeting, and she looks away, then back at you. You turn to follow the girls, and you are gratified that the other cat trots along with you.

As if sensing you, the brunette glances back and breaks into a grin. She elbows the blonde who also turns around. The girls smirk at each other.

"Okay," the blonde says, "guess we're not done yet."

The blonde picks you up and carries you against her shoulder while the brunette lifts the other cat into her arms. When you reach the street, they find their vehicle.

The next few hours are crazy. You and the other cat ride in the car while the girls go from place to place. They go somewhere, then stop. Then come back, and they drive someplace else.

The other cat isn't interested in any of this, and she sleeps in the back seat.

You on the other hand, love climbing around the car. You enjoy sinking your claws into the cloth backs of chairs and mounting the headrest. Then jumping down to the vacant still-warm seats.

Finally, late in the day, just as the sun is setting, the girls return.

"Okay," the brunette says. "What a day."

"Who woulda thought a police statement would take so bloody long," the blonde complains, starting the car into its low growl, and shifting into gear.

When the car stops next, the girls peer into the back seat and examine the other cat's collar closely.

"There's a number," the blonde says. "I can call while you're inside."

"Okay," the brunette nods and picks you up. "Say goodbye, kitten." She raises you to eye-level with the blonde and the blonde gives you a kiss on the forehead.

"I'll be right back," the brunette says, carrying you out of the car and into a building.

Inside, you're brought to a desk, and the brunette says to the attendant, "Hi, I found this kitten in an alley, and I didn't know what else to do with it so I..."

"Oh," the man says. "Well, did it have a collar or anything?"

"No," the brunette shakes her head. "Didn't see anything."

"So you don't know its name?"

A woman slides over with a clipboard. "Is this a new turn-in?"

The man nods. A phone rings and he picks it up.

"Name please?"

"Oh I — " the brunette begins. "I was just — holdin' onto him."

The man hands the woman a note and she glances at it briefly, before turning back to the brunette.

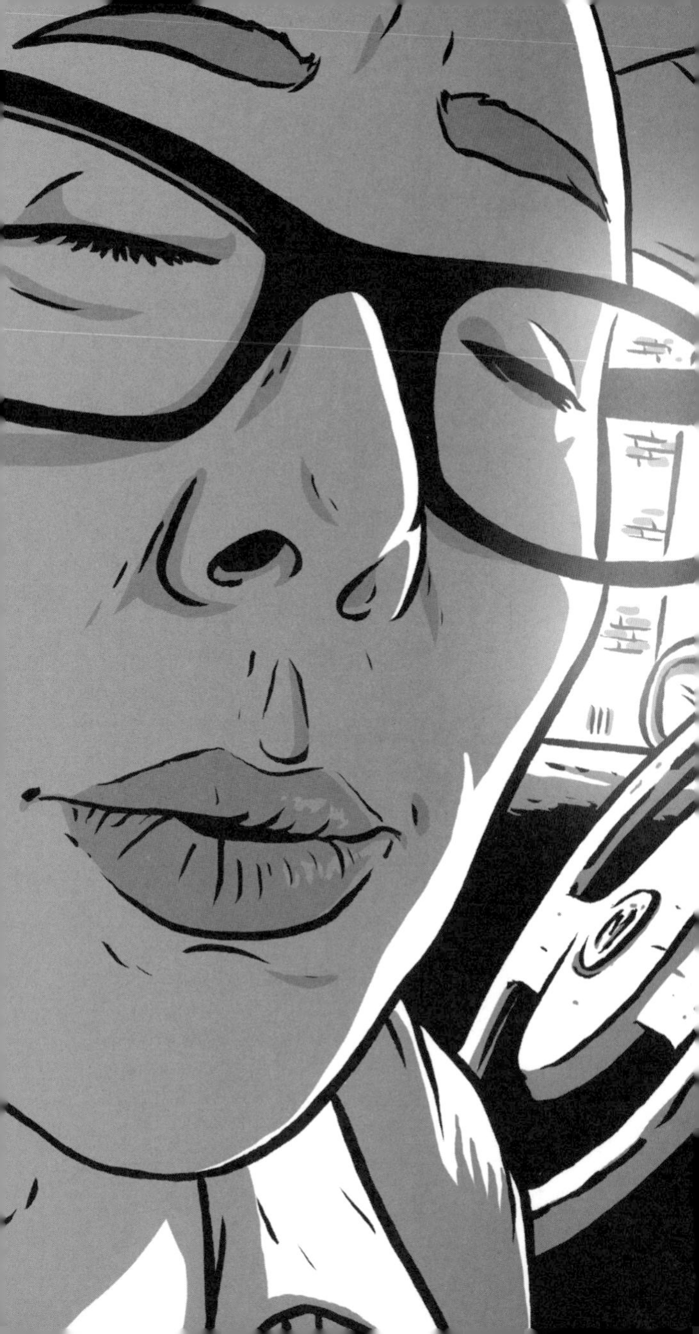

"I'm sorry. Did you say his name was Holden?" the woman asks.

"Um," the brunette half-smiles. "Sure?"

"Hand him here, please." The attendant puts on a pair of blue rubber gloves.

The brunette bends her head down to touch yours and whispers quietly to you.

"Well, little kitten. You've helped us a lot. And I'll never forget it. And don't worry about your new friend — we'll make sure she gets home safe. And you — you're going to get a new home soon yourself." She kisses you on the nose, which is a little ticklish, then she hands you over to the attendants.

You are placed in a cage and watch as the girl leaves.

Turn to page 246.

Just as you step over the fence and into the alley behind the yard, you see a man walk out of the house. Silently, you crouch down, and find cover behind a couple of trees.

The man looks around. He carries a bright light in his hand, and he shines it in your direction, then into the water bowl.

"Oh god!" he cries, and drops the light.

Then he runs and dives into the water bowl, working hard to pull the girl out and onto the paved tiles beside it.

Another figure emerges from the house — a woman. She takes a few halting steps to see what's going on, then runs back into the house. "I'll call for help!" she tells the man.

The girl lies face-up, and the man pushes on her chest repeatedly, then kisses her every once in a while.

"C'mon, Syd! C'mon!" he mutters, a note of desperation in his voice.

This is very exciting. The man and the woman's excited movements have excited you.

Do you hunt your new playthings?
Turn to page 232.

Or, you can still leave to page 224.

At the noise, the boy turns toward the shed, where he notices the brunette.

"Hey bitch!" he shouts. "Get that camera out of my face!"

"We're documenting all of this, asshole!" the brunette screams. "You're going to jail!"

"We'll you're going to die!" The enraged boy rushes at the brunette with his knife. But before he takes two steps, the blonde has snaked her arm around his neck, and pulls back with all her strength.

The boy tries to buck her off his back, clawing with his free hand to get some air, but the girl is relentless. Finally, he starts slicing at her forearm.

The blonde screams, but doesn't let go.

"Shit! Shit!" the brunette says. "What should I do?!" One hand clenched into a fist, she takes a step forward.

"Keep filming!" the blonde replies through gritted teeth. "Don't do anything. He's gonna..."

The boy drops down onto his knees, and then finally flops onto the ground face first, unconscious.

"...go out." the blonde finishes. She holds her chokehold for a second or two longer, then extricates her arm. Three short gashes spill blood along her forearm.

"Oh my god," the brunette says. She puts the camera down and tears off one sleeve of her long-sleeved shirt. "We've got to get you to a hospital."

The blonde nods and lets her friend tie the cloth around her forearm.

"What the hell was that move?" the brunette asks.

"Rear naked choke. Jui-jitsu."

Once the bandage is tied in place, the brunette tugs on the blonde's arm. "We should go."

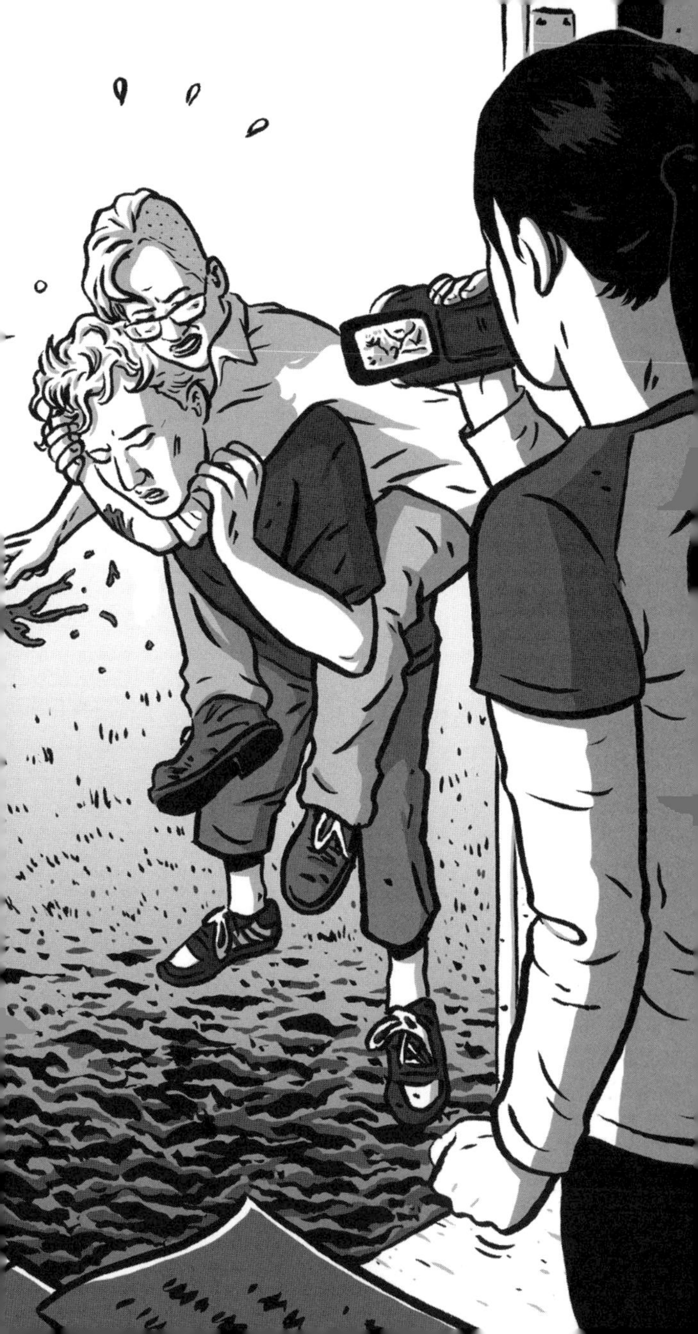

"Wait," the blonde says, returning to the shed. "I thought I saw something in here." The blonde taps the yellow label on the shelf in front of your cage and nods to herself. "He's an organized bastard. I want to see if..." She spots a binder sitting on another shelf. "A-ha."

The blonde opens the binder and stifles a cry.

"Oh god," she says.

Page after page of missing pet posters and yellow labels stare back at her.

"You gotta get this!" the blonde tells her friend. "Get your camera!"

The brunette films the blonde, flipping through the pages.

"This psychopath has been doing this for *years*. This is a full-blown *business*. And this is the proof!"

"Is..." the brunette begins haltingly, "is Olivia in there?"

The blonde flips methodically through the binder and stops at a photocopied colour poster. She nods. On its back, she finds a yellow label. At the bottom of the label is a red X with a date.

"Oh god," the blonde is crying. "What does this mean?"

"So," the brunette takes a deep breath, "you should tell the camera, for the record, what made you suspicious in the first place."

The blonde nods, swallowing heavily.

"Look at the camera," the brunette instructs.

"I'm trying to but I'm also keeping an eye on *that* asshole," the blonde nods towards the unconscious boy, "to make sure he doesn't *wake up*."

"Oh, good point."

The blonde talks to the camera as she flips

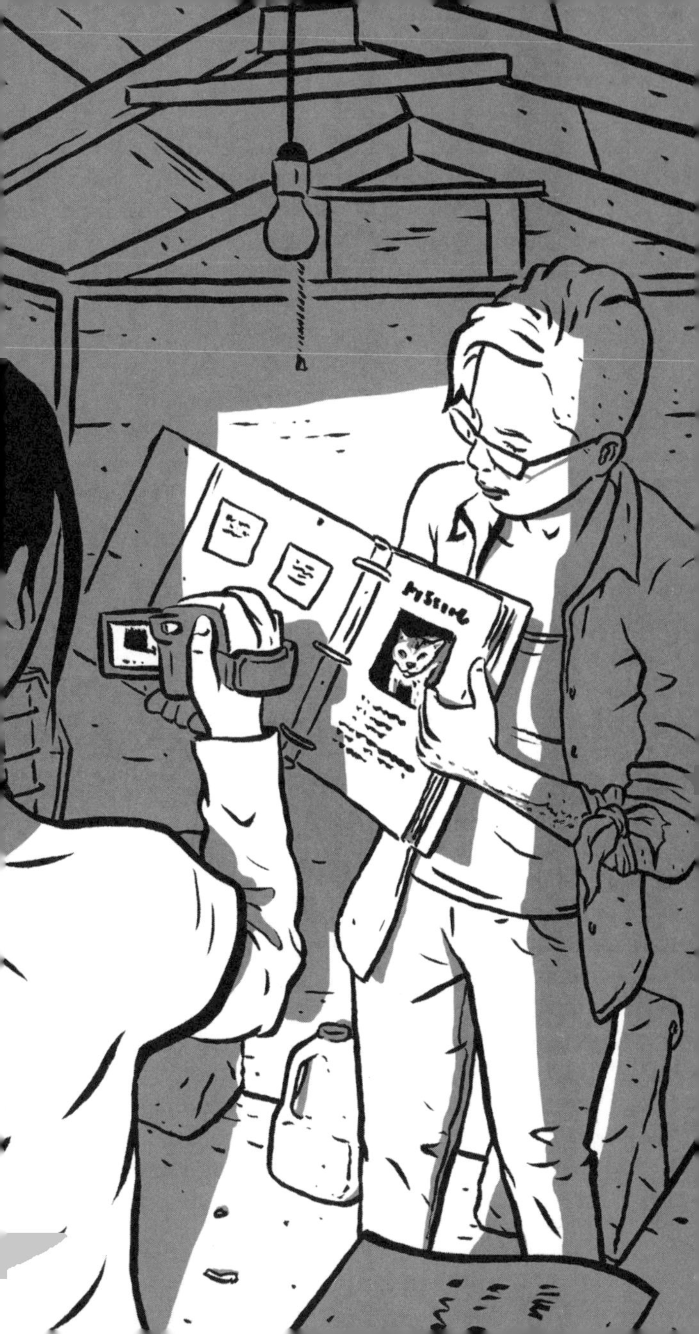

through the pages.

"Anyway, so a month ago, my cat Olivia went missing. And then my phone was stolen. Unrelated awful things, but anyway, finally I got a new phone, and I checked the messages. That asshole — " She points at the unconscious boy " — had called, saying that he had *found* Olivia, and that he wanted to bring her by for the reward. And he left me a number to call. But when I called him back, he denied *everything*. But it was his *voice!* Why would he have lied in the first place? That's when I got suspicious."

"Oh god!" the brunette points at the last page.

"What?" the blonde turns the binder around and inhales sharply.

The last page is a map of the backyard with various plots marked out, red X's and names on each of them.

The blonde looks out at the grassy yard.

"Olivia is *here.*"

Drops of blood now fall freely from the blonde's bandaged arm.

"Hey!" the brunette says with alarm, "we gotta get you to a hospital!"

"And then we're going to the cops," the blonde says.

The other girl nods, then moves deeper into the shed.

"And before I forget..." the brunette reaches down and unlocks the cage for the other cat, then reaches up to the high shelf and lowers you to the ground. "You've earned your freedom, kitten. And our thanks."

You watch as the girls leave.

As she passes the boy, the blonde gives him a

powerful kick in the ribs. He grunts, then coughs.

"Uh," the brunette says, "that was on camera."

"Well, we'll edit it out."

You're free again! But you're still only a kitten, and kind of helpless in the world.

If you follow the girls, trot after them to page 209.

If you decide you'd rather go your own way, turn to page 206.

Ignoring the fragrant smell of the tasty treats, you decide to try to escape, by any means necessary. You start by clawing your way up the side of the bag toward the exit.

The hole is tiny and, though you pull at it, remains stubbornly closed.

"67 Cosgrove Crescent," the boy sings to himself, "67 Cosgrove Crescent."

You need to escape. You begin yowling, and scrambling on the inside of the bag. You jump from side to side, clawing at the cloth. In a frenzy, you tear around, sending the treats bouncing everywhere.

"Whoa!" you hear the boy yell.

He drops the bag!

You are in mid-air for only a moment before the bag his the ground. You barely feel it, bouncing around the inside as you are.

Now you go for the exit. But try as your little paws might, the hole is difficult to widen. You poke your face into it, trying to squeeze out, but you only get the very tip of your nose and part of your mouth out into the open air.

And then you're forced to fall back to the bottom of the bag as the boy lifts you up again.

"Fuck," he says. "You're crazy. No way am I keeping you a few days. You'd bring the whole neighbourhood running."

Now comes a long walk.

You're exhausted from your outburst and discouraged by the results. You console yourself by eating the treats.

Finally, you hear the boy speak to someone. An older man.

"You can have the bag," he says. "Cat's inside."

"Thank you, Mr. Cotton," another male voice responds. "Here is your payment."

"Thanks, Doc."

"How's your mother?" the man asks.

"My mom's fine," the boy replies tersely.

"I trust these payments are helping with her health?"

"Yeah. Thanks for the business."

"Glad I can help."

You hear retreating footsteps and then you go somewhere inside. Finally, you're hung up. You feel a cool wall pressing against your side.

Then, from outside the bag, you feel a hand pressing against you. The probing fingers find your head, then your body. It feels for your legs.

Suddenly, there is a sharp pinch in your side!

Then the pain is gone, leaving only a dull, throbbing ache.

Moments later, you lose consciousness.

Turn to page 168.

You don't know where you're going. You're moving on instinct and scent. All you know is that bright lights have caused you problems so far.

You move easily over fences, and you duck under trees, when finally you spot something: a water bowl!

You step over a short wooden fence and bend down to lap at the water. A number of leaves sit in it, and you studiously avoid them. Not only is the water very cold, but it tastes weird. Still, it's better than nothing, and you slurp it greedily.

Then a light comes on in the building next to the bowl.

You freeze, and watch. A little figure moves into view, sliding open a glass door and stepping outside.

You back away, and your tail bumps into the low fence behind you.

The little figure approaches, taking tiny steps.

"Oh wow," she breathes. "Oh my god! Kitty! You're so big!"

The little girl, in her nightshirt, reaches out to touch your paw.

If you let her, turn to page 227.

If you don't want to be touched, turn to page 202.

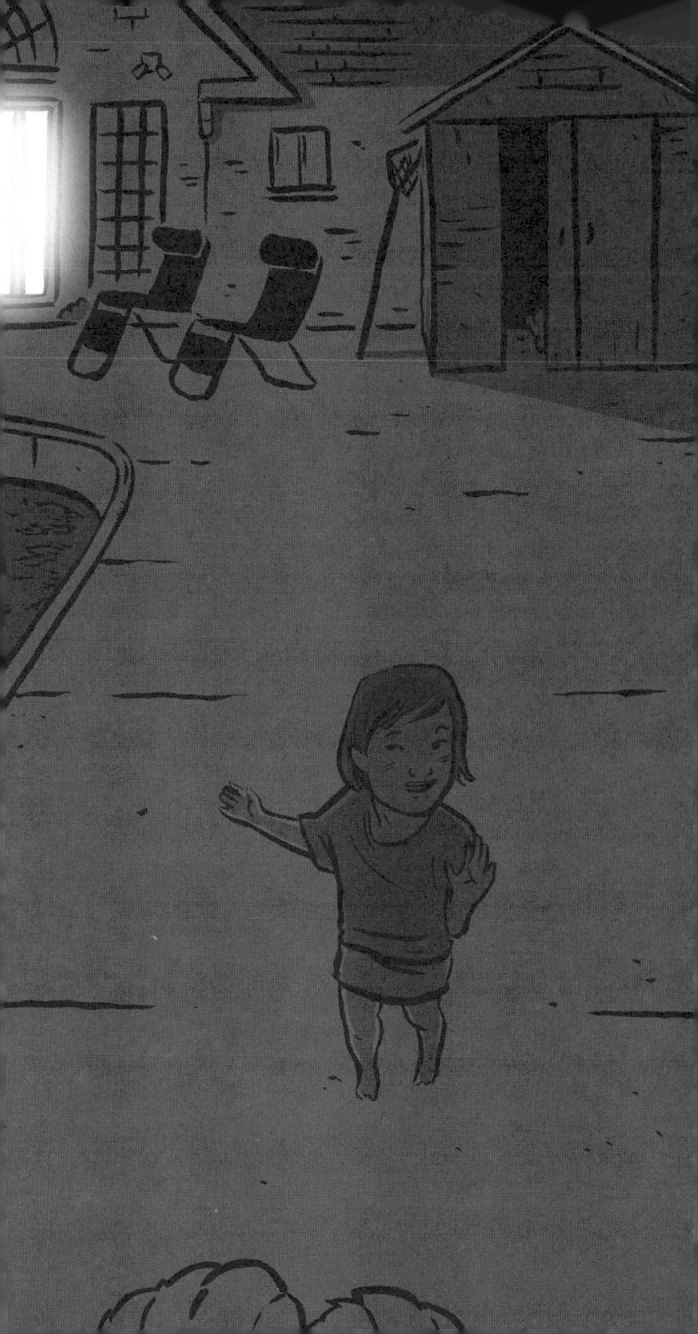

You're tired. You've had enough excitement for now. Enough of all this. You want to move to a quiet area. Someplace you can hide and feel safe.

You move through the night, finally arriving at a large parking lot that leads to a short fence which you hop over easily. Moving through a cramped tunnel, you find yourself in a wide area that's astonishingly quiet, as if insulated from the city's noise.

A large expanse of grass is surrounded on all sides by tiers of seats spreading up and out to other levels above. This should be safe enough.

You're not completely calm though — your skin is too tight, and you stretch your body, trying to ease its discomfort.

Settling down on the soft grass, you decide to go to sleep.

The last thing you see before you blink into unconsciousness are the stars, which seem closer to you than they ever have before.

Turn to page 124.

Leaving the cage, you just jump. You need to get out of here, away from all these crazy humans.

But it's a long fall.

Instinctively, you spread your body wide, stretching your arms and legs and tail out as far as possible, to try to slow your descent.

But you still slam yourself senseless into the ground. It's further than you've ever fallen. You try to hobble away from the shed, but your legs don't work. Or some of them do, but you're not sure which. Woozily, you try to move, but all you want to do is lie down.

"Oh no! Kitten!" the brunette exclaims.

Outside the shed, the boy takes the opportunity to run. He dashes into the alley and disappears.

"Fuck!" the blonde starts after him, but looks back. "He's gonna get away!"

"Come help me!" the brunette has her hand on you. "He's hurt."

The pain begins to radiate throughout your body.

"Did you get it? Did you videotape it all?" the blonde asks.

The brunette nods.

"Yeah, I got it. But we need to help him."

You lose consciousness.

When you wake up, both girls are there, watching you. It's very bright, and you can barely see.

"Hey kitten," the brunette smiles at you. "We're gonna help you, okay?"

"Soon it won't hurt anymore," the blonde massages your cheek with her thumb. "Thank you for everything."

"You helped us get enough evidence to get that

creep charged with fraud and cruelty to animals." the brunette kisses you on the forehead.

"And more — that knife he had is probably a felony."

"Thank you, kitten."

A third person enters the room. She is blurry.

"Is this it?" the brunette asks. "Is this the one?"

The blurry figure nods, and says, "The earlier one was a sedative and muscle relaxant. This one will stop the heart."

You don't even feel the needle puncture your skin.

With the two girls holding you and kissing you as you drift off, you just feel loved.

THE END

You have just used up one of your lives. You have eight more! Feel free to reincarnate on page 1 and make different choices! See another ending! Pick another plot!

The girl touches your soft paw, and a huge grin spreads over her face. Leaning in, she throws her arms around your arm, and she nuzzles against you.

You bend your head down, to rub your face against her, then you lick her.

A peal of laugher escapes her, and she digs her hands deep into your fur. Slowly, she manages to climb up your neck and get up on to your back.

"Mush!" she calls out. "Go!" She digs her heels into your neck.

You bend down to drink more water from the bowl.

"I'm calling you Falkor!" the girl says. "That means you're my dragon and you have to do what I say! Now c'mon Falkor! Go!"

A motion from the lit house catches your attention — a man in boxer shorts and a T-shirt steps out the sliding door and sees you and the girl.

"This is impossible. This isn't real," he mutters to himself, shaking his head.

"Bite his head off!" the girl whispers to you.

You back away from the man. He's grabbed a long pole from the side of the house and is swinging it slowly.

"Syd," he calls to the girl. "Come down. Please hon."

"No," the girl responds defiantly. "Falkor is my friend. And we're leaving now."

"Let her go!" the man screams, and rushes at you, swinging wildly.

You turn to run. But just as you're about to jump back over the fence, you feel the man grab your tail!

You swing it — slamming the man against the fence.

"Awright!" the girl cheers in your ear. "Now eat him! Munch him up!"

You run through the night. You're aware that something is wrong with you. You're constantly growing, and at a rate faster than you can adjust to. Even as you jump over backyard fences, you have a hard time assessing distance.

"Go left!" the girl bellows. "I wanna go to the water!"

The girl keeps yelling in your ear. She is getting annoying. Now she climbs closer to your right ear. "Didn't you hear me?!" she yells. She starts yanking on the fine hair that grows inside it.

If you scratch at her, like an itch, turn to page 251.

If you leave her be, figuring she'll stop, turn to 255.

You keep your nose close to the water, but it's blindingly apparent that you are growing at an uncontrolled and inexplicable rate.

The humans have sent airplanes and missles at you, and they hurt, but you are growing so large that they are little more than flesh wounds and stings.

Your tail, seemingly swishing of its own accord, takes care of most of the threats, batting these annoyances out of the air, or disturbing the atmosphere so much that the turbulence makes it impossible for aircraft to keep aloft.

Still, the crippling growing pains of your rapidly enlarging bones makes every second a painful journey into the next.

Even with your nose down below the clouds, it's hard to breathe. Your need for oxygen is using up the planet's entire precious reserve, and your shoulders and your backside actually breach the thin blue atmospheric membrane, allowing it to leak into space.

You have grown so large that your body spans an ocean, which is now little more than a puddle to you.

In a delerium of pain and hypoxia, it's hard to keep track of how big you're getting, but the Earth is like a wobbly ball underneath your massive mass.

From the center of your rapidly beating heart you begin to exert a gravitational pull on all the neighbouring celestial bodies, and the Milky Way galaxy stops what it's doing to take notice.

But now you can no longer breathe.

Finally, desperate, you wrap your arms and legs around the world. Your claws dig into the Earth like the opposite of mountains. It reminds you of your days in the playpen with the other kittens, dozing off with your arms wrapped around one of your sisters or brothers.

Behind you, the sun on your back is the last warm thing you feel.

With her trembling hand pressed against the rear window of the International Space Station, first science officer Sally Kimball stares in shock.

She wonders for a moment if the station has depressurized, or if there's an oxygen leak, because she is *seeing* things.

This is impossible.

She shuts her eyes, willing the scene to be different when she opens them.

If what she's seeing is real, then that means that everyone who she loves is now dead.

Her wife, their daughter Chloé, her family. Their cat Porkinsons.

All dead.

First science officer Sally Kimball opens her eyes again, only to see through the reinforced glass what she had witnessed a moment earlier — the spectacle of an impossibly giant kitten hugging its beautiful blue ball of yarn with a fierceness she could only interpret as love.

THE END

You have just used up one of your lives, and indeed all the lives of every being on Earth. You have eight more! Feel free to reincarnate on page 1 and make different choices! See another ending!
Pick another plot!

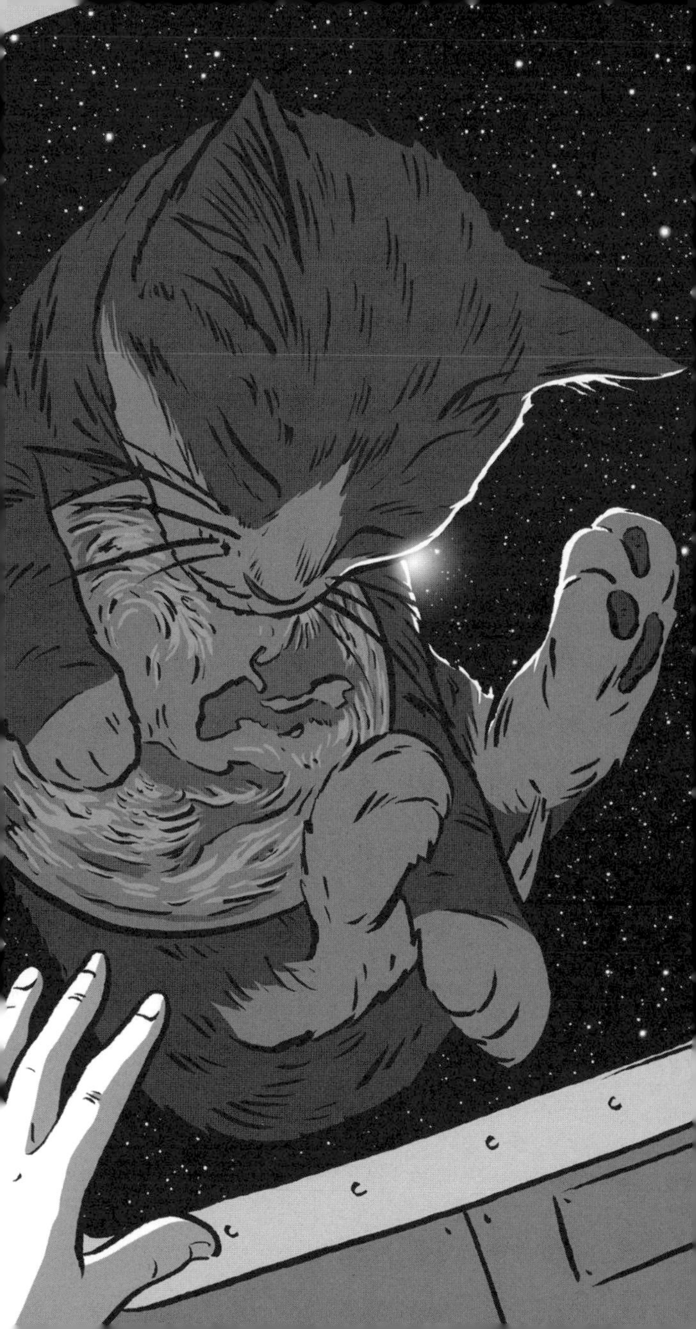

Silently, you jump back over the fence.

"My daughter," the woman is sobbing into her phone. "We found her in the pool. She's not breathing. No, she's not responsive. Please, send an ambulance!"

While the man is busy kissing the girl, you pounce over them, driving both forepaws into the woman. She drops, and the phone clatters to the ground. You keep one paw on her belly to keep her from going anywhere. She just stares at you. She makes no noise, though her mouth is agape.

"Ma'am? Ma'am?" a voice from phone. "Are you there? EMS is on its way."

You remove your paw, and she inhales audibly, but then you put your paw back on her.

Suddenly, the man is there, and he's wrapped his arms around your forearm.

"Get off of her!" he screams.

You jerk your arm back and forth to fling him off, and finally he's forced to let go, disappearing into the night. You think you heard him hit the ground, but you're not sure.

Meanwhile, the woman has gotten to her feet and is trying to get away! She makes her way to the door, but you snag her nightdress with your claw and haul her back.

She is screaming.

With both paws, you bring her to your mouth and bite down. She squeals even louder.

You munch down on her, feeling her chest bones break, and she's finally quiet. You work your jaws, chewing her up into something soft enough to swallow.

Then you lap up some more water to wash her

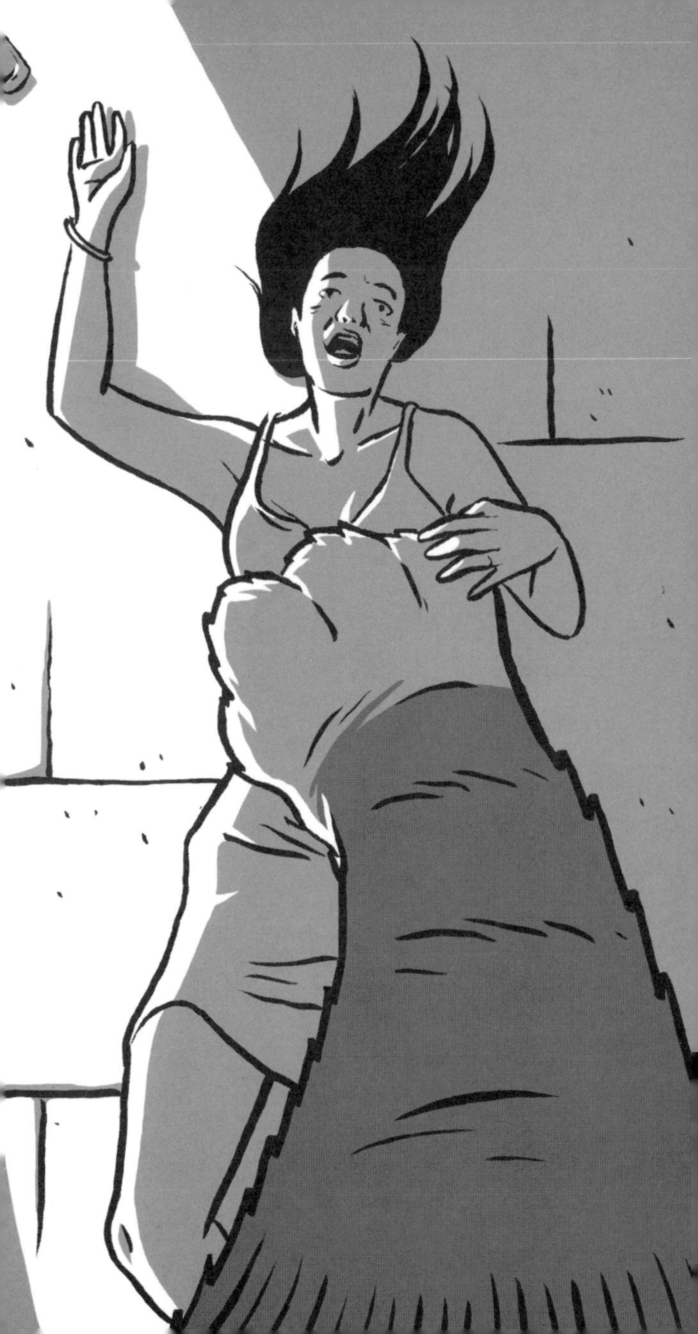

down.

Your ears prick up — sirens are approaching.

Now that your belly's full, you kind of want to find a place to rest.

Turn to page 224.

You don't like how the man is trying to goad you into something. You don't trust him. Instead, you turn back to the tunnel entrance and head outside.

The assembled onlookers back away, murmuring with uncertainty.

You squint into the bright light shining down on you, and the steady buzzing sound behind it. You leave the main road through a parking lot, your weight crushing cars as you move. You need to get to a dark area. You need to escape all this attention.

But you realize something horrible — no matter where you go, the bright light follows you! Normally you like a bright light. For instance, you love sunbeams. They are the embodiment of love for you. But this harsh, sharp light, accompanied by that relentless buzzing noise is terrible.

You climb up onto a building's rooftop and stare at the light, defiant. You yowl at it.

The light just stares.

You decide to take it down. With a huge push off the roof's edge, you pounce at the light —

But you miss it!

You actually reach above it, and something stings your paw! Ouch! You drop back to the ground, flattening some random cars.

You get back to your feet, ready to pounce again, but you notice that the buzzing has sputtered to silence, and the light is actually falling like a leaf from the sky. When it hits the ground, a huge explosion follows.

It scares you! You run off without any more lights chasing you.

Turn to page 224.

Everything is white. Where did everything go?

For a moment you panic, but soon, some of the clouds part and you can see again. You swipe at them, making the floating white mists move and swirl. It is like drawing your paw through water, but without getting wet! This is fun!

Your joy is interrupted by a piercing noise above you. Instinctively, you look up and you see a grey arrow zooming through the air. You reach for it, but it's too fast!

So many things to catch.

As it passes, it leaves a very loud noise in its wake.

Then you hear something else behind you —

Pain blooms in your back! You yowl in panic. You turn to face the threat, but it isn't from another being, or anything you can grapple with —

Your fur is on fire.

You scream and roll, the cool earth helping to put out the flames. But the pain remains, and you are wary of another attack.

The shooting arrow drifts lazily overhead, observing you.

This is terrible.

Do you fight them? Turn to page 204.

Do you run? Turn to page 259.

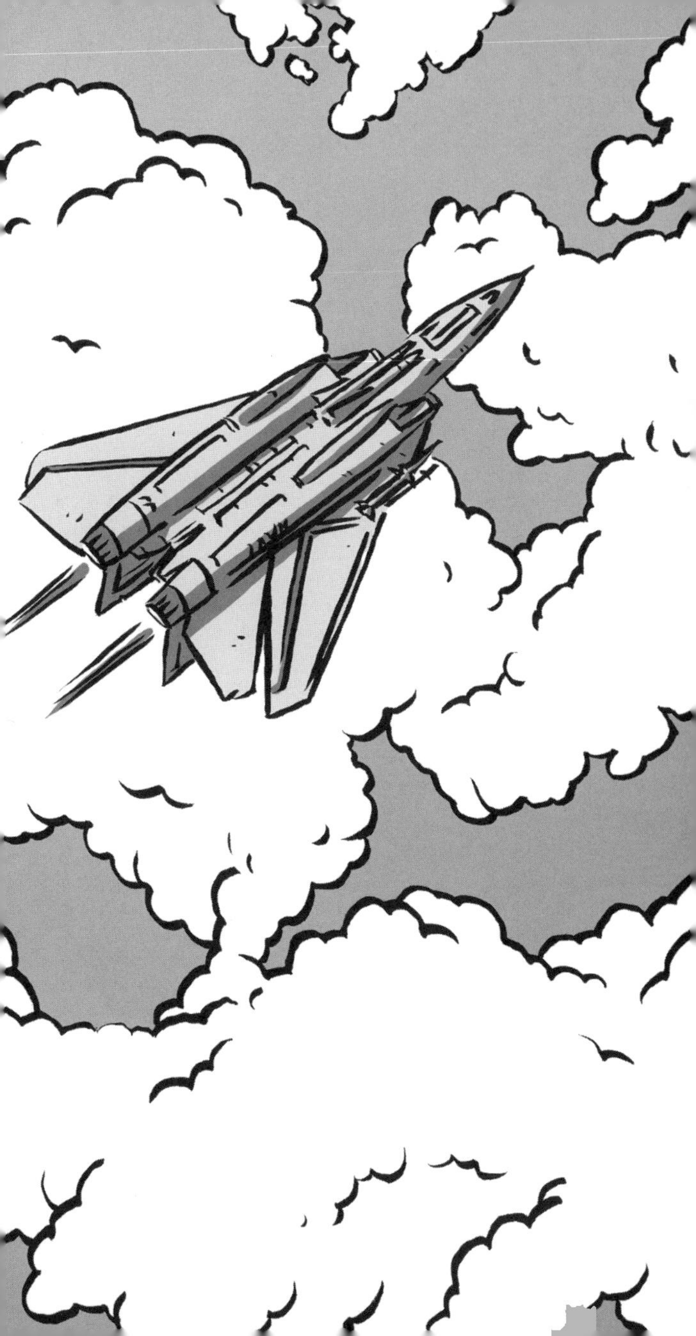

238

With a giant leap, you pounce onto the brunette's shoulder!

She yelps in surprise, but doesn't drop the camera. You start climbing down her body, but don't make it far.

"Kitten, I'm busy!"

With her free hand, the brunette manages to pry you off and stuff you back into the cage.

Turn to page 214.

You make your way along the water's edge, pausing to take a drink.

It's initially satisfying, but the water is very salty, and you smack your lips together and lick your whiskers to get the brine taste out.

Up ahead, you hear a noise.

A large fly veers out over the water. Amazingly, a voice emanates from it.

"Here boy!" it says. "That's a good boy."

Through the clouds, you witness a gargantuan puppy trot out into the water, sending giant waves everywhere, including some back onto shore. Its heavy, clumsy steps shake the ground around you.

You remember this puppy. Was it back at the lab?

But something else catches your attention — following behind the puppy, a giant turtle is hustling along as fast as it can. Behind it, small planes drop bombs on its back, near its tail, blackening the shell. The turtle is being prodded slowly, but irrevocably out into the ocean.

Past the turtle you see a giant rat! A bomber plane drops giant rolls of cheese out its bay doors, and the rat's sensitive nose, twitching even now, follows the smell of them, trying to catch them in its mouth. Even though the giant rolls are mere flakes compared to the rat, such is its hunger that it will follow the free food to the ends of the Earth.

You watch as the puppy scampers in the water. The mouse is at the edge of the ocean before it balks. The turtle has no choice, as the steady pain on its back and on its butt intensifies.

Suddenly, the dog turns and sees you, barking its head off.

Now the large fly that was speaking to the dog

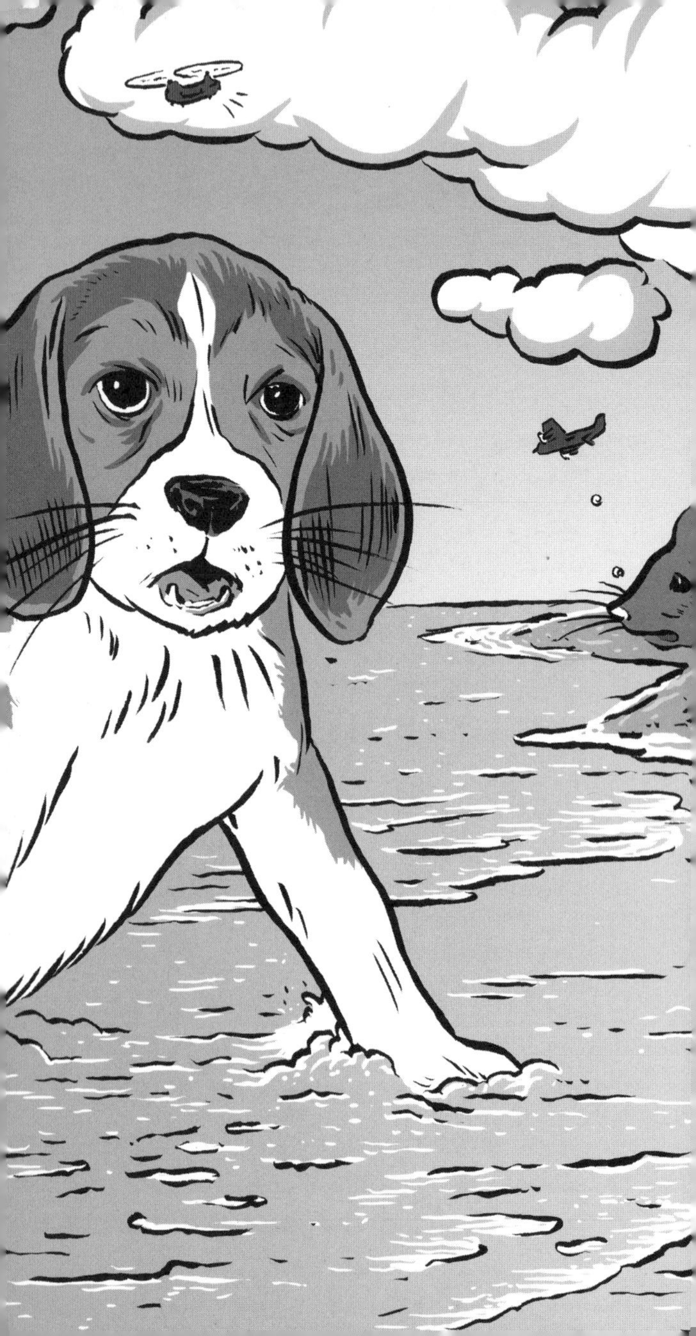

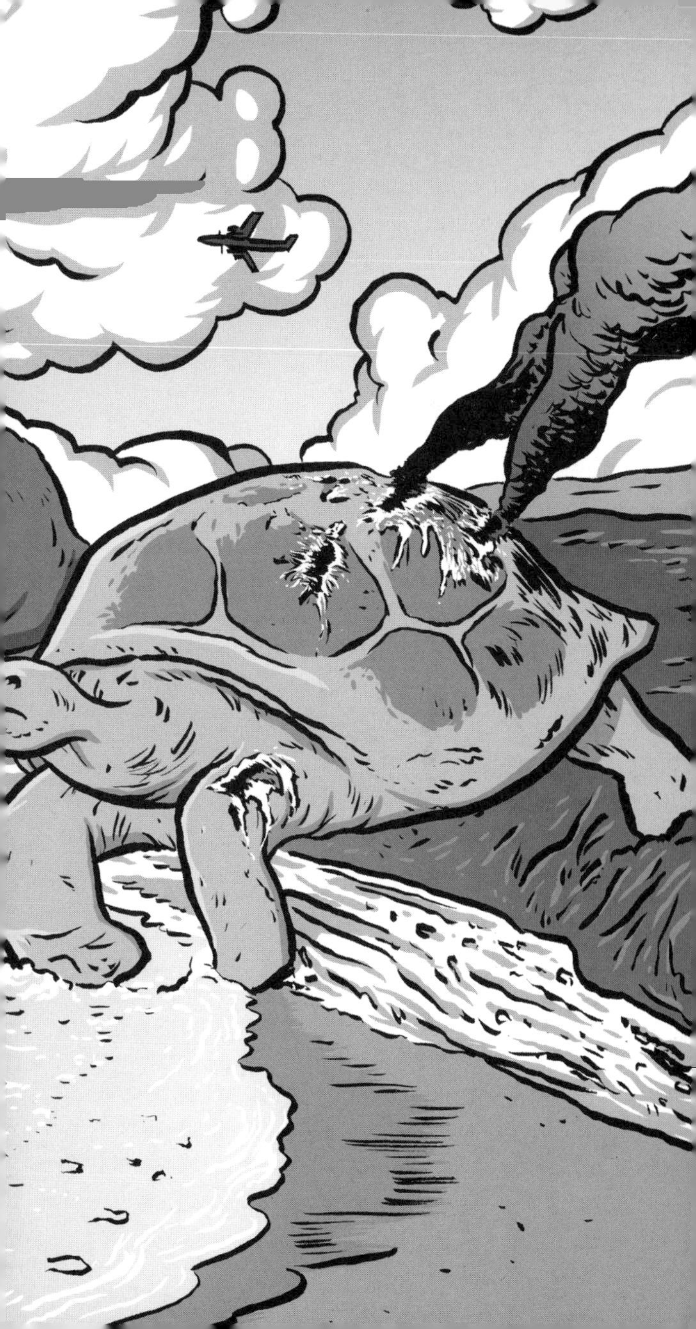

speaks again. "All choppers and other air support – area is hot. Evacuate the area! I say again: area is hot. Operation Mothra is commencing."

The fly zips off and you flatten your ears and arch your back as the dog approaches you, snarling aggressively.

The rat, for its part, starts scurrying down the shoreline, away from all of this. Perhaps it senses something that you don't.

The turtle has stopped moving, largely because the bombing raid on its back has mercifully stopped.

The puppy continues to bark so that you almost don't hear the high-pitched whistle.

But then the dog quiets, hearing it himself, and now you hear it more clearly too.

A lone, small dense thing drops down between you and the dog.

You almost want to swipe at it, but something nags at you. You are not sure you want to catch it.

You don't even see it hit the water. A white light blinds you, and a moment later your huge body is thrown into the air.

Your fur is stripped from your flesh, and your flesh is ripped from your bones, and your bones are separated from its marrow in the nuclear blast.

In the years to come, this whole incident will be known as the Attack of the Zillas, when all of the Earth's nations put aside their differences to wage war against an animal experiment gone wrong. It forces all of humanity to consider when (if ever) any animal experiments have gone right?

One of your giant bones is flung into the ocean and breaks down over centuries. Its internal spongy cancellous networks will one day become home to the

most amazing coral reefs that have ever existed.
A new kind of catfish will flourish there.

THE END

*You have just used up one of your lives. You have
eight more! Feel free to reincarnate on page 1 and
make different choices! See another ending!
Pick another plot!*

You make a move toward the motorcycle and the man takes off!

You gallop down the tunnel after him, hurdling over random cars that he must swerve around.

Repeatedly he slows and looks back to see if you're following him. He's *playing* with you! You played with Tupac this same way, hiding behind your other siblings, dashing around the playpen, the beautiful rhythm of kitten chasing kitten.

You deliberately slow your pace, so that he slows too — then you *swipe!*

At the last second, he guns it and jerks out of your range. You run after him.

More vehicles race into the tunnel, and you dodge their bright headlights, their squeal of brakes, their sustained honking.

Finally you're both out of the tunnel. You can really let loose here. You run as fast as you can to catch up and you dive desperately to grab at the man.

Your claw slices through his back wheel, and you watch him wobble as he fights to retain control — but he crashes!

When you catch up, you watch the man get up and try to find his footing, but he drops, and does not move. Red blood smears the entire right side of his face.

You roll him back and forth. You want him to get up and play with you some more.

But he's done.

And now maybe so are you.

Turn to page 224

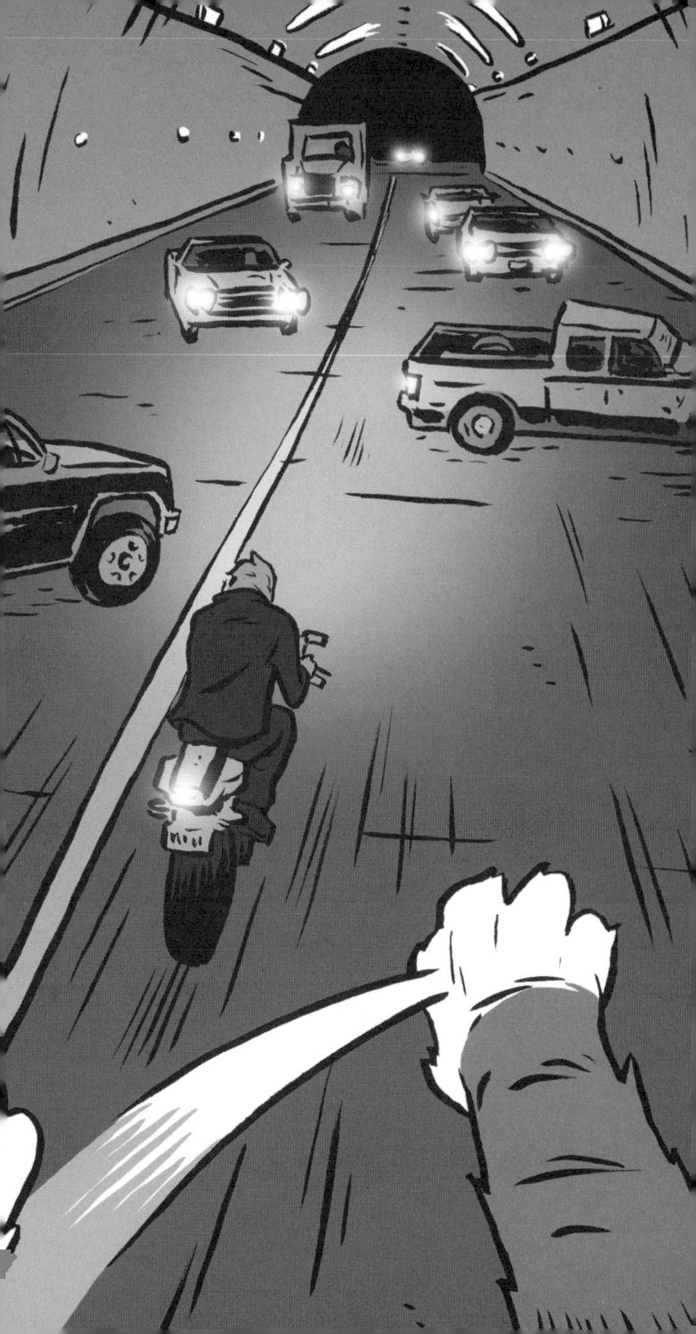

You are bored and upset. You've been in this cage for a long time. Furthermore, the scents of so many different animals cloud the room. It's stuffed with the stench of stress. Time passes very slowly, and the humans all ignore you. What is this place?

Finally, a woman in a white coat comes to your cage. She looks at you, glances at a tag on your cage, then reads a clipboard she's holding.

"Holden?" she says gently, then looks at another attendant at the desk. "His name is Holden?"

"I wasn't on shift," the man says. "Anyway, he's a drop-off."

"Okay."

The woman takes your cage into another room and lets you out. She shines a light in your eyes, and checks your ears, and moves your body around. It's sort of fun, but she turns your body without any affection. And the blue rubber gloves she wears have a very strong smell that you don't like.

"Lessee... no parasites," she notes.

Then you are put back in the cage and you never see the woman again.

More hours pass, and a man appears. This time, you're taken to a whole different room. It's empty save for a few items. He opens your cage at one end, and goes to sit on the floor on the other side. He pretends he's not watching you, but you can feel that he's watching you very carefully.

You don't like this room. There's no exit. Again, the scent of a billion different animals suffuses every surface. You walk over to the wall, where there is a blanket on the ground and sniff it.

"Holden," the man says. "Holden."

You look up at him. It's clear he's calling you. He

holds out his hand. First though, you check out another thing in the room — a small cloth tent. Just your size. You don't venture in, however. Some other cat has sprayed into a corner of it. It's his territory and you don't want to risk reprisal.

"Holden," the man calls again. He lifts a rectangular wafer to his face and speaks into it. "Cat is an orange tabby named Holden. Looks to be two to four months old. Holden is curious, actively investigating the room."

You wander over to the man and smell the hand he's holding out. There's no food, but the man is very calm and he smells okay. When he moves his hand up to your head, you are startled for a second, but then you let him stroke you. You climb up onto his lap and start smelling his shirt.

"Friendly to humans, as well. Very sociable."

But all too soon, you're back in the cage and placed in a whole other room.

Whereas before, humans were rather indifferent towards you, now — humans were all *too* curious. Faces peer in at you, all carefully examining you. They wave fingers and call to you, trying to get you to respond. Some of them tap the glass with their fingers. You find them interesting, but you're mostly busy playing with your toy. This small nubbly ball they left in the cage with you.

A blonde girl in a loose shirt holds a wafer to her ear.

"There's one here that's really cute!" she says. "If we want a kitten, we need to pick him up now. The lady at the counter says kittens go fast!"

An attendant shows another person into the room. This one is a tall bearded man. He makes a circuit around the room, looking at every animal.

"Hold on," the girl says, holding the flat part of the wafer up toward you. A bright light flashes in your face. You blink, annoyed. "I'm sending you a picture now. Show it to everyone. It'd be so cool to have a kitten around the apartment. Call me back."

The bearded man wanders over and looks at you.

"He's perfect," the girl says to herself.

"You're right about that," the man says. His voice is gruff and low. So low, it's hard to hear. "Hey look," he says to the girl, though his eyes never leave you, "I know you were here first. The thing is — my kids really want a cat. And I'm in the doghouse with their mum. No pun intended. And I really like this cat. I like the look of him. I like the calm way he sits, but at the same time, you can tell he's got energy."

"Wait, what are you — "

"You were here first," the man says, interrupting. "No question. I know that. And I respect that. This kitten by all rights is yours. And if you say no, I'll walk away. But I'll give you $200 right now — I have it in cash — to forget about this one. There are other cats here that could use a good home, and I think you can give them one."

The girl is quiet for a moment. Her phone sings a song, but she doesn't acknowledge it.

"Why this cat?" she asks.

"I dunno," the man rumbles. "I like him. I think I could live with him. He's probably a good listener."

"Make it $250," the girl says quietly.

The man thinks for a second, then nods. They shake hands.

As the man counts out the bills, the girl speaks into her wafer. "Hey, yeah, no. There was a problem.

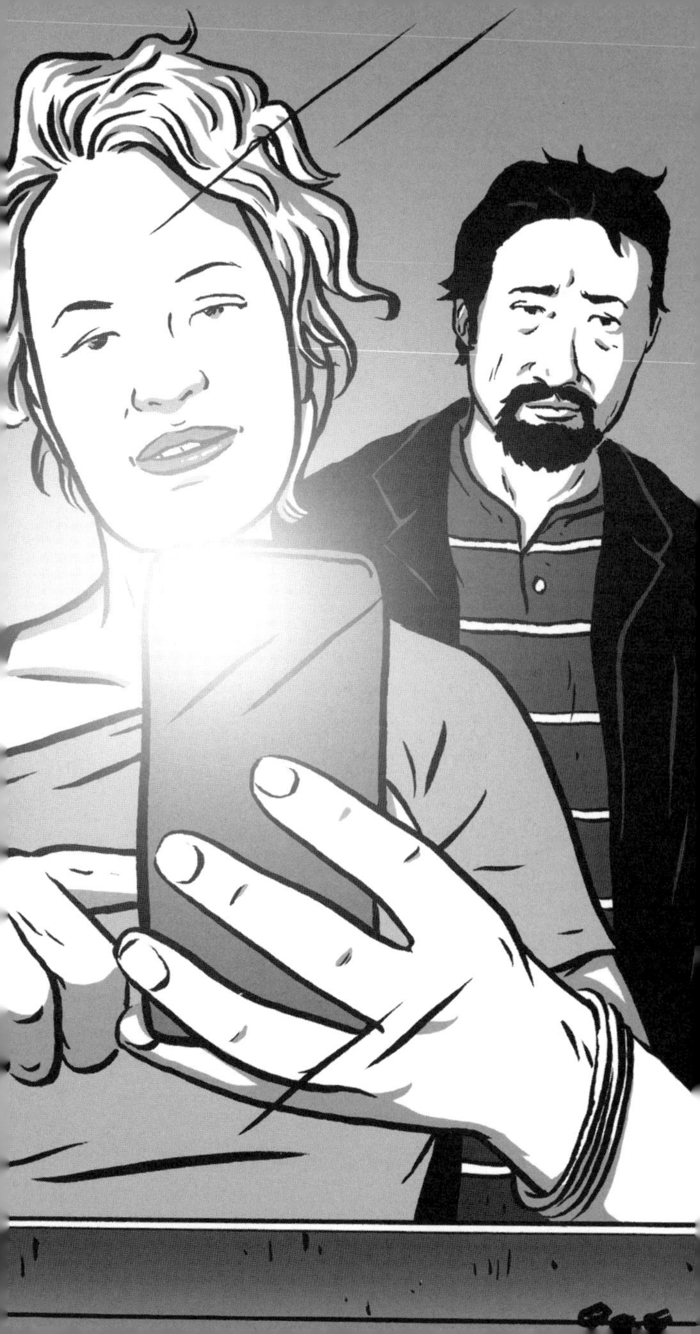

There was a mix-up. He's not the one. I'll come back another day. There's plenty of time. Yeah. Yeah. No, see you at home."

As the girl leaves, the man winks at you.

You spend a whole other day in the cage. They take you into another room, and the things that occur are a blur. You remember a sharp pinch, and falling asleep. Drowsy, you wake up and some sensitive parts of your body hurt. Additionally, there is a pain in between your shoulders. More sharp pinches, and then back in the cage.

Finally, a day after that, when you are feeling more yourself, the bearded man returns.

He puts a collar on you, then brings you out in his arms to a car.

It's a long drive, and you spend most of it asleep in his lap. You don't like driving — this weird movement you have no control over, but the low, ambient purring of the car soothes you.

A long time later, the car stops outside a house, and the purring ceases, and the man lifts you up.

"We're home," he says.

Turn to page 264.

You bring your paw up to your ear and try to pull her off.

"Ah!" the girl screams. "No! Don't do that!" Now she's even louder. "Fuck you, Falkor!"

It's very unsettling — the girl fell into your ear. Your turn your head, trying to shake her loose, but she's holding onto something. Some hairs, maybe.

You roll on the ground, flattening a few houses and trees, and bang your ear against the ground. Finally she lets go, and you see her on the grass.

Is she dead? You press on her to see, and she makes a choking noise, then is still.

You press down on her again. This time, no choking noise.

Maybe she's dead.

Turn to page 224.

You take a tentative step out into the infinite ocean, and as you wade in, you realize that it's not that deep. You move outwards, taking on a regular gait, and you surf through the clouds, which part for the girth of your shoulders.

It's quite beautiful up here, and you keep moving, aiming to drink in all the beauty you can. You stare at the low, fiery ball, falling fast into the ocean, offering you its last sunbeams.

Over time it gets harder to breathe, and you notice that the tips of your ears are cold.

But you keep going. You are looking for a peaceful place.

Soon, the clouds dissipate, and you can see clear to the horizon, which is dark.

By now, you find you have to bend your head down if you want to breathe, leaving your shoulders cold.

You peek up at the black sky, and see the pale white moon.

It is curved, like a claw.

You feel like maybe you can get to it — leap up and snag it with your own claw.

If you shoot for the moon, turn to page 260.

If you keep your head down and keep breathing, turn to page 229.

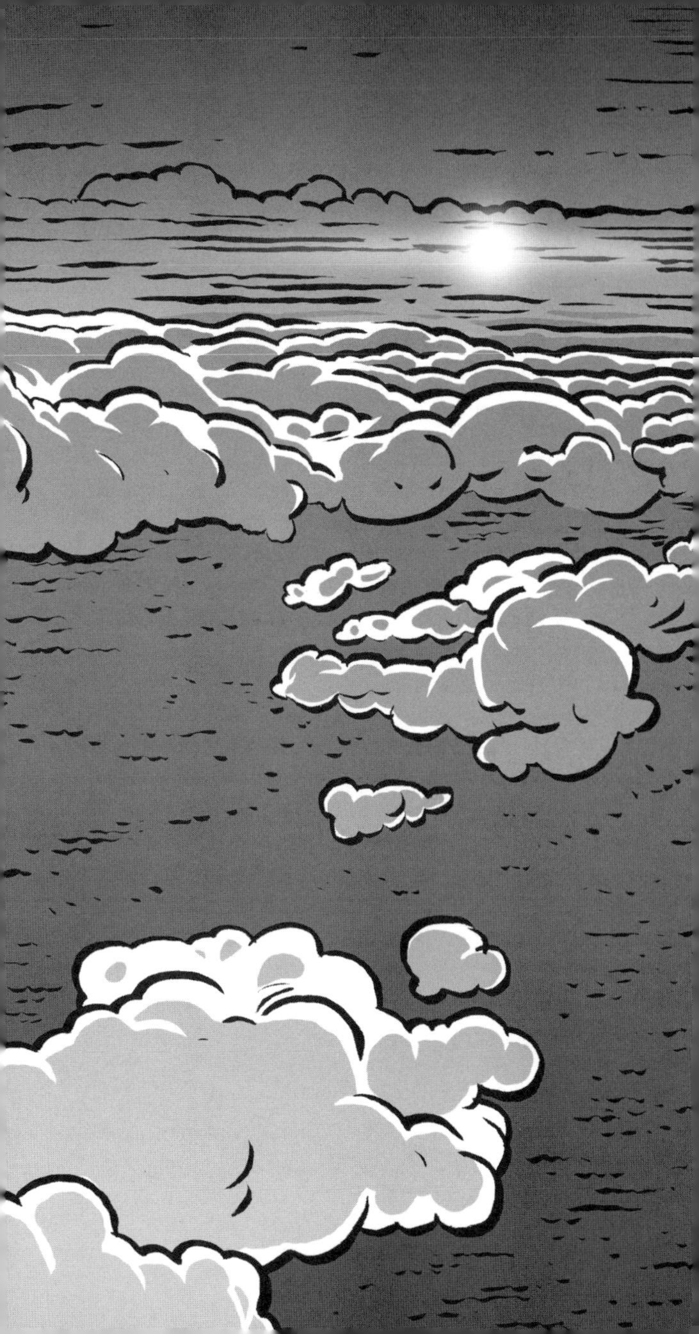

You get up and focus on the flies. They back off, drifting away.

You clamber up the side of the bowl, following them, but the sloped wall collapses under your weight! It looks solid, but isn't.

One of the flies takes off. You decide to chase it!

You leap over the top lip of the stadium and go after it. Seeing you, the fly increases its speed, but you are too fast for it. You launch yourself up and grab it between your paws.

It explodes, stinging and burning you!

You lick you paw, trying to take the pain away.

Now the other flies keep their distance — moving away. Down below, ants scatter. You reach down and squish a couple, making them still.

But suddenly you can't see!

Turn to page 236

Pretty soon, the girl manages to climb up the back of your head. Handful by handful, she grabs your fur and makes her way to the area in between your ears. Her weight isn't unpleasant. It reminds you of when your mom used to lick that exact place.

There is something going on in front of a house, and you settle on it, appreciating the rough roof tiles as you look down on the scene.

There's a white car with flashing lights on the top, and two men are standing with flashlights out, aiming into the dark alleys in between houses.

One of them touches a radio on his shoulder. "Central, this is 4-12. We're at the scene, but no sign of it. Complainant said a wild animal? Are they sure it wasn't just a raccoon or a cat? Over."

"Copy 4-12, this is Central. From their account, it might be a bear, over."

"A bear?!" the other man says to his partner. "Holy shit."

"4-12, air support is on its way."

"Copy, Central. We'll wait for backup."

One of the men opens the car's trunk and pulls out a shotgun.

"Will this even *stop* a bear?" he asks.

"That's got such a punch it'll even stop a *zombie* bear," his partner quips.

You rest your head on the roof, rubbing your cheek against the chimney. The oscillating lights simultaneously arouse but relax you. You curl your paws around the front edge of the roof.

Presently, you hear a buzzing in the air. You look up and see a steadily blinking, small yellow light approach. It floats like a hummingbird. Idly, you consider if you could catch it.

When it's right overhead, however, a bright flood-light washes the ground in a cold sunbeam.

You bring your paw up over your eyes. It's very bright.

As if noting your movement, the spotlight rises up the front face of the house and onto you.

The men on the ground follow its track, and they are momentarily flummoxed.

"Shoot!" one of the men raises his weapon.

Immediately you get up. You've seen this before.

"Wait!" the other man says, "There's a girl on his head!"

You don't like the light. You reach up and push the nose of the helicopter. It drifts off a bit, and rises into the air. But the spotlight stays fixed on your position.

"Oh no, Falkor! We're gonna be in trouble!" the girl yells.

"Honey," one of the cops has his hands out beseechingly, "please come down!"

"We need backup!" the other cop is saying into his radio. "All of it! Bring everyone!"

You swipe at the helicopter again, but you misjudge its distance, and don't manage to even touch it

One cop starts shooting at you! A pinch in your belly!

"Hey! Cease fire! Cease fire! There's a girl up there!"

"It just went for our air support!"

More gunfire.

You reach down and put your paw on the one making all the noise. He squirms, but your paw holds him in place. You flex your claws and he's suddenly wet.

The other cop now fires at you. It stings!

You jerk back, sending the girl on your head off balance. You feel her tumble forward, bouncing off your nose, and falling to the ground!

She screams.

The cop drops his gun, and sprints forward — arms out to catch her.

But he's short by a few feet, and the girl smacks the ground, bouncing a bit. The cop screams in anguish.

You run away through the night, though the spotlight follows you.

Finally, sick of the attention, you turn and reach for it. You snag a landing strut and yank it towards you, gnawing on it.

The propellers blow on your whiskers, and annoy you. Bringing it to the ground, you don't anticipate the huge fireball that erupts when it hits.

You back off, smelling something burning. Did it get your whiskers?

You run from the crazy scene.

Escape to page 224.

You keep licking yourself, the satisfying sound of your rough tongue scraping your dirty fur clean in your ears. But soon the buzzing intensifies — more flies arrive. There are several of them, all floating in place, surrounding you.

Annoyed, you stand and swish your tail at them. They veer away in a panic, but soon return.

You decide to get out of there, clambering over the stadium edge, but it collapses underneath you!

The sloped walls crumble under your weight when you press down with your feet.

The flies draw even closer when this happens.

Pulling your paws free of the wreckage, you venture outward. But just as you step into the world, you spot the most utterly compelling bright red dot on the ground!

It shimmers like a living thing.

If you follow the dot, turn to page 262.

If you'd rather just run away and escape the flies, turn to page 259.

You run.

You want to be left alone.

You are desperately hungry and thirsty and your body hurts.

You gallop over tiny structures that crunch under your feet.

You run through clouds. Most of them hover below your chin now, and you can see the sun. It is so bright and warm. You are so grateful for it.

For what seems like forever you run.

Until suddenly, your feet are wet!

You bend down below the clouds, checking your location.

The water seems to go on forever. What is this? You stare hypnotized at the ocean. You've created huge waves with your movements and the ripples spread outward forever.

It's so calm out there.

Do you venture out into the ocean?
Turn to page 252.

If you prefer to move along the
shoreline, turn to 239.

Gathering your legs underneath you, and taking deep breaths, you leap, pushing off from the muddy sea-bottom!

As you rise, there is a sudden shift in temperature. You stretch out your arms toward the moon, reaching for it. Maybe you can snag it before gravity brings you back in its embrace.

But gravity is gone.

You have left it behind.

You are *so* close.

The moon tempts you like the curled wing of an insouciant bird that needs taming.

You want to reach it and wrap your paws around it, squeezing.

You would hold it so tight it couldn't breathe — just as you are having trouble breathing right now.

And as you take a slow blink to say hi to the moon, your lids don't rise again.

Your choice to leave the planet saved it.

Over centuries, your giant kitten body will crystallize, continue on its trajectory, be pulled into a new, more expansive and elongated elliptical orbit.

You will become known as the Catzilla comet, which will be viewable from the Earth once every nine years.

THE END

You have just used up one of your lives. You have eight more! Feel free to reincarnate on page 1 and make different choices! See another ending! Pick another plot!

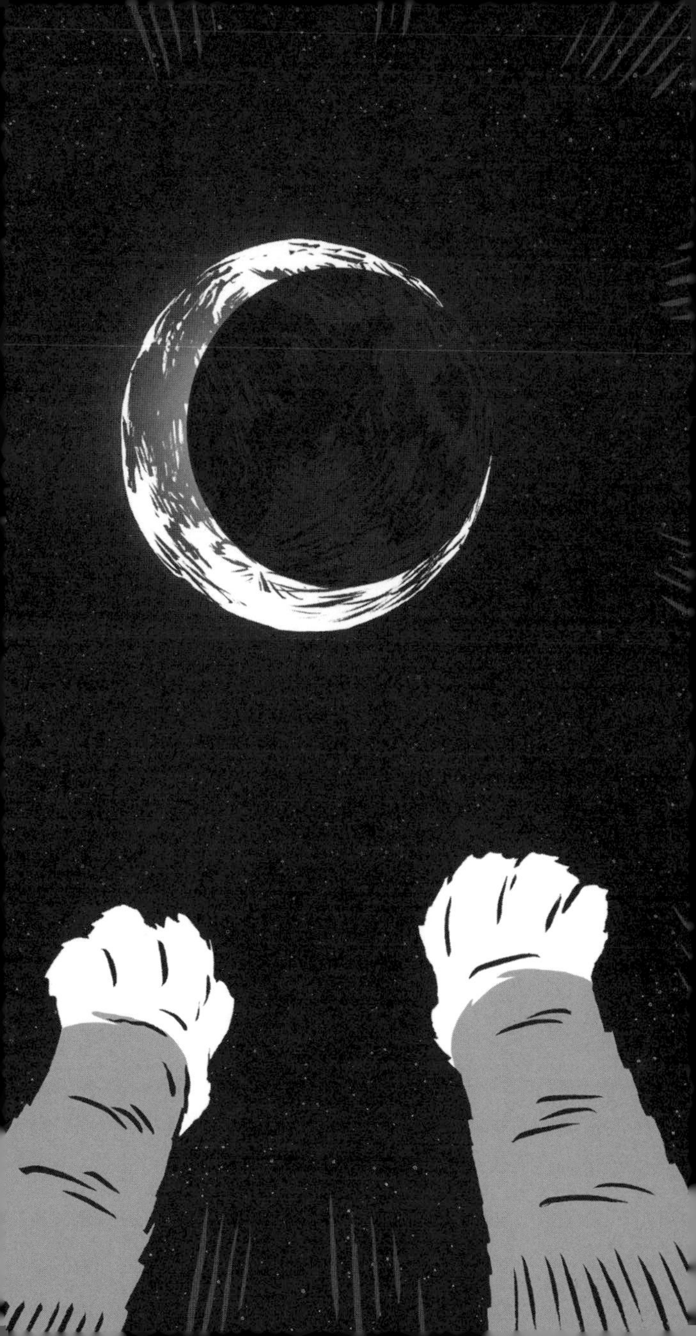

262

The red dot moves quickly, as if it notices you noticing it. What is it? Is it a fly? A bug? You try to pounce on it, but it zips along the ground, moving up a road. You follow as it dances away.

Sometimes it hides behind trees, and you lose it for a moment, but then it shows itself and takes off again!

You love this. It's playing with you!

Soon it leads you out of the city and towards farmland and empty fields.

You keep jumping on it, but it eludes you. Bah! You thought you had it but it escapes again! The bright glow of the red light is so compelling, the way it shivers and burns. More than anything you want to catch this magical thing and eat it.

In the background, you hear a low buzzing noise, but you ignore it, preferring to focus on the dot.

Finally you reach a large body of water, and the red dot ventures out into it, but you balk.

You are not fond of getting wet, and you are suspicious of how the water goes on forever.

You flick your tail back and forth nervously. Then, without warning, the dot disappears somewhere in the waves.

Where did it go?

You look all around for it, following along the water's edge.

Turn to page 239

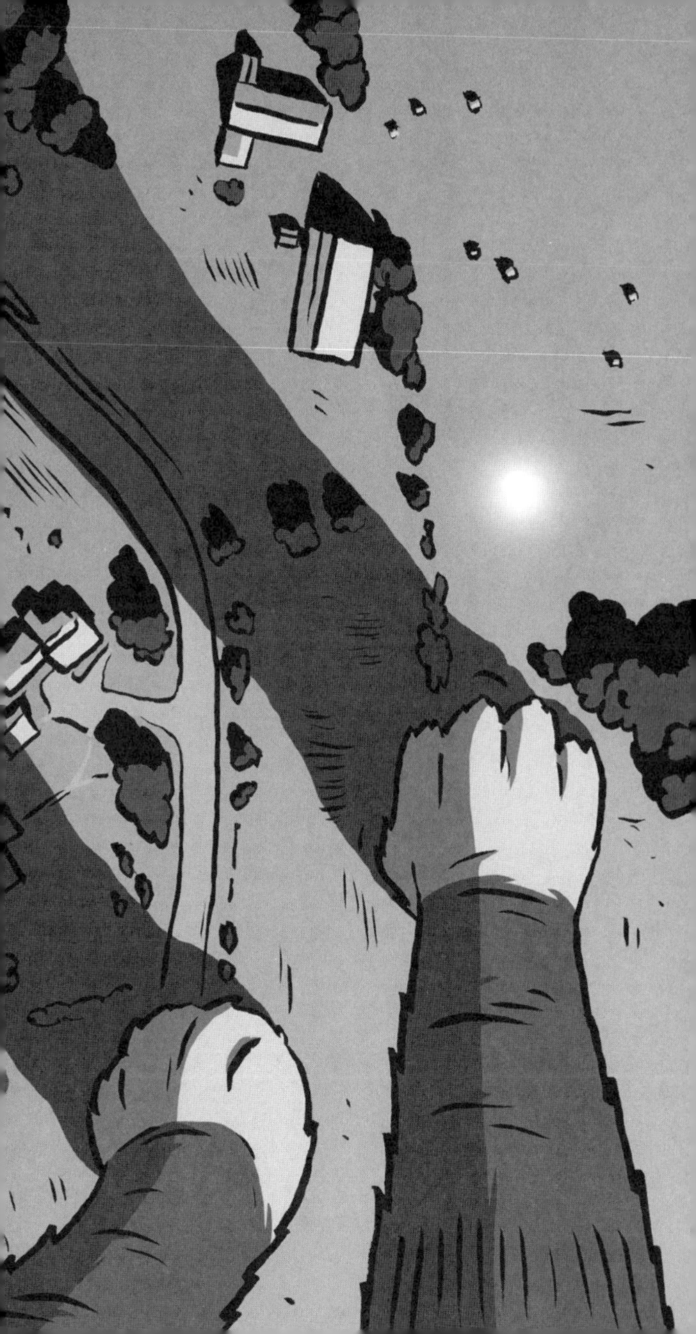

The bearded man drops you down in the house.

Your nose pulses as you take in the smell of it. There's no immediate danger — no other cats in the house. You just smell humans.

"Take a look around," the man says genially. "Make yourself at home." He kicks his shoes off and walks past you. His feet leave scent trails as he walks. "After all, it's your home now too."

You walk into another room and take it in, smelling the legs of couches and chairs, staying close to the walls.

What is this place?

"Wife's at work," the man says to you. "Kids are at school. Your litter box is here, just off the kitchen. I've also got you some food."

The man opens the fridge and pulls out a dark bottle. "I'm gonna have a beer. Do you want one?" He smiles at you. "But you probably want water."

The man fills a bowl from the tap and places it on the floor in the kitchen. You know that sound. You make your way there and lap from it.

The man tears open a giant purple bag and pours some kibble into another bowl, and places that beside your water. You sniff it, assessing. It smells pretty good and you take some into your mouth, crunching it.

"I'll get you some wet stuff tomorrow," the man says. "Maybe some toys."

You munch the kibble and the man takes a drink of his beer. "See this?" he uses his socked foot to point to a spot on the kitchen door not far off the ground. "Right here — this is where I'm going to install a cat door for you. So you can come and go as you like."

The man seems to be trying very hard to be re

sponsive to your needs, which is nice.

"Alright, I gotta get some work done. But you just look around."

Then the man heads to the basement, but you don't follow him. You walk to the living room and find a couch. Jumping up, you settle into a corner of it. Exhausted, you nap.

Later, more humans enter the house. You meet a boy and a girl. Both of them are way too excited to meet you, and you run, hiding underneath a dresser upstairs. But soon they approach again, this time slower and calmer and you come out.

"What's his name?" the boy asks.

"Holden," the man says, coming into the room behind them.

"Like Holden Caulfield? From *The Catcher in the Rye*? We're supposed to read that next year, for English," the boy says.

"What about Holden *Cat*field?" the girl squeals.

The man chortles. "Sounds good to me."

Later that night, as everything winds down, you meet the woman of the house. She is more reticent around you. You are not sure if she likes you. But that's okay. You're not sure yet if you like *her*.

That night, the girl of the house drags you into her room and makes you a small tunnel out of the duvet of her bed, which you appreciate. You nuzzle yourself in there and the warmth is overwhelming.

You think of your mom, and Tupac, and your littermates. You think about all the people you have met, and will miss. It seems a cat's life is all about change — and not always the kind of change that you can control.

In the morning, you awake inside the soft corner

the girl makes with her calves and her thighs. Getting up, you walk over to the edge of the bed and drop down. You take a firm grip of the carpeted floor and stretch.

Then, in the far corner, you see your favourite thing in the world: a small, but intense *sunbeam*.

You go over and dip your head in its brilliance. It warms your fur and your heart.

This might not be so bad after all.

THE END

This is the end of your very purrticular coming-of-age, but it's far from the end of Holden Catfield's journey! Continue Holden's adventures in Pick-a-Plot™ #1: "You Are a Cat!"

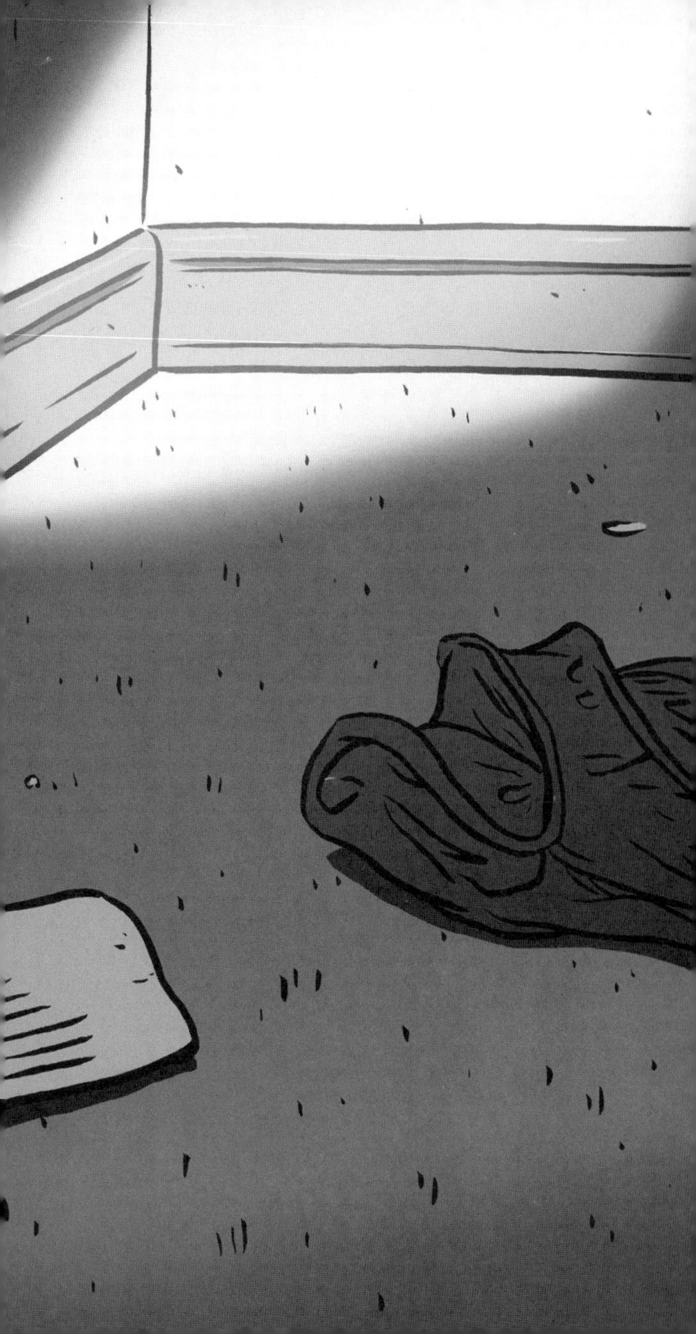

So You Want To Write Your OWN Pick-A-Plot™ Adventure?

What follows is a guide or how2torial for creating your own multiple-path, branching narrative work of fiction. I'm going to share all the tips and tricks I've picked up along the way. Making a gamebook isn't like writing a regular novel — it is its own genre and it comes with its own challenges and pitfalls. Hopefully this guide will help you bypass most of them. Keep in mind that this guide is only useful when making physical books like the one you hold in your hands. Making e-books, apps or hypertexts is beyond the scope of this guide.

1. The Premise

This is probably the most important decision you'll make. It took me years to arrive at my own premise. Though once I did, I practically kicked myself because it was so obvious. I love cats. What better book to write than one where I AM a cat? But I've already done it — so *you* have to come up with something else. Maybe write a book about being a dog. *I'm* never going to write that, so that territory is up for grabs. Try to arrive at a role-play that would be compelling not only to you, but to others.

Gamebooks allow you to pretend — to *be* someone or some*thing* you aren't. Don't go for something obvious, either. Think about the most powerful person you know. Now think about the most power*less*. But even the most powerless have choices, and even the most powerful are often constrained by invisible forces. These are ripe avenues for subverting expectations. Every time you meet someone new at a party, imagine writing a whole Pick-A-

Plot™ book of their week. Gamebooks are uniquely suited to putting you in someone else's shoes. They are empathy machines.

2. Brainstorming

Once you've decided on a premise, you'll want to brainstorm ideas, scenes, paths, events and themes about that premise. Imagine all the fun things about being that person. Now imagine all the awful or boring things. Try to come up with interesting ways for your character to arrive, interact and grapple with those things. In every situation, do your best to give your character a variety of choices. Offer the obvious one, but also offer its opposite. Then offer the offbeat and outlandish.

Try to offer choices that would appeal to different personality types. Try to see a situation from an extrovert *and* an introvert's POV. Also, try to create consequences for those choices. If your character double-crosses someone early on, try to funnel that someone back later to take revenge on your character. Bad things always happen in good stories. Do a lot of specific research about your premise, which should help spur new plot ideas.

Try to have characters change during the course of the book. Maybe a character is scared of everyone at the start of the book and by the end learns that everyone is just like them, and is similarly scared, but that being scared is okay, and that actually there's nothing to be scared of — so why not go for it? These are things to keep in the back of your mind.

3. Mapping

This is literally a map of paths. You introduce your reader to the world, then start giving them choices. Similar to how a porn movie uses narrative as the connective tissue between sex scenes, a branching narrative's meat is the ability to make choices. When I first started plotting my maps, I used regular paper and scotch-taped pages to it as needed, but I quickly developed this unwieldy document that actually began to take up as much space as an actual city map, so I abandoned that and started using these graph-paper books.

I give every narrative section a codename (ie. A12, F36, etc. Letters for plotline and numbers for section). This will be very useful later during the layout phase. It's necessary to give each written passage an individual name that isn't an actual page number

(ie. 52), but which is still easy to navigate and put in order. At this stage, you just want to sketch out the events in point form.

Don't go crazy with choice options at the start. This will quickly result in exponential branches, and too many options for you to keep track of. It may also result in a book that's 3000 pages long. Which would be cool, but possibly unpublishable.

You don't need to only branch outwards, either — funnelling can be your friend. That is, even if you have many branches at the beginning, you can corral them all back to one particular path later on in the book if you want. Instead of a tree as a model, consider capillaries and their path through your body as a possible model. They start off as this giant artery with many branches, which get smaller and smaller. But then they start linking up again, and form a giant vein, in order to move the deoxygenated blood back to the lungs and heart. Or think of rivers that become streams that become rivers again. Whatever branch you are mapping out, always see if you can create opportunities for a reader to get off that branch and to try another.

Try to have a good variety of deaths/endings, but not too many of them. It's too tempting to create a narrative path that you want the reader to walk, and the second they step off of that critical path to punish them by killing them. Try and Die™ is a poor branching path book. A good rule of thumb is that if one path ends in a death, have two choices that continue on. This will minimize railroading and reader frustration. Also, try to dream up the most interesting deaths possible. If the reader has to die, might as well make it awesome, or brutal, or disgusting, or bittersweet.

When you're done mapping your book, you may want to re-draw the thing on one page, to not only get a global sense of the narrative, but to ensure that you don't inadvertently create a logic loop, where a reader could end up going in circles. But really, you might want it all on one page because it's quite beautiful to see. It looks like arterial paths, or the lymph system.

4. Writing

This is where you add meat and muscle to the map's bare bones. Write everyday with a quota for yourself. I like to do a thousand words a day, but it doesn't matter the number. The most important thing is to do it every day until you're done. Even on days you don't feel like it, do at least a little. Start with section A1 and follow your choices. Try to have a good balance of action with dialogue and description. Never too much of one thing.

Don't be afraid to cut branches off if they aren't working. Don't be afraid to change your map if the narrative demands it. This is actually the *best* time to change your map. Like any map, it sets you off on your road trip, but you are the one who needs to assess your mood, the road, the weather. The map suggests a direction, but when you write you are the one responsible for every inch of movement. The map is a best laid plan that doesn't survive an encounter with the writing. Keep in mind that branching narratives need far fewer words than regular novels. Perhaps as much as a *third* fewer words than a regular book its size.

Once the first draft is done - congratulate yourself! Have a drink! Take a day off. But then print that sucker out and edit it. Go through it with a red pen. Unclunkify your clunky sentences. Maybe you use the word "suddenly" too many times. Perhaps you've repeated certain phrases. You'll discover all this and more when you edit.

The entire time, be on the lookout for astonishing scenes. Incidents that in your mind's eye are amazing, but which the writing might not do justice. These are possibilities for illustrations. Maybe do a thumbnail sketch on those pages. Try to choose images that offer a variety of scenarios, and which pique curiousity. If someone picks up your book, for example, try to have an image that plants a question in the mind of the browser, like, "How the fuck did we end up here?" which hopefully can only be answered by buying and reading your book.

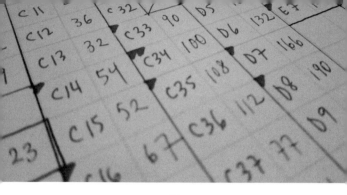

5. Layout

When I go to layout the book, I create a chart that has all my codenames for narrative sections, with a blank space next to them. This is because every narrative section doesn't have an address in the actual book yet. A1 is *probably* page 1, but that's about all I know.

I also do a page assessment. That is, once the typeface and size and page layout styles are decided on, I copy and paste the entire manuscript into a template. This is not the final layout — this is just so I can get a sense of how many pages the sheer text in my book requires, and how many pages I have left for illustrations. This can be massaged. Sometimes you can cut some text and gain yourself another page for an illustration.

Once you start your layout, the writing should be largely finished. The difficulty with any deep edit here is that every section is connected to one or more sections, and to start cutting sections becomes logistically complicated.

Illustrations are noted on my chart with a small red triangle in the corner. This lets me know that I have to reserve a page for it nearby when I am laying out the text. Try to have the illustration appear either concurrent with, or after that particular scene appears in the text. You don't want an illustration to spoil something for the reader.

Every time you place a section like 'B15' down, it will acquire a new page address in the book proper, like page '67'. You will need this for later on when you go to replace all the choices. So something like, "If you run, turn to page B15" will become "If you run, turn to page 67". I tend to lay the entire book out first, and acquire all the new page addresses before taking another pass and "translating" all of the new page numbers onto the old codenames in the choices. This is meticulous and terrifying work. After awhile, all the numbers begin to blur. It's very easy to fuck up here, so don't do this drunk, like I did.

Try to diversify where your choices lead the reader. It's not charming when the results of the reader's choice ends up next to each other (ie. "If yes, turn to page 22." "If no, turn to page 23.") It's too tempting for the reader to arrive at that branch and read a little bit of both choice to determine which path they want to go on. Try to choose pages that are far apart, to make the choice seem more indelible.

Try to place large chunks down first. You may have a longer scene that runs on for several pages. *More,* when we include the illustrations. Get these down first and fit smaller scenes in around them, all the while keeping strict note of every codename's new page number.

Occasionally, after all the pages are laid out you might discover that you have an orphan blank page in the middle of your book. This is a fun opportunity to write a weird, impossible scene, or embed a secret message for your reader. Since no other page links to it, the page may go unread except by completionists who are reverse-engineering and "mapping" your book themselves. I didn't have an orphan page in *this* book, but there is one in Pick-A-Plot #1 which I will leave you to discover.

Try to have your "happiest" ending end the book. You could be a rebel and follow your own rules and not do this, but there is a tendency by readers of books of this nature to want to get the "good" ending. This is only natural because a gamebook is a microcosm of our lives. We are always trying to make the choices that will lead to the "good ending" in our actual lives as well.

6. Illustrations

As mentioned, try to pick scenes to illustrate that generate a question in the reader's mind. You can't illustrate everything, so try to pick a nice diversity of images, and spread them out among all your narratives. Also try to pick scenes that are hard to describe in words.

For a book like this, told in the second person, you might want to do your illustrations in the first person. In your scene, portray what your main character sees. If your protagonist is stroking a koala, have their hands in the illustration! It's much more immersive.

At the end of the day, however, you'll want to pick the illustrations you personally *want* to draw. Passion and motivation are always good arbiters.

If you can't draw, consider hiring an illustrator, or taking staged photos, or getting a friend to help you out. Maybe your book doesn't need illustrations. Maybe it has cut-out finger puppets. Maybe it has instructions for origami sculptures. Maybe it has a blank page for the reader to illustrate.

7. The Cover

With a branching-path book, it's tough to decide on one definitive cover image. I have gone for a 70s "movie-style" adventure poster look for my books, but this is a personal decision. Look at the original posters for movies like *Star Wars* or *Indiana Jones* or *James Bond*. Large portraits surrounded by mini-scenes from the movies themselves. What I like about this format is that it evokes many emotions: suspense, romance, action. This is an opportunity for you to hint at scenes in the book without necessarily giving anything away. Try to go for bright colours, if possible. They are nice.

8. Branding

You'll need to concoct some way to let your audience know that your book is different than a regular book, that it's interactive fiction. I made up the "Pick-A-Plot™" brand because *Choose Your Own Adventure*™ was already taken, but the goal was to convey that genre. Make sure to check online to ensure you have a new umbrella brand name for your series and aren't stepping on anyone's creative toes. Often on books like this you'll see a byline that says "YOU are the hero!" or something like that.

9. Fun!

Remember that the goal is to have fun! I'm laying out the nuts and bolts here in a very matter of fact way, but make no mistake, I had an absolute blast making this trilogy. I basically cackled like a loon the entire time, and I write this guide in the hopes of inspiring more loons to share this genre with.

10. Final Thoughts

There's always a point in everyone's life when they notice the less fortunate — maybe you pass someone sleeping on the street — and you ask your parents why they're doing that. That is the awakening of empathy.

If the whole goal of a gamebook is to let you "walk a mile in someone else's shoes" then gamebooks are uniquely qualified to be immersive empathy engines because they *force* the reader to consider a world from someone else's *literal* POV. Gamebooks are also unique in that they allow the reader to game the gamebook — by keeping a finger in the book in case the choice they decide isn't the one they like, offering the reader agency they normally wouldn't have in a traditional narrative.

Quantum Leap, the TV show that ran from 1989 to 1993 is likely the closest analogue to a gamebook since it drops the protagonist's consciousness into different people's bodies and circumstances every episode. But in that case, there is a purported Good Ending that the protagonist must steer back towards, to "put right what once went wrong." What the show suggests is that sometimes, when we are steering our own gamelives, we are unable to see the choices available to us, or to write different ones.

Probably the most immersive gameworld is this life. You are the hero of your own life, and you make the choices that determine its outcome — always on the lookout for the Best Ending rather than The End. But unlike a gamebook, you can't commit a murder, end up in prison, and flip the page to another outcome; this life must be lived indelibly. The choices we make in this life really *matter.* You can't just cheat and take choices back. You are not a cat with nine lives!

Perhaps the greatest lessons of a gamebook — that we have the power to make choices, to see the world from someone else's POV, and that we are all looking for the Best Ending — can only truly take root when we strive to find the Best Endings not only for ourselves, but for everybody else as well.

Catknowledgements

I can't believe it's over. I didn't expect this: an actual trilogy of books that grew out of what seemed at the time an outlandish premise. As the last one, this book was particularly bittersweet to create, but also a ton of fun.

It was a delight to imagine this ultimate cat-crazy man, and then modelling him on myself. The rise of Kittenzilla. The pair of teen sleuths with their secret agenda. The puzzle & joy of joining this prequel up with the first book. I didn't anticipate any of this six years ago when I first started playing around with the idea.

Today it seems that every book is already the first in a series even *before* it comes out! But I couldn't see past the first one. I also didn't anticipate how cat culture has started to rule the world. During the last six years, internet cat video festivals emerged, museums are having cat shows & CatCons are now a thing.

A year ago I even put on my own little internet cat video screening of *my* favourites. The videos I like aren't the cute ones though. Well, not *only* the cute ones. I showed cat fights. Cats giving birth. Cats killing birds. A cat munching down on a still-squeaking mouse. I like the *totality* of catness. The reality of a cat's life is what I delight in. And like us, their reality is not always family-friendly. To say you only like a cat when it's cute does a disservice to the reality of their lives.

Over the last several years I've also seen a lot of other books with cats as main characters, but these are usually sentient cats, or talking cats. They're cats with weapons, or they're cats who are going to college. So they're not really cats at all, but humans, with cat-like qualities. Which I am okay with, as I *am* a human with cat-like qualities, but I was rather determined to keep Holden Catfield an actual cat, even though I take the occasional liberty, like I did in *You Are a Cat in the Zombie Apocalypse!*

What's next? Not sure. I feel like this trilogy has thoroughly explored Holden Catfield's life & times & End Times, from the mundane to the monstrous. I'm not ruling out any more Pick-A-Plot™ books, but I would need a concept that would really grab me, that would almost *pull* the story out of me.

So thank you for reading! Thank you for joining me on this journey. It was by turns ridiculous, raucous & absurd, but I hope it has entertained you, and warmed you, like a cat in a lap. It has certainly warmed me.

I couldn't have done it without you lovely readers, and I couldn't have done it without the following people.

I want to thank my family — my brother Sean, his girlfriend Steph, my mom and my dad, my uncle Sie Gie and my extended family for their support and love over the years and into the future.

I want to thank the following people, who, in very particular ways, contributed to the creation of this very particular book: Al L, Amber G, Amy B, Amy D, Andrea JR, Bess WK, Billy M, Dawn K, Elena T, Emilie O'B, Emma K, Farshid E, Geoff A, Glenna G, Ian SC, Ian F, Indigo E, Jenny L, Jim M, Joe O, Jo W, Joey D, Julia B, Julian P, Kimura B, Louis R, Luna A, Lynn C, Margaux W, Megan H, Michelle W, Miriam G, Patricia W, Robin H, Ryan K, Shay, Shie K, Sofi P, Stephen WW, Tif F, Tori A, and Vince T.

Thanks to Orion and Altaire and Roy and Jo, who, with their warm house full of animals, first lit for me my lifelong love for cats.

Thanks to James M, Jess A, Kailey B, Shawn L, Elena T, Ian F, & Emma K, for kindly and without reservation posing for the pictures which helped me work out numerous purrspective problems in the first-purrson pictures that finally appear here. Thanks also to Kimura B and Pangu! Thanks to Robin H & Blanche! Thanks to John Bartlett at the Critter Room! I am grateful for your help & purrmissions!

Thanks to Julian So, Carmen Ng, and Maf Alda who were so generous with their knowledge about various animal support groups!

Thanks to the cats who have taught me everything I know about verve, daring, calmness and patience: Kara and Cohen. Joe. Sully. JJ. Miccio and Gigi. Rosa. Ali, Rosa, Dirty, Gina and Gloria. Melon. Pinky. Rosie. Khan. Mia. Morris. Coco. Jingxi and Margaux. Blanche and Sophie. Genghis K the asshole cat. The late October.

Thanks to my Facebook "friends". I understand that a Facebook relationship is tenuous and complicated, and while some people find Facebook invasive and superficial, I have found it nothing but a scintillating revelation, and am proud to engage in this global village conversation every day with all of you.

Thanks to Andy B at Conundrum Towers for being my Q & MI6, granting me the legitimacy & leverage to spin this ridiculous web.

Thanks to Elena T for our continued madcap adventures.

Thanks to Kailey B, for the sunbeams.

About the Meowthor & Mewllustrator

Sherwin Sullivan Tjia is a Montreal-based writer and illustrator who has written nine books.

The World is a Heartbreaker, a collection of 1600 pseudohaikus, was a finalist for the Quebec Writer's Federation's A.M. Klein Poetry Award.

The Hipless Boy, a collection of short, interconnected stories told in graphic novel form, was a finalist for the Doug Wright Award in the Best Emerging Talent category, and also nominated for 4 Ignatz Awards.

His invention, *The E-Z-Purr: The Virtual Cat!* (an album with over an hour of cats purring) is available on the iTunes music store and its proceeds go to local cat shelters & adoption programs.

In his spare time, he organizes Slowdance Nights, Love Letter Reading Open Mics, Crowd Karaoke singalongs, and Strip Spelling Bees in and around Montreal and Toronto as *Chat Perdu Productions*. Occasionaly, he tours these events internationally at various art festivals.

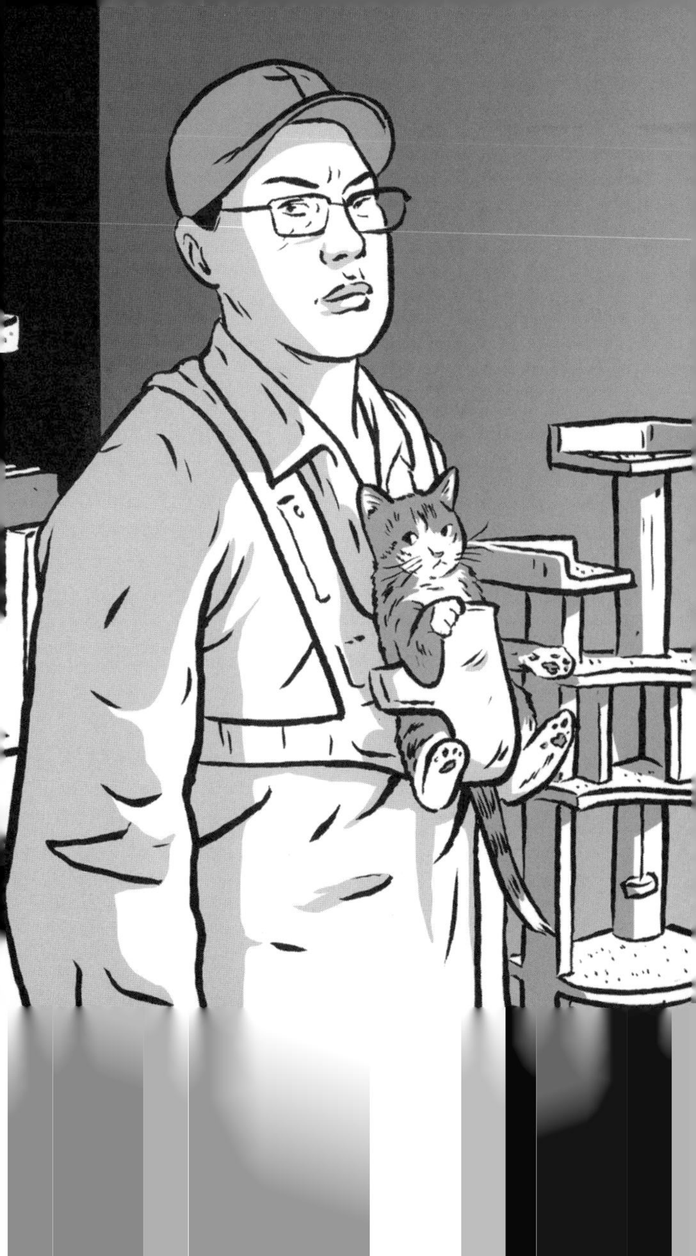

Purroducts & Purrchandise!

PICK-A-PLOT™ #1: You Are a Cat!
READ THE ORIGINAL and guide Holden Catfield as he stays in the house, or explores his neighbourhood. Hang out with the family! Play with your toy mouse! Take a nap or investigate the unusual sound coming from the upstairs bathroom! The choice is yours! Experience the book that started it all.

PICK-A-PLOT™ #2: You Are a Cat in the Zombie Apocalypse! THE EXCITING SEQUEL thrusts you into the end of the world as you know it! Take off on the road with the girls or stay in your neighbourhood and look for your girlfriend. The choice is yours! But some things aren't always up to you...

The EZ-PURR™: The Virtual Cat! THIS LANGUID AND luxurious album will sing and soothe you to sleep! An audible hug, this is purroma therapy! With over an hour of cats purring this hypnotic album is available for purchase right here: *https://itunes.apple.com/us/album/the-virtual-cat!/id509240768*